THE BROKEN CODE

WARRIORS

VEIL OF SHADOWS

THE BROKEN CODE

Book One: Lost Stars
Book Two: The Silent Thaw
Book Three: Veil of Shadows

THE BROKEN CODE

WARRIORS

VEIL OF
SHADOWS

ERIN
HUNTER

HARPER

An Imprint of HarperCollinsPublishers

Library of Congress Cataloging-in-Publication Data

Names: Hunter, Erin, author.

Title: Veil of shadows / Erin Hunter.

Description: First edition. | New York, NY : HarperCollins Children's Books, [2020] | Series: Warriors: the broken code ; book 3 | Audience: Ages 8-12. | Audience: Grades 4-6. | Summary: "With an impostor leading ThunderClan, threatening to exile any cats who challenge him, a small but growing group of cats must find a way to expose the truth and return ThunderClan's rightful leader—before the tensions among the Clans erupt into war"— Provided by publisher.

Identifiers: LCCN 2019033127 | ISBN 978-0-06-282368-7 (hardcover) | ISBN 978-0-06-282369-4 (library binding)

Subjects: CYAC: Cats—Fiction. | Fantasy.

Classification: LCC PZ7.H916625 Vei 2020 | DDC [Fic]—dc23

LC record available at https://lccn.loc.gov/2019033127

Typography by Jessie Gang

20 21 22 23 24   PC/LSCH   10 9 8 7 6 5 4 3 2 1

❖

First Edition

Special thanks to Cherith Baldry

ALLEGIANCES

THUNDERCLAN

LEADER **BRAMBLESTAR**—dark brown tabby tom with amber eyes

DEPUTY **BERRYNOSE**—cream-colored tom with a stump for a tail

MEDICINE CATS **JAYFEATHER**—gray tabby tom with blind blue eyes

ALDERHEART—dark ginger tom with amber eyes

WARRIORS (toms and she-cats without kits)

THORNCLAW—golden-brown tabby tom

WHITEWING—white she-cat with green eyes

BIRCHFALL—light brown tabby tom

MOUSEWHISKER—gray-and-white tom
APPRENTICE, BAYPAW (golden tabby tom)

POPPYFROST—pale tortoiseshell-and-white she-cat

LIONBLAZE—golden tabby tom with amber eyes

ROSEPETAL—dark cream she-cat

BRISTLEFROST—pale gray she-cat

STEMLEAF—white-and-orange tom

LILYHEART—small, dark tabby she-cat with white patches and blue eyes
APPRENTICE, FLAMEPAW (black tom)

BUMBLESTRIPE—very pale gray tom with black stripes

CHERRYFALL—ginger she-cat

MOLEWHISKER—brown-and-cream tom

CINDERHEART—gray tabby she-cat
APPRENTICE, FINCHPAW (tortoiseshell she-cat)

BLOSSOMFALL—tortoiseshell-and-white she-cat with petal-shaped white patches

IVYPOOL—silver-and-white tabby she-cat with dark blue eyes

EAGLEWING—ginger she-cat
APPRENTICE, MYRTLEPAW (pale brown she-cat)

DEWNOSE—gray-and-white tom

THRIFTEAR—dark gray she-cat

STORMCLOUD—gray tabby tom

HOLLYTUFT—black she-cat

FLIPCLAW—tabby tom

FERNSONG—yellow tabby tom

HONEYFUR—white she-cat with yellow splotches

SPARKPELT—orange tabby she-cat

SORRELSTRIPE—dark brown she-cat

TWIGBRANCH—gray she-cat with green eyes

FINLEAP—brown tom

SHELLFUR—tortoiseshell tom

PLUMSTONE—black-and-ginger she-cat

LEAFSHADE—tortoiseshell she-cat

SPOTFUR—spotted tabby she-cat

FLYWHISKER—striped gray tabby she-cat

SNAPTOOTH—golden tabby tom

QUEENS (she-cats expecting or nursing kits)

DAISY—cream long-furred cat from the horseplace

ELDERS (former warriors and queens, now retired)

GRAYSTRIPE—long-haired gray tom

CLOUDTAIL—long-haired white tom with blue eyes

BRIGHTHEART—white she-cat with ginger patches

BRACKENFUR—golden-brown tabby tom

SHADOWCLAN

LEADER **TIGERSTAR**—dark brown tabby tom

DEPUTY **CLOVERFOOT**—gray tabby she-cat

MEDICINE CATS **PUDDLESHINE**—brown tom with white splotches

SHADOWSIGHT—(gray tabby tom)

WARRIORS **TAWNYPELT**—tortoiseshell she-cat with green eyes

DOVEWING—pale gray she-cat with green eyes

STRIKESTONE—brown tabby tom

STONEWING—white tom

SCORCHFUR—dark gray tom with slashed ears

FLAXFOOT—brown tabby tom

SPARROWTAIL—large brown tabby tom

SNOWBIRD—pure white she-cat with green eyes

YARROWLEAF—ginger she-cat with yellow eyes

BERRYHEART—black-and-white she-cat

GRASSHEART—pale brown tabby she-cat

WHORLPELT—gray-and-white tom

HOPWHISKER—calico she-cat

BLAZEFIRE—white-and-ginger tom

CINNAMONTAIL—brown tabby she-cat with white paws

FLOWERSTEM—silver she-cat

SNAKETOOTH—honey-colored tabby she-cat

SLATEFUR—sleek gray tom

POUNCESTEP—gray tabby she-cat

LIGHTLEAP—brown tabby she-cat

CONEFOOT—white-and-gray tom

FRONDWHISKER—gray tabby she-cat

GULLSWOOP—white she-cat

SPIRECLAW—black-and-white tom

HOLLOWSPRING—black tom

SUNBEAM—brown-and-white tabby she-cat

ELDERS

OAKFUR—small brown tom

SKYCLAN

LEADER

LEAFSTAR—brown-and-cream tabby she-cat with amber eyes

DEPUTY

HAWKWING—dark gray tom with yellow eyes

MEDICINE CATS   **FRECKLEWISH**—mottled light brown tabby she-cat with spotted legs

FIDGETFLAKE—black-and-white tom

MEDIATOR   **TREE**—yellow tom with amber eyes

WARRIORS   **SPARROWPELT**—dark brown tabby tom

MACGYVER—black-and-white tom

DEWSPRING—sturdy gray tom
APPRENTICE, ROOTPAW (yellow tom)

PLUMWILLOW—dark gray she-cat

SAGENOSE—pale gray tom

KITESCRATCH—reddish-brown tom

HARRYBROOK—gray tom

BLOSSOMHEART—ginger-and-white she-cat

TURTLECRAWL—tortoiseshell she-cat

SANDYNOSE—stocky light brown tom with ginger legs

RABBITLEAP—brown tom
APPRENTICE, WRENPAW (golden tabby she-cat)

REEDCLAW—small pale tabby she-cat
APPRENTICE, NEEDLEPAW (black-and-white she-cat)

MINTFUR—gray tabby she-cat with blue eyes

NETTLESPLASH—pale brown tom

TINYCLOUD—small white she-cat

PALESKY—black-and-white she-cat

VIOLETSHINE—black-and-white she-cat with yellow eyes

BELLALEAF—pale orange she-cat with green eyes

NECTARSONG—brown she-cat

QUAILFEATHER—white tom with crow-black ears

PIGEONFOOT—gray-and-white she-cat

FRINGEWHISKER—white she-cat with brown splotches

GRAVELNOSE—tan tom

SUNNYPELT—ginger she-cat

ELDERS   **FALLOWFERN**—pale brown she-cat who has lost her hearing

WINDCLAN

LEADER   **HARESTAR**—brown-and-white tom

DEPUTY   **CROWFEATHER**—dark gray tom

MEDICINE CAT   **KESTRELFLIGHT**—mottled gray tom with white splotches like kestrel feathers

WARRIORS   **NIGHTCLOUD**—black she-cat

BRINDLEWING—mottled brown she-cat
APPRENTICE, APPLEPAW (yellow tabby she-cat)

LEAFTAIL—dark tabby tom with amber eyes

EMBERFOOT—gray tom with two dark paws

SMOKEHAZE—gray she-cat
APPRENTICE, WOODPAW (brown she-cat)

BREEZEPELT—black tom with amber eyes

HEATHERTAIL—light brown tabby she-cat with blue eyes

FEATHERPELT—gray tabby she-cat

CROUCHFOOT—ginger tom
APPRENTICE, SONGPAW (tortoiseshell she-cat)

LARKWING—pale brown tabby she-cat

SEDGEWHISKER—light brown tabby she-cat
APPRENTICE, FLUTTERPAW (brown-and-white tom)

SLIGHTFOOT—black tom with white flash on his chest

OATCLAW—pale brown tabby tom

HOOTWHISKER—dark gray tom
APPRENTICE, WHISTLEPAW (gray tabby she-cat)

FERNSTRIPE—gray tabby she-cat

ELDERS

WHISKERNOSE—light brown tom

GORSETAIL—very pale gray-and-white she-cat with blue eyes

RIVERCLAN

LEADER **MISTYSTAR**—gray she-cat with blue eyes

DEPUTY **REEDWHISKER**—black tom

MEDICINE CATS **MOTHWING**—dappled golden she-cat

WILLOWSHINE—gray tabby she-cat

WARRIORS **DUSKFUR**—brown tabby she-cat

MINNOWTAIL—dark gray-and-white she-cat

MALLOWNOSE—light brown tabby tom

HAVENPELT—black-and-white she-cat

PODLIGHT—gray-and-white tom

SHIMMERPELT—silver she-cat

LIZARDTAIL—light brown tom
APPRENTICE, FOGPAW (gray-and-white she-cat)

SNEEZECLOUD—gray-and-white tom

BRACKENPELT—tortoiseshell she-cat

JAYCLAW—gray tom

OWLNOSE—brown tabby tom

ICEWING—white she-cat with blue eyes

SOFTPELT—gray she-cat
APPRENTICE, SPLASHPAW (brown tabby tom)

GORSECLAW—white tom with gray ears

NIGHTSKY—dark gray she-cat with blue eyes

HARELIGHT—white tom

BREEZEHEART—brown-and-white she-cat

DAPPLETUFT—gray-and-white tom

QUEENS

CURLFEATHER—pale brown she-cat (mother to Frostkit, a she-kit; Mistkit, a she-kit; and Graykit, a tom)

ELDERS

MOSSPELT—tortoiseshell-and-white she-cat

EXILED CATS

SQUIRRELFLIGHT—dark ginger she-cat with green eyes and one white paw

THE BROKEN CODE

WARRIORS

VEIL OF SHADOWS

GREENLEAF
TWOLEGPLACE

TWOLEG NEST

TWOLEG PATH

TWOLEG PATH

CLEARING

SHADOWCLAN
CAMP

SMALL
THUNDERPATH

HALFBRIDGE

GREENLEAF
TWOLEGPLACE

HALFBRIDGE

CAT VIEW

ISLAND

STREAM

RIVERCLAN
CAMP

HORSEPLACE

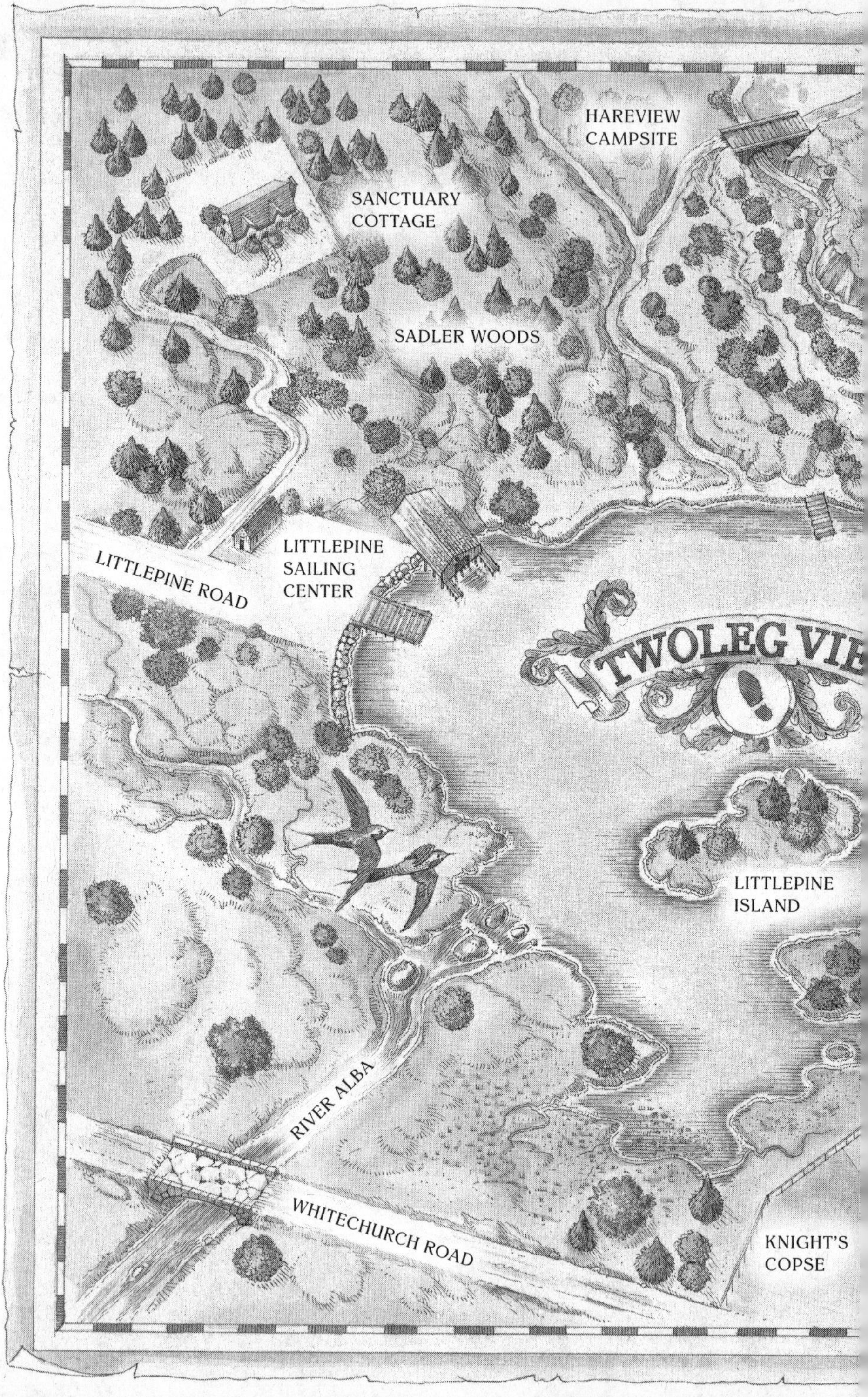
HAREVIEW CAMPSITE
SANCTUARY COTTAGE
SADLER WOODS
LITTLEPINE SAILING CENTER
LITTLEPINE ROAD
TWOLEG VIE
LITTLEPINE ISLAND
RIVER ALBA
WHITECHURCH ROAD
KNIGHT'S COPSE

PROLOGUE

Spiresight stretched himself out on a sun-warmed rock, enjoying the last rays as the sky above his head turned to scarlet. It was peaceful here, in the little clearing surrounded by bramble thickets. In fact, his whole existence had been peaceful since he had died. His last moons traveling with the ShadowClan cats, his death saving one of their kits, seemed almost like a dream. Even though Tigerstar had given him a warrior name and begged StarClan to admit him to their hunting grounds, he had chosen to remain a ghost, free to wander between the lake and the city without any cat to challenge him.

Spiresight had only known a small number of ShadowClan cats during his life, but since his death he had taken the opportunity to observe all the Clans, to try to understand them.

I have a pretty good idea of how they work now, he thought. *And the more I learn, the more I think something is wrong.*

The shiver that passed through Spiresight's pelt was not just because of the dying sun. His sense of unease deepened. It was more than just his fear that danger was lurking within the Clans . . . suddenly, he felt sure that a *specific* cat needed his help. *But who?*

Since he'd died, Spiresight had never felt such a strong sense of urgency. He jumped up and sped toward the lake, his ghostly paws skimming the surface of the ground. Something seemed to be tugging at him, opening up a path before him.

Twilight gathered around Spiresight as he ran; clots of deeper darkness formed beneath the trees. Before he reached the lake, he spotted a brown tom striding purposefully through the forest, the white splotches on his pelt glimmering eerily in the dusk. Spiresight took a sniff, but his instincts told him this was not the cat he was looking for. He ran on.

Soon he heard a rustling in the bushes and paused, all his senses alert. Just ahead of him he picked up the strong scent of crushed catmint. Taking a couple of cautious paces forward, Spiresight poked his head around a clump of fern and blinked in surprise.

Just off the path he had been following, a cat was rolling in a clump of catmint, working it thoroughly into his fur. By now it was too dark for Spiresight to make out any details, though he could see that the cat was a muscular, powerful tom.

Spiresight's sense of danger sharpened. *This is part of what has drawn me here,* he realized.

He doubted whether the other cat would be able to see him, but even so he moved as stealthily as he could as he drew closer. He was still a couple of tail-lengths away when the tom abruptly sat up, then settled into a hunter's crouch, peering into the undergrowth ahead of him. Almost immediately, he pounced, vanishing among the clustering ferns and bushes.

A cry split the silence of the night. Spiresight froze as he recognized the voice. *That's Shadowsight!*

Shadowsight had been only a kit when Spiresight died—in fact, it was his life that Spiresight had saved in his last moments. Even then, Spiresight could tell the kit was special. And now Shadowsight had grown into a gifted medicine cat. Spiresight pushed his way through the bushes to see the powerful tom attacking Shadowsight, raking his claws across the young medicine cat's defenseless back. As Spiresight watched in horror, he gripped Shadowsight by the scruff, gave him a vigorous shake, then slammed his body against a nearby tree trunk before letting him drop.

Shadowsight fell limply to the ground. His paws twitched briefly, then grew still.

Spiresight let out a yowl of shock and anger. He flung himself at the tom, clawing at his shoulder and throat, but his paws passed harmlessly through the tom's thick fur.

Spiresight flung back his head and let out a yowl, a desperate attempt to summon other cats to help. But there was no response. *I'm a ghost; I should have known no cat could hear me.*

The tom picked up Shadowsight's body and began dragging him deeper into the undergrowth. Spiresight followed, his eyes wide with dismay.

After a while, Spiresight realized that the tom was heading toward a rocky area on the border between ThunderClan and SkyClan. When he reached it, he scrambled among the rocks, dragging the motionless body of the young medicine cat between his forepaws. Suddenly Spiresight realized what he intended to do.

"No!" he snarled, leaping forward, but once again the tom didn't even flinch. Spiresight watched in horror as he swung Shadowsight by the scruff and tossed his body into a deep ravine. The limp gray form bounced off a jutting rock and landed beside the roots of a twisted thorn tree.

The burly tom gazed down at him for a moment, then whipped his head around in Spiresight's direction, his eyes wide and watchful. For a moment Spiresight froze, almost certain that the cat had spotted him. But a heartbeat later the large tom turned and raced away, vanishing into the undergrowth.

Spiresight gazed down into the ravine, his fear turning to despair; by now the darkness was so deep that he could hardly make out Shadowsight's body lying on the rocky ground. *I refused StarClan so I could watch over my friends. Why was I forced to witness this?*

Letting out a wail of anguish, he crouched down at the very edge of the gully.

Why did my instincts send me here, if I couldn't stop this? he asked himself in a storm of guilt and grief. *My friend is dead, and there's nothing I can do!*

CHAPTER 1

Rootpaw shuffled his paws nervously, darting glances at the medicine cats around him. Just being at the Moonpool spooked him: the spiral path stippled with the paw steps of cats so ancient that even their memory was lost; the continual gushing of the water that cascaded into the pool; the Moonpool itself, awash with reflected moonlight and starshine.

We don't belong here, he thought, his gaze catching briefly on his father, Tree, who was sitting beside him. *This place is only for medicine cats.* He remembered the last time he had been allowed to visit the Moonpool, when the medicine cats had tried to break the ice in the hope of helping StarClan reach them. *That didn't feel right either, and it didn't help us reconnect with StarClan.*

Even the medicine cats were looking anxious, Rootpaw realized. The medicine cats from all the Clans were here, except for ShadowClan. While they waited for Puddleshine and Shadowsight to join them, the half-moon rose higher in the sky, and Rootpaw's pelt tingled with mounting tension.

I just want to get on with it.

He and Tree had traveled to the Moonpool in the hope that they could make Bramblestar's wandering spirit appear to the medicine cats at their usual half-moon meeting. If they could, then every medicine cat would know that the cat inside Bramblestar was not the real leader of ThunderClan. And that would mean ThunderClan shouldn't follow his orders.

But it's a big if, Rootpaw thought gloomily. He knew that some of the medicine cats weren't happy allowing Tree to approach so close to the Moonpool. They couldn't accept the strange talents he had inherited from his kin in the Sisters, or his disregard for the warrior code. But for once Rootpaw was comforted by his father's presence. He hated to admit it, but the situation they were in now was bigger than the code.

"What's keeping the ShadowClan cats?" Kestrelflight muttered, rising to his paws and pacing from the water's edge to the bottom of the path and back again. "We're wasting moonlight," he added with a glance at the sky.

"They'll be here in a minute," said Tree. "We thought we heard a cat wailing in pain on the way here."

"Who was it?" Alderheart asked anxiously.

Tree shrugged. "We never found any cat. We kept on looking for a while, but then Puddleshine figured that the injured cat must have been able to get back to the ThunderClan camp. Shadowsight had stayed behind to gather cobwebs, so Puddleshine went back for him while we came here."

"I hope they haven't run into trouble," Alderheart responded. "We can't start without them."

Jayfeather let out a snort, the tip of his tail twitching irritably to and fro.

Before any other cat could speak, a rustling sound came

from the bushes at the top of the hollow and Puddleshine appeared, pushing his way through the thorny branches and running lightly down the spiral path to join his fellow medicine cats.

"Sorry I'm late," he panted. "I—"

"Where's Shadowsight?" Rootpaw interrupted. He had felt relieved at the arrival of the ShadowClan medicine cat, until he realized that Puddleshine was alone.

Puddleshine gave him a blank look, then glanced around in confusion. "Isn't he here?" he asked. "I thought he must have gotten ahead of me."

"He's not here," Mothwing meowed.

Puddleshine hesitated, blinking worriedly. "I looked for him, but when I couldn't find him, I thought he'd just decided to go on ahead." The fur on his neck and shoulders began to bristle. "Where can he have gone?" he asked.

"You must have missed each other," Mothwing meowed briskly. "We'll give him a little longer."

The other medicine cats murmured agreement, settling down again beside the Moonpool. Rootpaw could see their growing tension in their twitching whiskers and the impatient flicking of their tails. He felt even more strongly that he didn't belong here.

As the moments dragged by, an aching hollow of anxiety opened up inside Rootpaw. Puddleshine, too, was still looking confused, as if he couldn't imagine what was keeping Shadowsight.

Rootpaw's worry mounted until he couldn't bear it any

longer. Shadowsight was the cat who had first spread the news that StarClan was angry with the codebreakers, but he'd since changed his mind and begun doubting his own vision. *He has enemies now, throughout the Clans.* . . . "Something bad must have happened!" he burst out. "We should go and look for Shadowsight."

All the medicine cats turned to look at him with identical blank expressions on their faces. He was afraid that none of them would listen to an ordinary apprentice, but Frecklewish rose to her paws at once.

"Rootpaw is right," she meowed. "Shadowsight wouldn't keep us waiting like this if he had any choice."

"He'd better not," Jayfeather responded, a sarcastic edge to his voice. "If I find he's run off to chase moths, I'll claw his ears off!"

Puddleshine gave the blind cat a hard glare. "If Shadowsight has deliberately wasted our time, *I'll* be the one to deal with him," he snapped.

But Rootpaw could see from Puddleshine's hunched shoulders and the droop of his tail that he was genuinely worried. He was the first cat to bound up the path and thrust his way through the bushes, while the rest of the medicine cats streamed after him. Rootpaw and Tree brought up the rear.

"So much for calling up Bramblestar's spirit," Tree murmured with an anxious twitch of his ears.

"This is more important," Rootpaw insisted. He felt cold to the tips of his claws. *Could an animal have attacked Shadowsight?*

Or worse—could another cat have attacked him? He shivered at the thought of a Clan cat attacking ShadowClan's medicine cat. *Would any cat really do that? It's against the warrior code!* "I'm sure something bad has happened to Shadowsight. We have to find him!"

The group of cats climbed down the rocky slope and hurried across the moor, following the WindClan border stream until they reached ThunderClan territory. *Maybe we'll meet him on his way to the Moonpool,* Rootpaw thought hopefully. But there was no sign of Shadowsight by the time Puddleshine led them to the place where he had left the lakeshore and headed into the forest in search of the injured cat.

"This shouldn't be difficult," Mothwing mewed to Puddleshine. "Your scent is quite strong still, and so is Shadowsight's. We only have to follow it."

But not many fox-lengths into the forest, the scent trail led into a patch that smelled so strongly of catmint that the cats' scent was swamped by it.

"Weird . . ." Puddleshine shook his head in bewilderment. "This is where we heard the cat yowling. I remember, because I thought mint didn't grow in this part of the forest."

"That's because it doesn't. This isn't a catmint patch. Someone brought catmint plants here," Alderheart pointed out, giving them a good sniff. "And the stems of the grass below are crushed."

Rootpaw frowned, trying to work it out. "Maybe some cat—or even a fox—took prey here?"

"Or someone brought the catmint here to roll in it . . . and disguise his or her scent," Alderheart suggested, looking serious.

"I've found your scent, Puddleshine," Jayfeather reported from the far side of the catmint patch. "But not Shadowsight's. It's like he walked in here and never walked out again."

"But why?" Rootpaw protested. "Why would *Shadowsight* try to disguise his scent?"

"Shadowsight! Shadowsight!" Puddleshine's yowl shattered the silence of the forest, but there was no response.

"He can't be close by, if he didn't hear that," Mothwing pointed out. "We should split up and look for him."

Frecklewish nodded agreement. "We can organize another meeting at the Moonpool once he's found," she mewed.

But before any cat could move, Tree stepped into the middle of the group. "Wait," he ordered; Rootpaw blinked in astonishment at the authority in his father's voice. "Whatever happened to Shadowsight might be connected to what Rootpaw has to show us," Tree went on. "You all promised to listen—will you keep your word?"

"We can't trek all the way back to the Moonpool now," Willowshine protested.

"We don't have to," Tree told her, twitching his whiskers. "Rootpaw can show you right here."

With a wave of his tail he beckoned Rootpaw, who stepped forward. The medicine cats gathered in a ragged circle around him. He dug his claws nervously into the earth, sure that every cat must be able to hear the pounding of his heart.

Fixing his gaze on the branches above his head, Rootpaw reached out with all his concentration toward Bramblestar. *Come on,* he pleaded silently. *You* have *to come!*

For several heartbeats nothing happened, and Rootpaw began to wonder if he was doing this right. Then, from behind him, he heard a familiar meow.

"Greetings."

Rootpaw lowered his gaze to see the eyes of the medicine cats stretch wide in wonder as Bramblestar's spirit padded into the center of the circle.

Yes! It's working! They can all see him too.

Even Jayfeather gave a shudder; though he couldn't see Bramblestar, he clearly recognized his voice.

But Rootpaw's excitement didn't last long. When he took a good look at Bramblestar, he saw how hazy and indistinct his spirit form had become, much less solid than the last time Rootpaw had seen him. Rootpaw's pelt began to prickle with anxiety, and the sensation grew even stronger as Bramblestar began to speak.

"I'm thankful you have come," the ThunderClan leader began, gazing around at the medicine cats. His voice sounded distorted, so it was hard to make out what he was saying. "The longer I'm kept out of my own body, the weaker I'm getting. It's costing me a lot to appear like this, but I have to . . ."

On the last few words, Bramblestar's voice began to fade. His spirit form grew even more indistinct, no more than a smudge of tabby fur against the undergrowth.

"No!" Rootpaw choked out as the last vestiges of voice and body disappeared. "Wait . . ."

"Where did he go?" Alderheart demanded, gazing around in confusion. "Rootpaw, can you see him?"

Desperately worried and afraid, Rootpaw shook his head. "He's gone."

A shocked silence followed his words, broken after a few heartbeats by Fidgetflake. "What was that? Was it even Bramblestar?"

Kestrelflight let out a snort. "I could barely see or hear it. Rootpaw, are you playing some kind of trick?"

Rootpaw's indignant denial was swamped by Willowshine's sharp tones. "It looked pretty strange to me, too. Why are we worried about this weird Sisters talent, when we should be focused on getting back in touch with StarClan?"

"It's a waste of time," Kestrelflight growled, his shoulder fur bristling up.

"Now wait a moment," Alderheart meowed, raising one paw as he faced the RiverClan and WindClan cats. His eyes were deeply disturbed, but to Rootpaw's relief he didn't sound hostile. "Why *shouldn't* we listen to Rootpaw? Perhaps his talents will help us understand what's happened to Bramblestar."

"Alderheart is right," Mothwing added, with a severe look at her former apprentice, Willowshine. "I admit I didn't believe him at first, but now I have the evidence of my own eyes. That was Bramblestar who stood among us."

Jayfeather nodded. "I would know his voice anywhere." He

gave his pelt a shake; Rootpaw guessed he was trying to hide how uneasy he felt. "But if that was Bramblestar, who is the cat who's leading ThunderClan right now?"

"And what does it all mean?" Puddleshine asked.

No cat could answer him.

Rootpaw stood on the edge of the group, flexing his claws in frustration as the medicine cats continued to murmur among themselves, their heads shaking and their tails twitching as they tried to make sense of the vision they had seen. Tree came and stood beside him; for once, Rootpaw was glad of his solid presence and the warmth of his father's pelt touching his own.

Finally, Alderheart's voice rose above the other medicine cats'. "It's clear what Jayfeather and I have to do," he meowed. "And that's keep an eye on the Bramblestar who's still in ThunderClan."

"And StarClan help him if he's *not* really our leader," Jayfeather growled.

"That doesn't help the rest of us," Frecklewish pointed out. "What do we do? Do we tell our leaders?"

Mothwing shook her head. "I don't know. . . . It's a grave accusation to say that Bramblestar is not really himself—and we have so little evidence to prove it. Perhaps it would be better to keep this to ourselves until we're sure."

Kestrelflight hunched his shoulders, glaring around at his fellow medicine cats. "I don't know why you're all getting your tails in a twist," he rasped. "Bramblestar went on to his next life; it's that simple. And now he's going to lead the Clans to reconnect with StarClan. Do you, as medicine cats, want that, or do you want to sow suspicion and discontent by listening to this . . . this *apprentice*?"

Rootpaw took a step forward, jaws opening to defend himself, but Tree coiled his tail around his shoulders, drawing him back. "Let them go back to their Clans and think about what they've seen," he murmured into Rootpaw's ear. "Either they'll act or they won't, and arguing won't change their minds."

Rootpaw heaved a heavy sigh. He hated to admit it, but his father was right. He waited beside Tree while the medicine cats said their final farewells and turned toward their Clans.

"What about Shadowsight?" Rootpaw asked as they were about to leave.

"What more can we do?" Mothwing asked sorrowfully. "We've lost his scent, and if he were close by he would have heard us calling for him."

"But we can't just abandon him!" Rootpaw protested, his shoulder fur beginning to bristle indignantly.

Puddleshine flicked his tail. "Maybe he's gone back to ShadowClan," he suggested. "It's possible he made it to the Moonpool eventually and didn't find us there. Maybe we just missed each other?"

The medicine cats all exchanged glances. Rootpaw sensed their doubt, and he didn't feel optimistic, either. But it was clear that no cat knew what else to do.

Tree rested his tail lightly on Rootpaw's shoulder. "Let it go for now," he advised quietly. "If Shadowsight is anywhere nearby, we'll find some sign." To the medicine cats, he added, "All of you should stay alert for any sign of Shadowsight as you head for your camps."

Puddleshine nodded. "Yes, and if you find anything, send word to ShadowClan. But I'll hope to find him waiting for me back at camp."

The other medicine cats murmured agreement. That wasn't what Rootpaw wanted, but he had the sense to realize it was the best he could hope for. His paws dragging reluctantly, he followed Frecklewish and Fidgetflake on their way home to the SkyClan camp.

As he padded through the forest beside Tree, it wasn't only Bramblestar's fading ghost that weighed Rootpaw's belly down with dread.

Where is Shadowsight? What has happened to him?

Chapter 2

Bristlefrost slid between the branches of the warriors' den and into the silver wash of moonlight that filled the ThunderClan camp. Fluffing up her fur against the night chill, she cast a regretful glance over her shoulder at the warm nest she had left.

I wish I didn't have to go, but the dirtplace is calling. . . .

While she padded across the camp, Bristlefrost raised her head to see the half-moon floating in the sky, and the glitter of countless stars. But instead of rejoicing in the beauty of the night, Bristlefrost felt her belly begin to roil in apprehension.

Where was StarClan now? Why were they keeping silent?

As she walked back from the dirtplace, Bristlefrost spotted movement from the corner of her eye and turned to see two cats slinking quietly along the stone wall on the far side of the camp. At the same time, the scent of catmint drifted into her nose, so strong that she wondered whether the cats had been rolling in a patch of it on purpose. Tasting the air, she picked up another, fainter tang.

Could that be blood?

At first Bristlefrost wasn't sure which cats these were. They might even be interlopers, disguising their scent, though

Rosepetal, on guard beside the thorn tunnel, hadn't raised the alarm. Then, as the two cats drew closer, she recognized the impostor Bramblestar and the Clan deputy, Berrynose. Her first flash of relief was replaced by unease as she wondered why they were returning to camp so late and smelling so strongly of catmint.

Bristlefrost headed quickly back toward the warriors' den, hoping that her Clanmates wouldn't spot her. But before she could reach the shelter of the branches, she heard Bramblestar's voice behind her, quiet but insistent.

"Bristlefrost! Is all well?"

Turning to face him, Bristlefrost waited for the Clan leader to pad up to her, with Berrynose close behind.

"Yes, Bramblestar. A quiet night," Bristlefrost replied, dipping her head respectfully.

Bramblestar let out a huff of satisfaction. "Good."

His manner was normal—he even seemed to be in a good mood—but Bristlefrost felt uncomfortable talking to him. From this distance, she could see his chest fur matted with blood, dark in the silver moonlight. It had turned his pelt into sticky clumps, but there was no sign of a wound, and he was moving easily, with not a trace of pain in his voice. Bristlefrost opened her jaws to ask what had happened, then bit the words back. She was sure of one thing: Questioning the false Bramblestar would be a really bad idea.

"Good night, then," Bramblestar mewed, and headed toward his den on the Highledge, while Berrynose padded past Bristlefrost and thrust his way into the warriors' den.

Bristlefrost hurried after him, trying to tell herself that the two cats had simply been out on a moonlight hunt.

But a hunt for what?

The next morning, Bristlefrost woke to find that the clear night had given way to thick cloud and rain that battered the roof of the warriors' den. She flinched as an icy drop found its way through the interlaced branches and hit her on the back of her neck. She could hear wind, too, buffeting the trees at the top of the stone hollow.

"And guess what? I'm on dawn patrol!" she announced irritably as she hauled herself out of her nest and shook scraps of moss from her pelt.

She hadn't expected an answer, but Thornclaw looked up from where he was giving himself a quick grooming. "Like any cat would attack us in this weather," he mewed sourly.

Bracing herself, Bristlefrost headed out into the wind and rain. Her pelt was soaked in the first few heartbeats as she splashed her way to where Stormcloud was gathering the rest of the patrol together.

The night before, still and beautiful in the moonlight, seemed so far away that Bristlefrost almost wondered whether she had dreamed the encounter with Bramblestar.

But it was so real!

While she slogged around the border with Stormcloud, Molewhisker, and Poppyfrost, Bristlefrost's brief conversation with Bramblestar repeated itself in her mind. She couldn't forget the sight of his chest fur clotted with blood. By the time she returned to camp, drenched and shivering, she knew she had to tell some cat what she had seen.

As Bristlefrost emerged from the thorn tunnel, she spotted a hunting patrol just ahead of her, carrying their prey to the fresh-kill pile. Stemleaf and Spotfur were among them. Forcing her aching legs into a run, Bristlefrost crossed the camp and caught up to them, skidding to a stop and almost losing her balance on the muddy ground as they dropped a vole and two mice onto the pile.

"I have to speak to you," she murmured. "It's urgent."

Stemleaf turned to her, his eyes wide and questioning, but several cats were crowding around the pile, and he said nothing, only drawing her and Spotfur away from the others. They found a quiet spot beside the wall of the camp, beneath a jutting stone that gave them some shelter from the wind and rain. Spotfur glanced around warily, checking that no cat could overhear them.

"Tell us," Stemleaf mewed.

"Last night I went out to make dirt . . . ," Bristlefrost began, and went on to describe her weird encounter with Bramblestar and Berrynose, the overwhelming scent of catmint, and the blood clumping Bramblestar's chest fur. "I don't want to accuse a leader of something so serious," she added, "but I haven't been able to stop thinking about it. What do you think—am I making something out of nothing?"

Stemleaf blinked thoughtfully. "Maybe you are," he responded, "but given what we know about Bramblestar, it doesn't seem likely. I think he's up to something."

"We'll have to watch him even more closely," Spotfur put in.

"Yes," Stemleaf agreed. "But we know he sent dogs after Sparkpelt because she'd disobeyed him. And now he's coming back to camp covered with blood. What will we do if Bramblestar is up to something terrible?"

"I don't know," Bristlefrost admitted.

Neither of the others could suggest a plan, either. Still tense with anxiety, Bristlefrost returned with Spotfur and Stemleaf to the fresh-kill pile to choose some prey. They were sharing a squirrel when Bramblestar emerged from his den and stood on the Highledge, his amber gaze raking across the camp.

"Let all cats old enough to catch their own prey join here beneath the Highledge for a Clan meeting," he yowled.

The Clan began to assemble, those who had been sheltering in their dens hunching their shoulders against the driving rain as they ventured into the open. Bristlefrost made herself take a place at the front of the crowd, though she dreaded hearing what Bramblestar might be planning next.

"I have an important announcement to make," Bramblestar announced when the Clan had gathered. "Last night, Jayfeather and Alderheart returned from the medicine-cat meeting at the Moonpool. They brought the news that Shadowsight, the young ShadowClan cat whose visions have helped us face up to our codebreaking ways, has gone missing."

Bristlefrost's heart lurched at the news. Her forepaws kneaded the muddy ground as she remembered her meeting with Bramblestar the night before, and the blood clotting on his chest. She remembered too that Rootpaw and Tree had been planning to tell the medicine cats the truth about Bramblestar's spirit.

I wonder if they convinced them. Her apprehension swelled as she added to herself, *Does Shadowsight's disappearance have anything to do with their plan?*

"I believe Shadowsight has fled from the Clans," Bramblestar continued, his voice cold and severe. "I believe he couldn't cope with knowing that his mother, Dovewing, shared the blame for driving StarClan away, and that all codebreakers must be punished. Shadowsight was weak."

Bristlefrost stared at her leader in shock. *What is he talking about?* She didn't know the young ShadowClan medicine cat well, but she knew enough to believe there was no way he would have left his Clan—and his kin—willingly.

Bramblestar paused, gazing down at his Clan, and his voice grew warmer, trickling from his jaws like honey. "But of course, you, cats of ThunderClan—you are stronger. Those of you who need to atone will do so, and those who resist will be punished. In this way, we will set an example for the other Clans."

The Clan grew quiet and thoughtful as they listened to the impostor's words. Glancing around at her Clanmates, Bristlefrost thought that some of them seemed cowed, with their heads bowed, staring at their own paws, while others exchanged uneasy glances. She guessed they might be thinking of their past mistakes.

But Stemleaf and Spotfur, Bristlefrost noticed, had a glint of anger in their eyes, though they stayed silent and their shoulder fur remained smooth and flat.

Bristlefrost looked for Jayfeather and Alderheart. Did they know what had really happened to Shadowsight? She spotted them at the entrance to their den; Jayfeather leaned over to Alderheart and muttered something into his ear.

But the blind cat hadn't muttered quietly enough. Bristlefrost caught the word *nonsense*, and from his sudden sharp look she guessed that the false Bramblestar had heard it, too. Her belly cramped with fear.

Before Bramblestar could speak, Alderheart sprang to his paws, dipping his head to Bramblestar with the deepest respect. "Jayfeather says it's nonsense for a cat to have any reason to fear your orders, or try to escape atonement," he explained.

Oh, sure he does, Bristlefrost thought. From the look of anger in Bramblestar's eyes, and the snort he let out, she was pretty sure that he shared her skepticism.

But to her relief, Bramblestar said nothing. Instead he drew himself up, standing tall and straight, and let his gaze travel once again over his Clan. "Shadowsight's cowardice has convinced me that we must act swiftly and openly," he meowed. "We must deal with the codebreakers. I am not afraid to show StarClan that ThunderClan wants to make up for their mistakes. Therefore . . ."

He paused, and Bristlefrost's belly clenched again in fear for what was coming.

"Therefore," Bramblestar went on, "Jayfeather, Lionblaze, and Twigbranch, step forward."

Jayfeather rose to his paws at once and took a pace forward, his tabby fur bristling with a kind of angry pride. Lionblaze and Twigbranch hesitated for a few heartbeats, glancing at each other uncertainly, before stepping out from the crowd of their Clanmates and facing Bramblestar where he stood on the Highledge.

"I haven't broken the code," Lionblaze protested.

"Maybe not," Bramblestar responded. "But you and Jayfeather are half-Clan cats. The result of codebreaking. And while you live in ThunderClan, your very existence displeases StarClan."

"What?" Jayfeather snarled. He took another pace forward, his tail lashing in fury. "How am I to blame for the way I was born? I wasn't around to be given a choice!"

Alderheart slipped to his side and rested a tail-tip on his former mentor's shoulder, but if he had hoped to restrain Jayfeather, the gesture was useless. Jayfeather shook him off, all his attention still focused on the false Bramblestar.

"We all know," he continued, "that my mother, Leafpool, who deceived the Clan about our birth, is in StarClan now. If my so-called codebreaking existence bothers StarClan so much, why did they forgive the cat who was *actually* responsible?"

For a moment Bramblestar seemed to be caught off guard. Bristlefrost watched, fascinated, as his jaws flapped like a gasping fish. "StarClan works in mysterious ways," he mumbled at last. "I know very well that they don't always explain themselves clearly."

"I know more about StarClan than you ever will!" Jay-feather retorted. "And I know that you're lying. You're not even—"

Bristlefrost's ears twitched forward. *Does Jayfeather know that Bramblestar isn't really Bramblestar?* Ice-cold panic flooded through her, as she realized that Jayfeather might be about to reveal the truth to the whole Clan. She recalled that Root-paw and Tree were meant to tell the medicine cats about Bramblestar's ghost at last night's half-moon meeting. But the resistance had discussed the danger of letting all the Clan cats know too soon, before they had evidence to prove it. It would be a rash step to accuse a leader of being an impostor. *I can't imagine the chaos. . . .*

"I don't always understand StarClan's meaning," she mewed, feeling awkward at interrupting the medicine cat in front of the whole Clan. "They *can* be confusing sometimes."

Jayfeather shot her a sour look and muttered something too softly for Bristlefrost to catch.

But she was pleased to see a look of surprise spread over Bramblestar's face, and to hear some of her Clanmates yowl their agreement.

"StarClan!" Mousewhisker exclaimed. "Why can't they just say what they mean?"

"Half the time, even the medicine cats don't understand them," Sparkpelt added.

"I'm just repeating what the young medicine cat told all of us," Bramblestar told Jayfeather sternly. "However it hap-pened, you and your brother are half-Clan, which means you are codebreakers. As for you, Twigbranch," he continued, turning his attention to the young she-cat, "you changed Clans several times, and you even convinced a SkyClan-born cat to come with you. That is how you violated the code. All three of you were named in Shadowsight's vision, and you must be exiled."

Jayfeather let out an angry hiss as the whole Clan gasped in consternation at Bramblestar's decree. Lionblaze took a step back, angry resignation in his face, drawing level with his mate, Cinderheart, who gazed at him, stricken and worried. Twigbranch, however, sank down on her belly and gazed up at the Clan leader pleadingly.

"Please let me atone instead," she begged. "I know I'm a ThunderClan cat in my heart. That's why I came back. I'll prove my loyalty any way I can!"

Bramblestar hesitated. Bristlefrost thought he was enjoying the sight of Twigbranch prostrated in the mud in front of him. "Very well," he meowed at last. "But your atonement will be very difficult, because I have to be hard on you to please StarClan."

"I'll do anything!" Twigbranch promised eagerly.

"Then I want you to spend half a moon away from the Clans," Bramblestar went on, "and when you come back, you must bring twenty pieces of prey to feed your Clanmates."

What? Bristlefrost stifled a gasp of astonishment. *Every cat praises my hunting skills, but I can't imagine catching all that on my own.*

"Twenty!" Twigbranch exclaimed. "I know it's newleaf, but I'll be working alone. . . ."

"If that's the only way to prove to StarClan that you're a loyal warrior," Bramblestar responded, his eyes hard and implacable, "surely you can make it happen."

Twigbranch let out a long sigh, then scrambled to her paws, her head hanging. "I'll do it, Bramblestar," she mewed. She stepped back, trembling, mud dripping from her belly fur, and her mate, Finleap, pressed himself against her side and nuzzled her shoulder comfortingly.

"Half a moon isn't very long," he whispered.

Meanwhile Alderheart had padded forward to stand below the Highledge and face Bramblestar. "How can it be StarClan's wish for cats to be punished for their parents' mistakes?" he asked. "If that's true, is *any* cat innocent?"

Though Alderheart hadn't named any names, Bristlefrost could hear murmurs of understanding coming from some of her Clanmates. She understood, too. Though Bramblestar's own father, the first Tigerstar, had died long before she was born, she had heard stories about him from her father, Fernsong. In his quest for power, Tigerstar had betrayed his Clan and almost destroyed them all. He had left his son Bramblestar a terrible heritage.

But this isn't the real Bramblestar, Bristlefrost reminded herself. *I don't suppose he cares what Tigerstar did.*

"Enough!" Bramblestar snapped at Alderheart. "These are the codebreakers who StarClan chose to show Shadowsight in his vision. I'm aware—*very* aware—that others in the Clan have broken the code, but first we must expel the cats StarClan has pointed out. As for you, Alderheart, make sure you don't show disloyalty to your leader or try to get in the way of StarClan's wishes."

Or you'll be next. Bristlefrost supplied the words Bramblestar had not spoken. She was sure that every other cat in the Clan could fill them in, too.

"Leave now," Bramblestar continued, gazing down at Lionblaze and Jayfeather. "And don't look back. The rest of you, turn away from them."

Mews of dismay came from some of the Clan, but Bristlefrost forced down her protest. She longed to disobey the order, but it was vital for her to convince the false Bramblestar that she was loyal, so that she could go on passing information to the cats who were working against him. She sprang to her paws at once and made sure she was the first to comply.

She could hear the paws of the exiled cats splashing through the mud, then pausing as Jayfeather spoke. "You may think all of ThunderClan is taken in by your performance," he spat. "But it's not true, and you'll find that out very soon."

Bristlefrost froze. *So Jayfeather does know.* Rootpaw and Tree must have succeeded after all. But how would the false Bramblestar react to being very nearly exposed?

She glanced at the leader, but couldn't read anything in his gaze beyond his usual annoyance with the blind medicine cat. Bramblestar let out a growl from deep within his chest. "Hurry up and leave," he ordered.

He didn't pick up on it, she thought with relief.

"Come on, Jayfeather," Lionblaze meowed. "There's nothing we can do here."

Bristlefrost longed to speak to the exiled cats before they left the stone hollow, but she didn't dare, only standing with her back to them and listening as their paw steps faded away. She could feel the tension in the camp gripping every cat like a set of massive claws.

When Lionblaze and Jayfeather were gone, Bramblestar bounded down the tumbled rocks to the floor of the camp. To Bristlefrost's consternation, he stalked straight toward her.

"Make sure Twigbranch begins her atonement at once," he instructed, jerking his head to where the young she-cat still stood beside Finleap. She looked small and miserable, her gray fur plastered to her body by the pouring rain.

Why me? Bristlefrost wondered, though she had enough sense not to protest. "Of course, Bramblestar," she murmured, dipping her head.

She felt as though every cat in the Clan was staring at her as she padded over to Twigbranch. "It's time for you to go now," she meowed awkwardly. "Twenty pieces of prey is a lot for any cat . . . you'd better get started, I think."

"You don't have to be so unkind about it!" Finleap began hotly.

Bristlefrost wanted to murmur reassurance, but she knew that she couldn't let any cat see how she really felt. She hardened her expression, even though her heart was throbbing with pain.

Twigbranch stretched out her tail and rested the tip on Finleap's shoulder. "Don't," she murmured. "If this is truly what will bring StarClan back, then . . ." She broke off, her voice shaking, and leaned closer to Finleap to give his ear a farewell lick. Turning to leave, she added, "I'll see you in half a moon."

Her head held high, Twigbranch strode toward the thorn tunnel. A few cats called good-bye to her, but she didn't look back. Bristlefrost watched her go until she disappeared into the forest.

Turning, Bristlefrost found herself face to face with Finleap.

"I hope you're satisfied!" the brown tom hissed, fixing Bristlefrost with a hostile glare.

Startled by the force of his anger, Bristlefrost could find no response. She could only stand in stony silence as he whipped around and stalked away from her.

Though by now the rain was easing, most of the Clan headed for their dens as the meeting broke up. Glancing around, Bristlefrost realized that no cat was paying any attention to her. Swiftly she bounded across the camp and dived into the thorn tunnel.

If any cat asks, I'll tell them I'm going hunting.

In spite of the rain, Lionblaze's and Jayfeather's scents still lingered strongly in the grass. Bristlefrost followed them easily; they were heading for the edge of the territory, in the direction of SkyClan. The scents grew stronger still as she brushed through the wet undergrowth, and soon Bristlefrost realized that she had caught up to them; they were only just ahead of her, on the other side of a bramble thicket.

Why are they still here? she wondered. *There'll be trouble if Bramble-star sends out a patrol.*

Then she heard their voices rising above the brambles, and she understood. Lionblaze and Jayfeather were in the middle of an argument.

"... about as useless as a day-old kit!" Jayfeather was snarling as Bristlefrost came into earshot. "You gave in to Bramblestar far too easily!"

Lionblaze's voice in reply was far calmer, but Bristlefrost could discern the anger beneath his level tone. "Maybe you didn't realize we were heavily outnumbered. What were we supposed to do, attack our father?"

"Bramblestar isn't our father," Jayfeather scoffed. "And what's more, *that's not Bramblestar!*"

Bristlefrost took in a deep breath. *I was right—he knows. And if our medicine cat knows the truth, then maybe there is hope.*

She swiftly skirted the bramble thicket and joined her two Clanmates. "Greetings," she meowed.

Startled, both cats turned toward her. Bristlefrost forced herself not to flinch at the deep distrust in Lionblaze's eyes.

"What are you doing here?" he growled. "Has our glorious leader changed his mind, or has he sent my own kin to drive us out of the territory?"

"I know about Bramblestar," Bristlefrost explained quickly. "I know our leader isn't really himself. I'm here to help you, if I can."

Lionblaze let out a sigh, half irritated and half confused.

"Jayfeather has just been trying to explain that, but if you ask me, it's all a load of mouse droppings. How can that not be Bramblestar?"

"I know Bramblestar when I hear him," Jayfeather snapped. "Besides, last night that weird little SkyClan apprentice showed me and Alderheart and all the medicine cats that Bramblestar is currently a spirit, haunting the forest, and not the cat who's leading ThunderClan at all."

"I'm glad you and Alderheart know the truth," Bristlefrost mewed, massively relieved. "Tigerstar knows the truth, too. Squirrelflight is living with ShadowClan. If you follow me, I'll take you to her."

"Really?" Lionblaze's amber eyes reflected Bristlefrost's own relief. "Then lead on!"

The three cats headed through the forest and crossed the border into SkyClan territory, listening warily for SkyClan patrols as they padded through the trees. Rustling in a clump of ferns alerted Bristlefrost; she spun around to face the sound and spotted Twigbranch's face peering out nervously between two arching fronds.

"Come this way!" she called softly, beckoning with her tail.

"What are you doing here?" Twigbranch asked Bristlefrost as she emerged into the open and bounded over to the others. "Did Bramblestar exile you, too?"

"No," Bristlefrost replied. "And I have something to tell you, but we'd better keep going. SkyClan might not welcome us here."

Lionblaze took the lead, and Bristlefrost padded beside

Twigbranch as she told her everything she knew about the false Bramblestar. Twigbranch's eyes widened as she listened.

"I knew it!" she exclaimed, joy flooding into her gaze. "I knew StarClan didn't blame me for breaking the code. Only that . . . thing that's inside Bramblestar."

Bristlefrost nodded. "Of course. But it may be some time before we can convince every cat that that's true. Meanwhile, you can go and live in ShadowClan, if you want to, until your atonement is finished."

"I'd like that," Twigbranch responded.

At the ShadowClan border, the group of cats waited until they could scent that a ShadowClan patrol was approaching. A few heartbeats later Snowbird, Whorlpelt, and Slatefur appeared from behind a clump of hazel saplings. "What are you doing here?" Snowbird challenged the ThunderClan cats.

Bristlefrost dipped her head respectfully. "These three cats have been exiled from ThunderClan," she explained. "They'd like to join Squirrelflight."

Slatefur rolled his eyes. "What, more of you?"

Bristlefrost could see Lionblaze's shoulder fur begin to bristle at the comment, but to her relief the golden tabby warrior had the sense to keep himself under control. She was thankful to see that none of the ShadowClan cats looked particularly hostile.

"Come on, then," Snowbird meowed. Turning to her Clanmates, she added, "You two finish the patrol. I'll take these waifs and strays to Tigerstar. StarClan knows how many more cats we're supposed to take in to our territory."

Neither Jayfeather nor Lionblaze looked pleased to be called *waifs and strays*, but they followed Snowbird without protest. Bristlefrost brought up the rear with Twigbranch. *The ShadowClan cats know it's not our fault,* she thought. *It's the false Bramblestar they have to blame.*

As soon as Snowbird led the ThunderClan cats through the bushes and down into the hollow where ShadowClan had its camp, Tigerstar emerged from his den, took one look at them, and raced across to meet them at the foot of the slope.

"Have you seen Shadowsight?" he demanded, his dark tabby fur bristling. "Do you have any news about him?"

Bristlefrost was tempted to tell Tigerstar how Bramblestar had returned to camp on the previous night, his chest fur soaked in blood. But she kept her jaws shut. *I'm not sure it has anything to do with Shadowsight. And if I tell Tigerstar, there's no going back. . . .* If she accused Bramblestar of attacking Tigerstar's son, ShadowClan would have every reason to start a war. She remembered again what Bramblestar had tried to do to Sparkpelt. *What if Shadowsight is dead?*

Squirrelflight came bounding up to join them, her green eyes flaring in surprise as she recognized her two foster sons. Her purrs sounded half pleased and half anxious as she nuzzled them close to her.

"We don't have any news of Shadowsight," Jayfeather explained when they'd finished their greetings. "But Bramblestar has used his disappearance to crack down even harder on the codebreakers. He sent me and Lionblaze into exile because of what Leafpool and Crowfeather did, and Twigbranch has to atone for half a moon because she changed Clans."

Tigerstar's shoulders sagged as soon as he heard that there was no news about his son. "All right, you can stay," he mumbled.

At the same moment, Squirrelflight drew Bristlefrost aside. "Hurry back to ThunderClan, as fast as you can," she meowed. "Bramblestar mustn't suspect that you're helping the exiles."

Bristlefrost nodded. "I'll make sure he doesn't," she responded.

"I can't thank you enough," Squirrelflight went on. "You and the others who know the truth might be all that stands between ThunderClan and total chaos. Whatever happens, you must not let ThunderClan fall completely into darkness."

"I won't," Bristlefrost promised fervently.

But as she raced back through the forest toward the ThunderClan camp, her promise weighed on her as if she were trying to lift the Great Oak on her shoulders.

CHAPTER 3

Rootpaw scrambled out of the apprentices' den. Leafstar had called a Clan meeting, and most of his Clanmates were already gathered in a ragged circle around their leader as Rootpaw pattered up to sit with his parents, Violetshine and Tree.

His sister, Needlepaw, was standing there, too, her claws working nervously into the ground. Her black-and-white pelt was glossy and well groomed, and her eyes shone with a mixture of joy and apprehension.

"Good luck," Rootpaw whispered into her ear. "You deserve it."

Needlepaw turned to him, but she couldn't reply as Leafstar began to speak.

"Cats of SkyClan, we have gathered here for one of the happiest occasions in the life of a Clan," the leader began. "The making of a new warrior. Needlepaw, step forward."

Taking a deep breath, Needlepaw padded into the center of the circle and stood in front of her Clan leader.

"Reedclaw," Leafstar continued, turning toward Needlepaw's mentor, "has your apprentice, Needlepaw, learned the skills of a warrior, and does she understand the meaning of the warrior code?"

Reedclaw dipped her head respectfully to her leader. "She has and she does, Leafstar," she replied. "She's one of the most patient cats I've ever met, and that has done wonders for her hunting technique."

"Good," Leafstar meowed. "Then I, Leafstar, call upon my warrior ancestors to look down on this apprentice."

But are our warrior ancestors listening? Rootpaw asked himself, his pelt prickling uneasily. *Do they even know that Needlepaw is becoming a warrior?*

"She has trained hard to understand the ways of your noble code," the Clan leader continued, "and I commend her to you as a warrior in her turn. Needlepaw, do you promise to uphold the warrior code and to protect and defend your Clan, even at the cost of your life?"

Needlepaw raised her head, and her response rang out clearly across the camp. "I do."

"Then by the powers of StarClan I give you your warrior name. Needlepaw, from this moment on you will be known as Needleclaw. StarClan honors your skill and your patience, and we welcome you as a full warrior of SkyClan."

Leafstar stooped to rest her muzzle on Needleclaw's head, and the new warrior gave her leader's shoulder a respectful lick, then took a step backward. All the Clan burst into yowls and caterwauls to welcome their new warrior.

"Needleclaw! Needleclaw!"

Tree and Violetshine were both purring loudly as

Needleclaw faced her Clan as a warrior for the first time. Rootpaw thrust aside his doubts and joined in the acclamation. He was truly happy for his sister, but even so, he couldn't help feeling a little envious. Between his encounters with Bramblestar's spirit and worrying over the Clans being cut off from StarClan, he hadn't been able to focus on finishing his own training.

I've had more practice at trespassing on ThunderClan territory than learning my warrior skills.

As the caterwauls died away, Rootpaw caught Dewspring's gaze. His mentor gave him a stern look, and Rootpaw knew he wanted to say that his apprentice should be there beside his sister, receiving his Clan's welcome. Hot shame scoured through Rootpaw, and he hung his head, knowing that Dewspring was right.

But how can I keep my mind on my training when the stuff that's distracting me is so important for every cat in every Clan?

Two nights had passed since Shadowsight had disappeared, and so far no cat had the slightest idea what had happened to him. As if that weren't worrying enough, Rootpaw hadn't seen Bramblestar's spirit again since that same night.

Rootpaw shuddered. He knew that Bristlefrost, at least, believed that the false Bramblestar had tried to lead dogs to attack Sparkpelt. Sparkpelt had gotten away, but didn't that prove how ruthless the impostor was? If he'd wanted to get rid of Shadowsight, he might have done something terrible.

As he headed toward the medicine cats' den to collect their soiled bedding, Rootpaw couldn't get Bramblestar's last message out of his head. The spirit had seemed so faint. Maybe it was becoming harder and harder for him to communicate with living cats.

What will happen if Bramblestar's spirit fades away? Rootpaw asked himself. *Will he die for good? What about his nine lives? And if he dies, will ThunderClan be stuck with that intruder in his body forever?*

Rootpaw shuddered to think what that evil presence might do to ThunderClan if he was left in charge for much longer.

"Greetings. Please take me to your Clan leader."

Rootpaw froze at the sound of that hauntingly familiar voice, letting his claws sink into the ground. Had Bramblestar's spirit returned after all? Relief bubbled up inside his chest. *He's a pain in the tail, but I have kind of missed him. But then, why is he asking for Leafstar . . . ?*

Rootpaw whipped around to see that it wasn't Bramblestar's spirit who had spoken. It was Bramblestar's *body*. The interloper was here, in the SkyClan camp!

Sneaking closer, Rootpaw ducked behind two warriors crouched near the fresh-kill pile and watched as Bramblestar approached across the camp. Sparrowpelt was leading him toward Leafstar's den. Two ThunderClan warriors flanked their leader. The small white she-cat closest to Rootpaw was Whitewing, and on the other side of Bramblestar, Rootpaw recognized the pale gray pelt of Bristlefrost.

Rootpaw's pads prickled with excitement when he saw her, but he forced himself to stay calm and out of sight. This wasn't the time to start padding after a cat from another Clan. This looked serious. There was no threat in the gaze or demeanor of any of the three cats, but Bramblestar had clearly come to speak to Leafstar, leader to leader. *That wouldn't happen unless it was* really *important.*

Rootpaw remembered anxiously that he hadn't told Leafstar that the creature leading ThunderClan wasn't the real Bramblestar. After the encounter in the forest, he had left it up to Frecklewish and Fidgetflake, as the SkyClan medicine cats, to enlighten their leader, but he was sure that so far they hadn't done so. As far as he knew, the medicine cats hadn't spoken privately with Leafstar since that night, and Leafstar hadn't said anything to warn her Clan about strange happenings beyond their borders.

As if his thoughts had summoned them, Frecklewish appeared out of the medicine cats' den, with Fidgetflake close behind her. Rootpaw spotted them exchanging a glance, and saw how awkward and frustrated they both looked.

I guess they wish they had told Leafstar before this. . . .

Rootpaw's pelt itched with the need to find out why Bramblestar had come to the SkyClan camp. He scuttled rapidly across the open ground between him and Leafstar's den and skidded into cover around the back of the stump. Angling his ears forward, he listened as hard as he could, at the same time patting the debris around the oak roots with his paws.

If any cat asks, I can say I'm tidying up around the leader's den.

Ruefully he recognized that this wasn't exactly how a warrior should behave, but he knew that what he was doing was more important.

Though Rootpaw couldn't see Leafstar from where he was

hiding, he could tell that she had emerged from her den in the split at the bottom of the Tallstump and was standing in the entrance. Bramblestar and his escort were close by.

"I have called an emergency Gathering for tonight, because of Shadowsight's disappearance," Bramblestar announced, his voice carrying clearly to Rootpaw. "We in ThunderClan have stepped up our punishment and exile of the codebreakers who were named in his vision, and we think all the Clans must do the same. If Shadowsight is not strong enough to enforce his vision—"

"What makes you think Shadowsight isn't strong enough?" Leafstar interrupted. "Do you have any idea what happened to him?"

"Yes, I have an idea," Bramblestar responded. "And I'll share it at the Gathering tonight. In the meantime, Leafstar, you should make sure that you punish any codebreaking cats in your own Clan. It's vital for us all to do that, so that StarClan will know we're serious about following the warrior code."

I wonder how Leafstar will react to that, Rootpaw thought anxiously. His paws went still as he strained to hear his leader's answer.

Leafstar's tone was distinctly chilly as she responded. "With respect, Bramblestar, who are you to come here and tell me how to run my Clan?" Rootpaw had to slap his tail over his jaws to stop himself yowling in glee, hearing his leader stand up to the interloper. "For a start," Leafstar went on, "none of my warriors were named in Shadowsight's vision. For another thing, breaking the code has *always* been serious to SkyClan. Nothing has happened to change that, and I will continue punishing any culprits just as I always have."

Bramblestar's only reply to that was a dismissive grunt. "Tension between ThunderClan and ShadowClan was high at the last Gathering," he continued. "And I've heard rumblings that Tigerstar is quite distraught about Shadowsight's disappearance. What if he uses it to accuse other Clans of wrongdoing, or suggest that we don't enforce the code as good leaders should?"

The impostor paused, waiting for a reply, but Leafstar said nothing. After a few heartbeats Bramblestar spoke again.

"Eventually the Clans will need to take sides," he growled. "Those who are willing to commit to getting StarClan back no matter the cost . . . and those who are not."

Still there was no response from Leafstar. Bramblestar let out an angry snort. "Be there tonight!" he snarled.

Rootpaw heard his paw steps retreating, and Bristlefrost and Whitewing following. When he was sure they had left the camp, he slipped out of his hiding place to see Leafstar sitting at the entrance to her den, her tail wrapped around her forepaws and a thoughtful look in her eyes.

As Rootpaw watched, she rose to her paws and let out a commanding yowl. "Let all cats old enough to catch their own prey join here beside the Tallstump for a Clan meeting!"

Confident now that no cat would ask where he had been or what he had been doing, Rootpaw strode out into the center of the camp and sat beside Tree and Violetshine, who glanced at each other warily as they reappeared from the warriors' den. "Another meeting?" Tree asked in a hushed voice. "What now?" Rootpaw could see his father's confusion reflected in the expressions of several of the gathering warriors.

Needleclaw bounded over to join them. The two medicine cats left their den to sit near Leafstar, while the apprentice Wrenpaw scampered up to the side of her mentor, Rabbitleap. More warriors emerged from their den until almost the whole of SkyClan was assembled. The deputy, Hawkwing, was the last to appear, and padded over to sit at his leader's side, glancing at Leafstar with a questioning look.

"Some of you know that I have just had a visit from Bramble-star," Leafstar began, her gaze traveling seriously around her Clan. "He has called us to an emergency Gathering tonight, and he also tells me we must punish the codebreakers in our Clan so that we can reconnect with StarClan. If any of you have any thoughts about that, now is the time to share them with the rest of us."

"Do we *have* any codebreakers?" Plumwillow spoke up from somewhere behind Rootpaw.

"Of course not!" Sagenose replied indignantly.

"I don't know. . . ." Plumwillow's voice went on, and Root-paw glanced over his shoulder to see the dark gray she-cat working her claws worriedly into the ground. "We *must* recon-nect with StarClan. It's been moons since we last heard from them, and the frost seems to be over. So maybe we should investigate whether there *are* any codebreakers in our Clan."

"Yes, and if there are, exile them!" Plumwillow's mate, Sandynose, asserted.

"Fox dung to that!" Macgyver snarled. "Exile our Clanmates on the say-so of another Clan leader? Maybe ThunderClan is just trying to make trouble in the other Clans. Every cat knows how they like to interfere."

"Yes, we never had trouble reaching our ancestors in StarClan when we still lived in the gorge," Sparrowpelt agreed.

Leafstar blinked, still thoughtful, not giving away anything of what she felt. After a moment she turned to Hawkwing. "What do you think?" she asked him.

The dark gray tom dipped his head. "I think that causing trouble isn't like ThunderClan," he meowed. "Sometimes they like to have a paw in every cat's business, but as far as I know they've never been *destructive*. I'd like to find out what Bramblestar hopes to achieve."

Rootpaw's belly tightened. Should he tell them what he knew? To his surprise, before he could speak, he saw Frecklewish rise to her paws and pad forward to stand beside Leafstar.

"There's something I should have told you before," she confessed, "but I was afraid of what it might mean for all the Clans." She paused, looking around at the gathered cats with trepidation. "The truth is . . . Bramblestar is *not* the Bramblestar we all know. I saw the real Bramblestar on the night Shadowsight disappeared. He was a ghost, wandering far away from his body."

Admiration tingled through Rootpaw as he listened to the

medicine cat. Frecklewish was taking a brave step, telling the whole Clan even though the other medicine cats had been unwilling to tell even their leaders. *But I can't blame her. . . . She's doing what's best for our Clan.*

As Frecklewish finished speaking, the Clan remained in a stunned silence for several heartbeats, cats blinking in confusion and trying to make sense of what they had just heard.

"Have you got bees in your brain?" Sparrowpelt growled at last. "Whoever heard of a cat's spirit wandering out of his body?"

As if the senior warrior had given a signal, the Clan erupted into yowls of protest, disbelief, and fear. Leafstar let the noise continue for a few heartbeats, then raised her tail for silence. "Enough!" she meowed sternly.

"How could this be?" she wondered when the Clan was quiet enough for her to make herself heard. She directed her amber gaze toward Tree. "Did you have something to do with this?" she asked.

Rootpaw was aware of Frecklewish's gaze on him. She expected him to speak up, he realized. For a moment he hesitated, still reluctant to admit in front of every cat that he was as weird as his father.

Before he could, Tree stood up with a brief nod toward Leafstar. "I've seen Bramblestar's ghost, too," he meowed.

That isn't a lie, Rootpaw thought. *Tree saw Bramblestar at the medicine-cat meeting.* But it wasn't the whole story, not by a fox-length.

"Oh, so he's another of your ghosts, Tree," Sagenose mewed with a long, elaborate yawn. "Thought so."

The mockery in Sagenose's words gave Rootpaw the courage he needed. He was ashamed and grateful that Tree had tried to shield him from the Clan's scrutiny, but he knew he couldn't sit still and let his father take all the criticism. He sprang to his paws.

"Actually, I was the one who saw the ghost first," he announced. "I've been seeing it for moons now, ever since Bramblestar died in the cold and Shadowsight tried to bring him back."

"Yeah, sure, and hedgehogs fly," Harrybrook sneered.

A few of the others murmured agreement with the gray tom. Rootpaw tried to read Leafstar's expression, but she was giving nothing away. He closed his eyes, concentrating hard to focus on Bramblestar and call out to his spirit, hoping that he might be able to appear again.

That might be the only way to prove what Frecklewish and I are saying.

But no ghost responded to Rootpaw's call. He could feel that Bramblestar was far away from the SkyClan camp. Rootpaw could only hope that the ThunderClan leader was still out there somewhere.

"Why would Bramblestar appear to you?" Macgyver asked. He wasn't mocking Rootpaw like Harrybrook, but he couldn't hide the fact that he didn't believe a word Rootpaw had said. "If he had to come to a cat with the Sisters' blood, why not Tree?"

"I don't know!" Rootpaw retorted. He faced Macgyver, his pelt bristling with indignation. "But I'm telling the truth. I saw him!"

"So did I," Frecklewish asserted, while Fidgetflake nodded agreement.

"And me. Seeing ghosts is very different from the visions of the medicine cats," Fidgetflake went on, with a hard look at the cats who had voiced their disbelief. "But that doesn't seem to make it any less real."

The SkyClan cats were muttering together, exchanging uneasy glances as if none of them knew what to make of Rootpaw's story. Rootpaw stood listening, his belly roiling with tension as he wondered what their verdict would be, and what Leafstar would decide. He gave a start of surprise as he felt a tail rest on his shoulder, and turned his head to see his mentor, Dewspring, standing by his side.

"There's one thing that occurs to me," Dewspring began, raising his voice to be heard over the chattering. "Bramblestar has always been an honorable cat in the past. Does any cat feel that this recent behavior is *like* him?"

Warm with gratitude, Rootpaw realized that his mentor must believe him, and the rest of his Clanmates were listening, thinking over what he had just said.

Maybe now Dewspring will understand why my mind hasn't been totally on my training. . . .

Eventually Leafstar waved her tail to quiet the Clan once more. "I don't know what to make of any of this," she admitted. "I trust my medicine cats, and I know that Tree and

Rootpaw are loyal Clan members. I want to believe them, but I *don't* want to believe that some mysterious spirit cat is driving ThunderClan to exile its warriors." She paused for a moment to give her chest fur a thoughtful lick. "The stakes of being wrong are so high," she continued. "SkyClan is still the new Clan around the lake; if we accuse Bramblestar of being an impostor, we could start a war."

"Maybe we should do just that!" Sandynose put in. Plum-willow gave him an irritated nudge.

Leafstar gave Sandynose a chilly nod, as if she had heard his suggestion but didn't think much of it. "SkyClan lived alone for a very long time," she went on. "We haven't faced as many battles as the cats who have been living by the lake for all these moons—and in their old forest for seasons before that. In battle many cats die—not just the bad ones. I believe that Tree and Rootpaw are trying to help, but I haven't seen enough yet to risk cats' lives."

The hope that Rootpaw had begun to feel faded abruptly at his leader's decision. *But it's true, what she says,* he admitted to himself. *It must be really tough for a leader to lead her cats to their death.*

"Then what are we going to do?" Sparrowpelt asked.

"No matter what, there is one thing SkyClan will always do," Leafstar replied. "We will protect one another."

The decisiveness in Leafstar's voice made Rootpaw think that the meeting must be over, until Violetshine rose to her paws. "Of course you are right," she began, dipping her head toward Leafstar. "But if Bramblestar is violent toward other cats, especially those in his own Clan—cats he is supposed to care for—then he must be stopped." Her voice shook a little as she added, "I learned about that from Darktail."

Rootpaw stared at his mother. *She must feel very strongly to mention Darktail. Normally she never talks about that part of her life.*

Leafstar met Violetshine's gaze thoughtfully. "That's true," she meowed at last. "So it's decided. We will protect one another. And we will keep our eyes and ears on Bramblestar, and do our best to prevent him from hurting any other cat."

The Clan leader half turned away, perhaps to go back to her den, then swung around to face her Clan again. "There's one more thing," she added, beckoning with her tail to the two medicine cats. "Frecklewish, you said that Rootpaw's and Tree's ghost-seeing is as true as medicine-cat visions. So it seems obvious to me we should be asking ourselves: Should Rootpaw be apprenticed to you to become a medicine cat?"

Rootpaw let out a gasp, too shocked by the suggestion to comment on it. Frecklewish was shaking her head uncertainly. "I've never heard of a medicine cat with his abilities. . . ."

"That doesn't mean there can't be one," Leafstar told her briskly.

"Of course we could always use another medicine cat," Frecklewish responded. She gave Rootpaw a look from narrowed eyes, as if he were an unknown herb that might be good for healing or might turn out to be poisonous. "But I can't say Rootpaw has ever shown much interest in the job."

At last Leafstar turned to Rootpaw. "What do you think, Rootpaw?" she asked. "Would you be willing to try?"

Rootpaw realized he was gaping at his Clan leader. "I—I'm

not sure," he stammered. "I'd rather be a warrior, but if I'm needed as a medicine cat, I'll serve my Clan the best way I can."

Maybe this is a good thing, he tried to tell himself. *At least being a medicine cat is a sort of okay way to be weird!*

Leafstar turned back to her Clan and raised her voice once again. "Then it is decided. Rootpaw will become a medicine-cat apprentice," she announced.

At her words, Rootpaw's belly felt like it had fallen out past his paws and down into the earth. An image of Bristlefrost flashed into his mind, her sleek gray fur and graceful movements, and he suddenly remembered the drawbacks of what he had just promised to do.

My apprenticeship will last even longer, *and I'll be further behind Needleclaw. And maybe even worse—I'll never be able to take a mate. . . .*

CHAPTER 4

❧

Bristlefrost plodded through the mud, following Bramblestar and Whitewing through the thorn tunnel and back into the ThunderClan camp. Bramblestar didn't bother to dismiss them; without a word he headed across the camp and up the tumbled rocks to his den on the Highledge.

Whitewing exchanged a friendly glance with Bristlefrost. "You'd better go and help yourself to fresh-kill," she suggested. "You deserve it after that."

Bristlefrost nodded in gratitude. She felt every muscle in her body relax at the relief of getting out of the rain and away from Bramblestar for a while. Ever since he had exiled Lionblaze and Jayfeather the day before, he had been poking his nose into the business of every cat in the Clan: not just keeping a paw on their welfare, as a Clan leader should, but popping up inside their dens or listening in on conversations, looking for excuses to send more warriors away.

Meanwhile, Bramblestar had spent a lot of that time with Bristlefrost, but the attention he paid her seemed different. It was like she was exempt from his suspicion. He treated her like a cat he could trust to do as she was told. Now that he had gone for a rest, Bristlefrost felt as if she had escaped from a fox's den. She spotted Stemleaf and Spotfur sharing tongues under a tree beside the fresh-kill pile, and bounded over to join them.

"Thank StarClan that's over!" she mewed with a gusty sigh as she flopped down beside them.

"What happened in SkyClan?" Spotfur asked, while Stemleaf snagged a vole from the pile and pushed it over to Bristlefrost.

Bristlefrost took a hungry bite and mumbled her reply through a mouthful of delicious vole. "I'm not sure." After swallowing, she went on. "Leafstar didn't seem convinced by Bramblestar urging her to exile more cats."

"Good for her," Spotfur commented.

"But it doesn't help much," Stemleaf reminded his mate. Under his breath he added, "There's still no sign of Shadowsight. Could Bramblestar have *killed* him?"

"No cat has found his body, or any blood," Spotfur pointed out, while Bristlefrost shivered at having her worst fear put into words. "If Shadowsight was dead, there would be some evidence of it, surely?"

Stemleaf shook his head slowly. "It could have been covered up. Or maybe he's being kept prisoner somewhere."

"One thing I'm certain of," Bristlefrost meowed. "Bramblestar is wrong when he says that Shadowsight ran off."

"He would never do that," Spotfur agreed. "He—"

She broke off as Stemleaf stretched out his tail to touch her shoulder, giving her a warning glance. Bristlefrost glanced around to see Stemleaf's father, Thornclaw, bounding over to join them.

Has Stemleaf told Thornclaw what we suspect about Bramblestar? she wondered. *No, he can't have, or he wouldn't have hushed Spotfur.*

Bristlefrost's muscles tensed briefly as she reflected on how many ThunderClan cats knew nothing about the false Bramblestar. She and the other rebels didn't know which cats they could trust. Seeing Stemleaf so tense around his own father, she was reminded how easily the Clan could be divided if they revealed their suspicions too early, without proof. *ThunderClan could be torn apart,* she thought with a shiver. *We must all tread very carefully.*

"Greetings," Thornclaw meowed cheerfully as he sat beside them and chose a mouse from the fresh-kill pile. "The prey was running well today, despite the weather," he continued. "I'm sure now that newleaf is here, things will start to get better."

"I hope so," Stemleaf commented, though Bristlefrost thought he looked dubious. "Might be nice to see the sun again, though."

"Are you worried that StarClan is sending this terrible weather, too?" Thornclaw tore off a mouthful of mouse and swallowed it. "I gather you're not alone, but don't read too much into it. I admit I don't always understand StarClan, but they'll explain themselves sooner or later, you can count on it."

"But do they really want us to exile our own Clanmates?" Bristlefrost asked. As soon as the words left her mouth, she wondered if she had been too daring. *What if Thornclaw reports what I said to Bramblestar?*

But Thornclaw didn't seem at all worried about her question. "You're young, and of course you worry about these sorts of decisions," he purred. "But after what I experienced in the Dark Forest—well, I'm willing to do what's necessary, and now I'm sure things will settle down. StarClan will be back soon, you'll see."

Bristlefrost narrowly avoided rolling her eyes, while Stemleaf and Spotfur exchanged another uneasy glance.

"I'm sure you're right, Thornclaw," Stemleaf meowed.

Quickly finishing her vole, Bristlefrost excused herself and bounded back to the warriors' den. Outside, she spotted her brother, Flipclaw, who was balancing precariously halfway up the outer wall; water dripped from his nose as he wove a bramble tendril into a gap that had opened up in the high winds the night before.

"Hi!" Bristlefrost called up to him, pleased to see a familiar and friendly face. "That's a great job you're doing."

Flipclaw glanced down at her, and the look in his eyes wasn't friendly at all. "You wouldn't know a great job if it sat up and bit you," he mewed coldly. "Or you wouldn't have been so eager to turn your back on Jayfeather and Lionblaze, after all they've done for the Clan."

The barbed comment shocked Bristlefrost so much that for a few heartbeats she couldn't find words to reply. Her brother leaped down from the den wall and stalked past her before she recovered. Bristlefrost gazed sadly after him.

I should have told him what I did for the exiles, she thought. *But he didn't give me the chance.*

She wanted to curl up in her nest and sleep, forgetting all her problems for a while, but as she was padding up to the entrance of the den, she spotted Finleap. The brown tom was crouching with hunched shoulders underneath an elder bush that grew in a crack in the den wall below the Highledge, avoiding the rain. He looked so unhappy that Bristlefrost felt sorry for him, and she trotted over to sit beside him.

"Twigbranch will be okay," she murmured in an attempt to comfort him.

"I know she will," Finleap responded, "but that doesn't make it all right. Why should we expel our Clanmates like this? Why should I have to lose the cat I love because Bramblestar says so?"

His voice rose on the last few words; Bristlefrost felt all her muscles tense, and she glanced around to see if any cat might have overheard him. She touched her nose to his shoulder in a warning gesture, but Finleap hardly seemed aware of her.

"Why would StarClan want this?" he asked, growing even more impassioned. "I did the same thing—I left the Clan I was born in—and I wasn't named as a codebreaker!"

"For StarClan's sake, be quiet!" Bristlefrost hissed. She didn't want to sound so fierce, but for Finleap's own sake he had to stop protesting so loudly. "Remember, it's Bramblestar's order, and the code tells us we have to do what he says."

Finleap gave her a long, melancholy stare. "I'm disappointed in you," he mewed. "We might not know each other well, but I always thought you had a mind of your own."

Before Bristlefrost could respond to the accusation, an

irritated yowl came from the Highledge above. "What cat is screeching down there when I'm trying to rest?"

Horrified, Bristlefrost leaped to her paws. She had forgotten how close she and Finleap were to the Clan leader's den; now she looked up to see Bramblestar peering blearily down from the Highledge. Beside her, Finleap was standing stiff-legged, his ears laid back and his shoulder fur bristling. Bristlefrost was terrified that he would challenge their leader.

"I'm sorry, Bramblestar!" she called quickly. "It's okay. Finleap and I were just having a stupid argument." She paused for a moment, then added, "May I please speak to you in private?"

Bramblestar hesitated, then replied with a grunt and jerked his head to invite her to come up. Finleap relaxed his hostile stance and gave Bristlefrost another disappointed look before turning his back on her and heading toward the warriors' den.

Bristlefrost climbed up the tumbled rocks and onto the Highledge. *I'd better think of something to talk about—and fast,* she told herself, her thoughts whirling uselessly like a startled nest of bees.

Bramblestar had returned to his den; when Bristlefrost reached the entrance, she saw that he was sprawled out on the heap of moss and bracken against the back wall.

"Come in," he growled. "What do you want?"

Bristlefrost had only asked for the meeting to separate Bramblestar and Finleap.

"I just wanted to ask if you're okay," she meowed. "It's great that StarClan will be back with us soon."

Bramblestar flexed his claws. "I'm doing fine," he rumbled.

"But what can you tell me about the rest of the Clan?"

"Oh, they're doing fine, too," Bristlefrost assured him, desperately eager. In reality she was finding it hard to carry on the conversation—she was too distracted by the terrible state of the den. "You know, they're all a little wet, but in good spirits."

Bramblestar's bedding was lumpy and smelled stale. It looked as if it hadn't been changed for a moon, and there were prey bones and scraps of fur scattered everywhere. They were giving off a reek, too.

It was never like this before Squirrelflight left, Bristlefrost thought. *Has Bramblestar been forbidding the apprentices to clean it up? Why would he do that?*

Even while Bristlefrost was talking to him, the false Bramblestar seemed listless and lethargic, stretching his jaws in a massive yawn instead of paying attention to her.

Bristlefrost couldn't think of any reason for this unknown spirit cat to have taken over Bramblestar's body, except to become leader of ThunderClan. But now that he had achieved what he wanted, he didn't seem to be hopeful or pleased about it. Instead he seemed depressed, like he had lost interest in what it meant actually to *be* a leader.

Most of the ThunderClan warriors hadn't noticed Bramblestar's apathy, because Berrynose had made sure that the routine duties of the Clan were taken care of.

He may be a real pain in the tail, but he's not a bad deputy.

Several times Bristlefrost had overheard Berrynose giving orders to other warriors, claiming that they came from

Bramblestar, when she knew that Bramblestar hadn't given any orders at all. Stemleaf, Spotfur, and Alderheart had noticed the change, too, but what could so few cats do about it?

A chill like the tapping of icy claws ran down Bristlefrost's back as she met the hard amber gaze of the impostor. *Who is this cat?* she asked herself. *What does he really want?* The code-breakers Shadowsight had named were gone from the Clan. That had seemed to be the false Bramblestar's goal, but now that he had achieved it, his success clearly wasn't making him happy. *So why is he doing it? Who is this?*

Bristlefrost could find no answer to her questions.

The night sky was blotched with clouds as Bristlefrost padded beside Bramblestar and Berrynose on their way to the emergency Gathering. Fitful gleams of moon and starlight struggled to break through the covering, and the forest lay in deep darkness as the ThunderClan warriors brushed through the undergrowth.

Every step was an effort, and Bristlefrost would have much preferred to curl up in her nest and forget her troubles for a while in sleep. Her kin and most of her friends were still keeping their distance from her; clearly they assumed that she supported Bramblestar and his harsh punishments.

From the looks they're giving me, you'd think I'd rolled in dog dung!

Before they had left the stone hollow more than a few fox-lengths behind, Bristlefrost realized that Bramblestar was paying keen attention to the forest around them, his eyes wide and his ears pricked alertly. He was completely different from the listless cat of earlier that day.

Now what does he think he's doing?

Soon Bramblestar halted and plunged his nose into a thick growth of moss on the root of an oak tree, sniffing deeply. Turning to Bristlefrost, he asked her, "Is that Squirrelflight's scent? Has she been here?"

Bristlefrost wasn't sure how to react. She knew very well that far too many days had passed since Squirrelflight's banishment for her scent to have survived on ThunderClan territory. But why was Bramblestar asking? Was he looking for reassurance that the exiled deputy was gone?

Hoping to please him, she took a sniff of the moss. *It smells like . . . moss.* "I'm not sure," she replied to Bramblestar. "It could be."

Bramblestar gave her a curt nod and continued toward the lake, but he was still watchful, and a few paces farther on he stopped to sniff at the debris beneath a holly bush and asked Bristlefrost the same question. There was a strange, wistful look in his eyes. Bristlefrost tried to keep her answers vague. She knew that Squirrelflight was living on ShadowClan territory, but she dared not give the interloper the least hint of that.

Even when Bramblestar and the rest of the cats reached the lakeshore and crossed into WindClan territory, the impostor still kept up his search for Squirrelflight.

Why? Bristlefrost wondered. *Does he feel threatened by her? Does he think she might come back and try to take leadership of the Clan?* Then she saw how Bramblestar's tail began to droop with disappointment when he couldn't find any definite traces of the former deputy. Bristlefrost realized there must be something more behind his search. *He misses her.*

But then why had he sent Squirrelflight away in the first place?

As soon as she pushed her way through the bushes into the clearing around the Great Oak, Bristlefrost was aware of tension in the air. Cats were glaring at one another, their shoulder fur twitching and their tail-tips flicking back and forth. She realized that one wrong word could break the Gathering truce and lead to all-out fighting.

We couldn't be more jumpy if we were gathering in a badger's den!

Because Bramblestar had paused so often in his search for Squirrelflight, the ThunderClan cats were the last to arrive. Tigerstar was scraping his claws impatiently on the bark of the Great Oak as Bramblestar hauled his way up the trunk and settled himself in a fork between two branches.

"You took your time," Tigerstar snapped. "Why did you call this Gathering just to keep us all waiting?"

Bramblestar ignored the question, and after a couple of heartbeats the ShadowClan leader rose to his paws and addressed the Gathering.

"Shadowsight is still missing," he announced. "If any cat has seen or scented him, for StarClan's sake tell me now."

A sympathetic murmur arose from the cats in the clearing. Bristlefrost, who was sitting close to the oak roots with Stemleaf and Spotfur, wished that she could tell Tigerstar something that would help, but she knew that there had been no trace of Shadowsight on ThunderClan territory since the night he disappeared.

As Tigerstar waited for a response, he flexed his claws in and out, his ears flattened in distress. The loss of a young cat was a terrible burden for any Clan, and this was not just any cat: This was a ShadowClan medicine cat, and, more important still, Tigerstar's son.

"Something *happened* to Shadowsight," Tigerstar went on, his voice distraught. "He wouldn't just leave without telling any cat. That means something—or some *cat*—attacked him."

Tigerstar's accusation was met with a thick silence. The tension in the clearing mounted until Bristlefrost could feel it in every hair on her pelt, as if a whole nest of ants were crawling through her fur. She clamped her jaws tight shut to stop herself letting out a yowl of fear and frustration.

Her thoughts flew back to the night when she had seen the false Bramblestar returning to camp, his chest fur matted with blood. It hurt like a fox's fangs to suspect that the ThunderClan leader had had something to do with Shadowsight's disappearance. But she stood by her decision not to accuse him. She had no evidence; if she brought this up, she would give away her hostility to Bramblestar for nothing. If the false Bramblestar stopped trusting her, how would she be able to work against him? Without proof, would any cat in ThunderClan believe her? The real Bramblestar would never have hurt a medicine cat.

Bramblestar let the silence drag on for several heartbeats before he rose to his paws and advanced along the closest branch until he could easily look down on the cats in the clearing. He surveyed them all calmly, and when he began to speak, his tones were clear and decisive. Bristlefrost felt a shock of surprise contrasting this cat, in command of himself and the situation, with the miserable lump of fur she had encountered earlier in his den.

"Tigerstar," Bramblestar began, "it's time to stop looking for Shadowsight." He raised a paw as Tigerstar opened his jaws to protest. "I understand you don't want to believe your son would leave," he continued kindly, "but there's no evidence of an attack of any sort. There's no sign of him or his corpse. We must assume that he has run away from the Clans. Probably he has gone to be a kittypet, where he can forget all about the difficult job of speaking for StarClan."

Bristlefrost's heart sank as she listened to Bramblestar. *He makes it sound so reasonable!*

She saw Tigerstar's shoulder fur began to rise at the suggestion that his son would ever want to be a kittypet, but when he replied to Bramblestar, his voice was tightly controlled.

"Why would Shadowsight do that?" he asked. "He loved being a medicine cat."

"He *did*," Bramblestar agreed. "Until one of his parents was named as a codebreaker."

Now all of Tigerstar's fur bristled, and he dug his claws hard into the branch where he was standing. Bristlefrost's belly lurched in fear that the ShadowClan leader would leap at Bramblestar and tear his throat out, right here at the Gathering.

Is that what Bramblestar wants? she asked herself. *Does he want to start an all-out war among the Clans, and have Tigerstar disgrace StarClan as well?* No cat knew how StarClan would react to some cat breaking the Gathering truce.

She glanced upward to see if clouds were covering the moon as the sign of StarClan's anger. But the sky had not changed: Faint gleams of light were still struggling through the cloud covering. *Maybe an emergency Gathering is different,* she thought. *There's no full moon. And anyway, it's been so long since StarClan gave us any sort of sign. . . .*

Tigerstar held himself very still, fixing Bramblestar with an icy glare and keeping a tight grip on his self-control. "You're wrong, Bramblestar," he rasped.

Bramblestar dismissed his words with a flick of his tail. "Cats of all Clans," he began, addressing the Gathering, "you no longer have a choice. Moons have passed since StarClan last communicated with us, and their intent could not be clearer. Their demands are hard to bear, but there's no doubt that obeying them is the right thing to do. We must exile each and every one of the named codebreakers. They must leave the lake, or StarClan will never return to us. I have already sent Jayfeather and Lionblaze away."

Bristlefrost noticed that Bramblestar didn't mention Twigbranch, and she wondered if he was hiding the fact that he had given her the chance to atone.

As the impostor finished speaking, yowls broke out among the cats in the clearing: some protesting, while others sounded simply confused. Bristlefrost saw many cats glancing around, and she knew they were trying to work out which of their Clanmates they would have to send away.

She noticed that Crowfeather and Mothwing were both there in the clearing; they would be among the first cats who had to leave if the Clans agreed to exile their codebreakers. Dovewing wasn't there, but she too was a cat who had broken the code in the most flagrant way possible.

Meanwhile, Harestar of WindClan had risen from the branch where he was sitting, a tail-length above Bramblestar. His chest was heaving, and his voice was unsteady as he spoke.

"Crowfeather was named as a codebreaker," he began, "and he's my deputy. I can't lose him to this! Many of the codebreakers are good cats. And Shadowsight's vision is the word of one cat, a cat who—no offense, Tigerstar—seems to have left the Clans. Can this truly be what StarClan wants?"

Bramblestar tilted his head to one side as he looked up at Harestar. "Shadowsight's disappearance is proof that this has to be done," he responded calmly. "Clearly, he ran away because he saw the truth. His own mother, as a codebreaker, must be exiled. It's difficult and painful to do StarClan's bidding, but we have no alternative, if we're to have any hope of seeing the spirits of our warrior ancestors again. Shadowsight understood that. He gave us our orders, but he left because he wasn't strong enough to see it through."

At his words, Tigerstar let out a growl, positioning himself to launch his body at Bramblestar. The impostor seemed unaware of the younger leader's hostility—or perhaps, Bristlefrost thought, he simply didn't care.

She knew that she had to stop a fight breaking out. She didn't dare speak, but she leaped to her paws and took a pace or two toward the Great Oak so that Tigerstar could look down at her. Gazing up at him fervently, she tried to tell him, *Stop! You have to play along for now, or all our plans will fall apart!*

Tigerstar's eyes widened in understanding. He shook his head slightly but retreated a pace, keeping his gaze firmly fixed on Bramblestar.

"I don't want to do this," Harestar went on, regaining some control over himself. "But WindClan is suffering. This recent wind and rain is driving prey from the moor, and my cats are hungry."

Bramblestar nodded, a gleam in his amber gaze. "Of course they are! This is StarClan's punishment for not following their wishes." Glancing around at the assembled cats, he added, "WindClan's woes are a warning to all of us. If we don't enforce the code and send the codebreakers away, things will get worse, not better! Every cat here must realize that we need StarClan's guidance more than ever. And that means we have no choice."

The impostor bent his head and directed his gaze downward to where Crowfeather was seated with the other deputies on the roots of the Great Oak. As the dark gray tom looked back at him, a growl rose from deep within Crowfeather's chest, though he said nothing.

Crowfeather's son Breezepelt rose to his paws. "Harestar, you can't seriously mean to exile our deputy," he protested. "WindClan needs him."

"And we don't have to do it now," Breezepelt's mother, Nightcloud, added. "We can try to contact StarClan again and make sure it's the right thing to do."

Harestar let out a yowl of frustration. "We *can't* contact StarClan. That's the whole problem!"

Nightcloud let out a hiss and turned her back on her Clan leader.

Before any other cat could speak, Crowfeather rose and leaped down from his position on the gnarled oak root. "If I have to leave to save my Clan from conflict, then I will leave," he announced to the whole Gathering. "But I tell you this: It won't bring StarClan back. Today it's me, and the other cats named in Shadowsight's vision. But what happens when we're exiled and StarClan doesn't return? Who will be next?"

Without waiting for a response, he stalked across the clearing, his head and tail held high, and disappeared into the bushes, heading for the tree-bridge. Bristlefrost watched him go, doing her best to hide her admiration.

Crowfeather is putting his Clan first. And he's right: I'm sure exiling all these cats won't bring StarClan back.

Bristlefrost turned back to the Great Oak as she heard Mistystar begin to speak. The RiverClan leader was looking sorrowfully down at her medicine cat, Mothwing.

"I'm sorry, Mothwing," she meowed. "Your mother was a rogue and your father was the first Tigerstar, who, whatever he was, was not a RiverClan cat. I must send you into exile."

"But—" Mothwing began to protest, while her former apprentice, Willowshine, glared up at Mistystar with narrowed eyes and teeth bared in a snarl.

"We must try," Mistystar interrupted. "These heavy newleaf rains have brought flooding and mudslides to RiverClan, and prey has not been running well. I need StarClan's guidance, but StarClan has turned away from us. Perhaps Bramblestar is right; perhaps we have been too lax in following the warrior code, and that's why StarClan is angry with us. I have no choice but to exile you."

Mothwing rose to her paws. Bristlefrost was close enough to see the hurt in her eyes as she responded to her Clan leader. "I've been devoted to RiverClan ever since my mother brought me to you," she pointed out. "My own mother decided to leave the Clan, but I chose to stay!"

"You don't even follow StarClan," some cat muttered from among the RiverClan cats.

Mothwing's head whipped around in the direction of the voice. "That doesn't matter," she snapped. "I've proven my loyalty to my Clan many times over." She gazed up at Mistystar, not pleading any longer, but Bristlefrost could see how much she loved her Clan, and how crushed she was at the thought of exile.

"I'm sorry," Mistystar repeated. "Perhaps when all this is over, you will be able to return."

Mothwing's chest heaved in a deep sigh, and she bowed her head to her leader without any more protest. Then she turned and headed out of the clearing, following in Crowfeather's paw steps.

All around Bristlefrost the assembly broke up into small groups of cats, arguing whether it was right to exile the code-breakers. Dread swelled in her belly as she listened to the furious yowls and snarling.

This isn't a war between Clans, she realized. *It could be even worse.*

Each Clan seemed to be splintering into different factions, allying themselves with cats from other Clans, even if all they had in common was their feelings about the codebreakers. Bristlefrost could see the strength of five united Clans slipping away like water soaking into dry ground.

She noticed that Bramblestar had leaped down from the Great Oak and was circling the camp, listening to the chaos he had unleashed. Now and again he would speak up to defend Mistystar or Harestar against their own warriors.

In the confusion, Bristlefrost noticed Stemleaf creeping away, following Mothwing and Crowfeather. A spark of hope lit inside her that he would be able to find them and tell them that Tigerstar had offered refuge to the exiles in ShadowClan.

I just hope he doesn't get caught. . . .

CHAPTER 5

Rootpaw scrabbled uncertainly at the pile of dried leaves lying in front of him on the floor of the medicine-cat den. "Comfrey?" he guessed.

Fidgetflake rolled his eyes. "It's *tansy*, for StarClan's sake! Can't you smell the difference?"

Rootpaw nodded obligingly, but inwardly he was thinking that all these dried herbs smelled the same—dry and dusty. Suppressing a sigh, he reminded himself that being a medicine cat was a very important job. His Clan needed him, and he liked the way that every cat treated him with respect. But at the same time, he couldn't get rid of the nagging feeling that it would be a lot more fun to be out hunting on such a sunny day.

I want to do what's right for my Clan, but maybe I didn't think this whole medicine-cat thing through. This . . . isn't how I imagined my life would be.

Frecklewish turned from the back of the den where she had been sorting a pile of freshly gathered herbs. "While it's quiet, we should take advantage of the sunshine," she meowed, "and spread these herbs out to dry. It could start raining again at any time."

At once Rootpaw sprang to his paws. "Sure, I'll help," he offered, pleased at the chance to get out of the medicine cats' den.

"Not you, Rootpaw." Frecklewish ordered him back with a wave of her tail. "You need to keep memorizing those herbs!"

While she and Fidgetflake began transporting the fresh herbs out into the sunlight, Rootpaw headed for the niches at the back of the den where the dried supplies were kept. He tried to remember what the medicine cats had taught him about how to identify each herb, what it was used for, and where it was stored.

He sniffed doubtfully at the dried leaves in the first niche. *Marigold, maybe?*

At the same moment, Rootpaw heard stumbling paw steps as some cat entered the den. Turning, he saw Rabbitleap, and froze at the sight of his Clanmate's chest and muzzle covered with blood.

Rabbitleap's voice was surprisingly calm as he began, "Rootpaw, I need you to—"

Rootpaw didn't hear anything else as panic swept over him. *I need to take care of him, but what am I supposed to do?* "Frecklewish! Fidgetflake!" he yowled. "Help!"

Frecklewish immediately slipped back into the den. "He has a thorn in his paw, Rootpaw," she explained. "I thought you would be able to cope with that." She sighed. "Sit down, Rabbitleap."

"But . . . the blood!" Rootpaw exclaimed as he watched Frecklewish lick Rabbitleap's paw until she could grip the shank of the thorn in her teeth and draw it out.

"I'm sorry, Rootpaw," Rabbitleap mewed. "I didn't mean to scare you. I just caught a squirrel, and I didn't realize how much of the blood is still on my fur."

Every hair on Rootpaw's pelt grew hot with embarrassment. *What kind of medicine cat freezes at the sight of blood?*

"Don't worry, Rootpaw," Frecklewish reassured him. "Rabbitleap was only your first patient. It'll get easier as you learn more." She gave Rabbitleap's paw one final swipe with her tongue. "There. You'll be fine, Rabbitleap, but stay off that paw for the rest of today. And don't go treading on any more thorns!"

Rabbitleap ducked his head. "Thanks, Frecklewish. I was so keen to catch that big squirrel that I didn't have time to look where I was putting my paws." He smoothed his whiskers with one forepaw. "But I'm proud that I brought back such a good addition to the fresh-kill pile."

Rootpaw struggled with a sudden stab of jealousy. *I miss hunting for my Clan so much!*

As Rabbitleap left the den, Fidgetflake returned from his task of spreading out the herbs and began testing Rootpaw once again on what he had learned. Rootpaw did his best to concentrate, but he was thankful for another interruption as Puddleshine, the ShadowClan medicine cat, appeared at the entrance to the den, escorted by Plumwillow.

"My patrol found Puddleshine at the edge of the camp," Plumwillow explained. "He says he's looking for Rootpaw."

As soon as Plumwillow spoke, Rootpaw remembered that today there was a meeting of the rebel cats. *I almost forgot! And it will be harder to sneak out now that I'm a medicine-cat apprentice.*

Fidgetflake gave Puddleshine a curious look. "Why do you want our new medicine-cat apprentice?" he asked.

Puddleshine looked flustered, giving his chest fur a couple of awkward licks. "I . . . er . . . oh. Well." Rootpaw shot the medicine cat an apologetic look. *Clearly my new role is news to him.*

But Puddleshine stood up straight, recovering. "Actually . . . I want to consult him about a sick cat in ShadowClan."

"What?" Fidgetflake sounded confused. "Why would ShadowClan's medicine cat want help from Rootpaw? He isn't even officially an apprentice yet."

Puddleshine didn't have an answer to that, and Rootpaw couldn't think of any better excuse. Fortunately, Frecklewish came to their rescue.

"I expect he wants to help Rootpaw get more experience," she mewed smoothly. "Puddleshine, suppose I come to help you, and Rootpaw can come with us so he can learn. Fidgetflake, you can take care of any emergencies in SkyClan while we're away."

Fidgetflake still looked puzzled, but he didn't object, and retreated toward the herb stores, shaking his head as he went.

Frecklewish took the lead as she and Rootpaw left the camp with Puddleshine, heading toward SkyClan territory.

"Has there been any sign of Shadowsight?" she asked Puddleshine.

The ShadowClan medicine cat let out a long sigh. "No cat seems to know anything," he replied sadly. "We're all worried about him."

Rootpaw felt sickness rising in his belly as he thought about the friendly young medicine cat and all the terrible things that might have happened to him. It still pained him to wonder whether a cat could have hurt Shadowsight. In the past, it would never have occurred to him that any warrior would attack a medicine cat, but everything was so different now. And he didn't believe Shadowsight would have left the Clans on his own. Puddleshine seemed really concerned for his former apprentice, but what if he wasn't the kind cat that he appeared to be?

What if he knows something he's not telling us?

"Do you know anything you haven't told us about Shadow-sight?" Rootpaw asked Puddleshine, not caring that he was a lowly apprentice making blunt demands of an experienced medicine cat. *I'm worried about Shadowsight, so who cares what Puddleshine thinks?* "Perhaps we should have looked harder for him before we went to the Moonpool . . . if there was no reason for him to leave."

Puddleshine didn't seem offended at Rootpaw's abrupt words. "We did look around," he replied. "But when we didn't find him, I thought he had gone on ahead." He heaved another deep sigh. "Shadowsight has always been an unusual cat . . . a special cat. At first I hoped he had just wandered off and would be back soon, but that seems less and less likely now." He gave his tail a single lash, and his voice was unsteady as he went on. "You might blame me for not doing more, but you can't blame me more than I blame myself. I shouldn't have left him alone. And I should have given him better support when he was . . . when he was here."

Hearing the pause, Rootpaw realized that Puddleshine believed Shadowsight was probably dead. His suspicions of the medicine cat faded; hearing him now, no cat could doubt that Puddleshine was truly upset.

But is he right? Rootpaw wondered. *Is Shadowsight dead?*

It was terrible, but Rootpaw kept coming back to the dreadful possibility that another cat had killed Shadowsight. And the obvious culprit was the false Bramblestar. Rootpaw believed that the false Bramblestar had tried to kill Sparkpelt by having her attacked by dogs, because she had defied him. Shadowsight was the cat who had received the codebreaker visions, and so he supported the impostor's efforts, but recently he had begun to back away from the idea of exile. Did Bramblestar believe that he could get his way more easily if Shadowsight wasn't around?

Rootpaw shivered as if he had suddenly walked into a shower of icy rain. *Would the fake Bramblestar really murder a medicine cat? And if he did, am I in danger too? What would he do if he discovered that I can see the real Bramblestar's spirit?*

Together the three cats padded on through the trees until they reached the ShadowClan camp. As soon as they pushed through the bushes and brambles at the top of the hollow, Rootpaw could see how many cats were crowded into the space, and how tense they were feeling.

Squirrelflight and Cloverfoot were both trying to assign cats to hunting patrols, and as Rootpaw padded closer he could hear how icily polite they were being to each other.

"Remember that the exiled cats can't hunt near the borders," Cloverfoot meowed. "There's too much risk that they'll be spotted."

"Of course," Squirrelflight replied through clenched teeth. She looked like she wanted to say, *Tell me something I don't know.*

At the far side of the hollow, loud yowls of complaint were issuing from the warriors' den.

"Get your paw out of my ear, you stupid furball!"

"You can't put your nest there—that's my space!"

"Leave my bracken alone!"

Puddleshine let out a sigh and exchanged a glance with Frecklewish. "You can't blame them," he mewed. "There isn't enough room here for so many cats."

Frecklewish nodded. "And with Bramblestar acting so unpredictably, who knows whether he's going to stop with the codebreakers? I fear it's only going to get worse."

Near the entrance to Tigerstar's den, Crowfeather stood by himself, his disapproving gaze raking across the camp. "I should have expected that ThunderClan and ShadowClan wouldn't be able to get along," he meowed, not speaking to any cat directly, but loud enough for several cats nearby to hear him. "Not even when it's in every cat's best interest. I ran things much better as WindClan's deputy, but I won't poke my whiskers in if no cat cares to ask for my help."

While he was speaking, Tigerstar emerged from his den,

casting an annoyed glance at Crowfeather as he padded past him to greet Frecklewish and Rootpaw.

"This won't do," he began abruptly. "I can't put up much longer with ShadowClan being the shelter for all the outcast warriors. There are just too many cats in the camp." With a brusque nod to Frecklewish, he continued, "What's the news in SkyClan? Leafstar's the only other leader with enough sense not to listen to Bramblestar's demands. Do you think she'd be able to give shelter to some of these cats?"

Frecklewish exchanged a doubtful glance with Rootpaw, then shook her head. "Leafstar has decided that SkyClan will go along with Bramblestar for now," she replied, "as long as there's no evidence of Bramblestar hurting any cat. That means that, officially at least, it's four Clans against one. I'm sorry, Tigerstar, but this isn't a good time to try to move the exiled cats out of ShadowClan territory."

For a moment Rootpaw was afraid that the ShadowClan leader would explode in a burst of fury. But then Tigerstar's tail drooped with frustration and weariness, and Rootpaw noticed for the first time how thin and anxious he looked. Glancing across the camp, he spotted Dovewing near the fresh-kill pile; she looked just as ill as her mate.

I know how worried they must both be about Shadowsight.

As the hunting patrols finally headed out of the camp, Squirrelflight and Cloverfoot padded over to stand beside their leader.

"Are we going to have this confusion every day?" Squirrelflight asked. "I don't want to tread on your tail, Cloverfoot, but some of the exiles don't know which of us they should listen to."

"I'm not one to stay where I'm not wanted," Crowfeather meowed, stepping forward to join the group before Tigerstar could respond. "But why can't the exiled cats move to the old SkyClan camp that's now on ShadowClan territory? I know no cat has lived there for a while, but we could fix it up." He tilted his head toward the warriors' den, from where loud sounds of squabbling still split the air. "It would solve that problem, for sure."

Tigerstar looked worried for a moment; Rootpaw guessed that he didn't like the idea of cats from other Clans setting up their own camp on his territory. Then his expression cleared, and he gave a brisk nod. "You're right, Crowfeather. This can't go on. We'll give it a try."

"The rebel cats could meet there, too," Squirrelflight suggested. "That would make it less likely for outsiders to find out that ShadowClan is involved."

"Excellent," Crowfeather meowed with a satisfied flick of his ears. "I'll call the exiles together." He disappeared into the warriors' den, and Rootpaw heard his voice raised in a commanding yowl. "Cats who are not in ShadowClan, come here to me!"

"I know where the old camp used to be," Cloverfoot told Tigerstar. "I'll lead the exiles there."

"Some of them are out hunting," Squirrelflight pointed out. "I'll wait here until they're all back, and then bring them along."

Tigerstar waved his tail in agreement and let out a sigh of relief. "Then maybe we'll get a bit of peace around here."

But Rootpaw saw the anxiety still lurking in Tigerstar's eyes, and knew that there would be no peace for the Shadow-Clan leader until he knew what had happened to his son.

Cloverfoot took the lead as the exiled cats emerged from the warriors' den, and they climbed the slope in a straggling line, moving toward the bramble barrier that edged the camp. Crowfeather brought up the rear.

As Rootpaw watched them go, he realized that Squirrelflight was standing beside him. She bent her head and spoke quietly into his ear. "Rootpaw, can you help me see Bramblestar again?" she asked, her green eyes gleaming with eagerness. "I have a lot I need to discuss with him."

Rootpaw looked around, but there was no sign of Bramblestar's spirit. Since his last appearance to the medicine cats, Rootpaw had hoped that he might be sticking close to Squirrelflight. *But if he's not here . . .*

"I'm sorry," he replied reluctantly. "It's been a while since I've seen his spirit."

He hated to see the light die from Squirrelflight's eyes, to be replaced with an anxiety that reflected his own. *If Bramblestar isn't with Squirrelflight, and I haven't seen him in days,* Rootpaw asked himself, *then what could have happened to him? How long can a spirit linger outside its body?*

And how will the Clans ever return to normal if the real Bramblestar is truly gone?

CHAPTER 6

✦

Bristlefrost glanced around curiously as she padded through the fern tunnel into the old SkyClan camp. The morning sunshine had given way to a heavy shower of rain around sunhigh, and gray clouds still hung low over the forest. All the undergrowth was drenched, and Bristlefrost shivered as she paused to shake moisture from her fur.

Stemleaf and Spotfur pushed through the tunnel behind Bristlefrost and came to stand by her side. "What a great place for a camp!" Spotfur exclaimed. "SkyClan must have been sorry to leave it."

"They didn't have much choice," Stemleaf mewed drily. "It *is* on ShadowClan territory, after all."

Bristlefrost had to agree with Spotfur: This had obviously been a good camp. A stream ran through the middle of it, overhung by vegetation, with flat rocks here and there that would be great places for cats to sun themselves. At the far end was an old cedar tree with a hollow that Bristlefrost guessed had been the Clan leader's den. The ferns that surrounded the clearing were reinforced by brambles, though gaps had opened up since the camp had been abandoned. The bushes that must have sheltered the various dens needed work, too, before they would keep out the wind and the rain.

Bristlefrost and her Clanmates had arrived for a meeting of the rebel cats, but so far the only cats she could see in the clearing were the exiles who had moved in there. Not far away from her she could see Crowfeather and Lionblaze facing each other with glaring eyes and fur bristling.

"You and Twigbranch need to get on with repairing the apprentices' den," Crowfeather snapped.

Lionblaze rolled his eyes. "It may have escaped your notice, but we don't *have* any apprentices," he pointed out. "Or kits, either. It's far more important to plug the gaps in the warriors' den, and fetch moss for nests."

"We might have apprentices soon," Crowfeather argued. "If Bramblestar keeps going, we can expect more exiles—I don't think even the apprentices are safe."

"Bramblestar *can't* keep going—"

Crowfeather interrupted Lionblaze's protest. "Don't be naive. We might be here so long that we need a permanent camp, with kits being born here and becoming apprentices."

Bristlefrost stifled a gasp of horror at the thought that the crisis in the forest might go on for so long. But the squabbling toms seemed unaware of her.

"You might be right," Lionblaze meowed. "But that's not happening right now. The first thing we need to do is make sure the warriors who are here *now* have a place to sleep. Besides," he went on when Crowfeather looked as if he would go on arguing, "you might be a Clan deputy, but you're not *my*

Clan deputy, so don't give me orders."

"Fine!" Crowfeather whipped around and stalked away, his tail held high. Lionblaze picked up a heap of moss he had let fall by his side, and headed off in the opposite direction.

"Is it true that Crowfeather is Lionblaze's father?" Bristlefrost murmured.

Spotfur nodded, letting out a small *mrrow* of laughter. "They don't get along very well, do they?"

Bristlefrost could see that some of the exiled cats who had heard the quarrel were looking troubled. "Will we really be here long enough for kits to become apprentices?" Twigbranch asked.

"I'm sure we won't," Squirrelflight reassured her, resting her tail on the younger cat's shoulder. "You can always trust Crowfeather to see the worst in any situation."

"You *certainly* won't be here that long." Tigerstar had entered the camp, followed by Dovewing and Tawnypelt, in time to hear Twigbranch's words. "Don't forget this is ShadowClan territory, and using this camp is only a temporary solution."

Twigbranch dipped her head in acknowledgment, but Bristlefrost wasn't sure she looked convinced.

By this time, more warriors were arriving for the rebels' meeting. As the crowd gathered, Bristlefrost realized that some of their original supporters hadn't appeared, and wondered if they were too afraid to come, especially now that the WindClan and RiverClan leaders seemed to be in agreement with Bramblestar. However, she was cheered to see some younger cats there for the first time, including Dappletuft from RiverClan, Kitescratch from SkyClan, and Conefoot from ShadowClan.

More SkyClan cats appeared with Kitescratch: Violetshine and Tree, with Needleclaw and Rootpaw. Bristlefrost carefully avoided catching Rootpaw's gaze.

"Oh, no—Twigbranch!" Violetshine exclaimed as she spotted her sister. "Are you exiled too?"

Twigbranch ran across and touched noses with Violetshine, letting out a welcoming purr. "For now," she explained. "But Bramblestar will let me back into the Clan when I've atoned."

Other cats, including Frecklewish and Puddleshine, trickled into the camp, but at last it was clear that no more were coming. They gathered with the exiles beside the old cedar tree.

Squirrelflight beckoned to Bristlefrost with a wave of her tail. "I think it's up to you to speak first," she meowed.

Bristlefrost looked at the assembled cats, her heart pounding. She was nervous about addressing so many cats, most of whom were far more experienced warriors. But she was also worried about telling this many cats the truth about Bramblestar. In a way, it would be a relief, but she also feared what might happen if not all the cats believed her, or if they couldn't agree about what to do. Still, with Squirrelflight nodding at her encouragingly, she braced herself and padded up to the front of the group. "I know this sounds crazy," she began, "and I have no idea how it can be happening, but we're sure now that the cat leading ThunderClan isn't really Bramblestar at all.

He's some other cat—or something—living in Bramblestar's body. Rootpaw," she continued, turning toward the SkyClan apprentice, "can you tell every cat what you have seen?"

Rootpaw ducked his head, seeming nervous, and came forward to stand beside Bristlefrost. "I've seen Bramblestar's spirit in the forest," he told the assembled cats. "Many times now. Tree has seen him, too, and the other night he appeared to me and the other medicine cats."

Murmurs of shock and protest broke out at Rootpaw's revelation. Bristlefrost wondered if the medicine cats had shared their news of the vision with their leaders, as Rootpaw and Tree had planned to encourage them to do. *I can't blame them if they didn't,* she thought. *It's so weird!*

"I find that very hard to believe," Crowfeather meowed. "Why would Bramblestar appear to you, and not to a cat of his own Clan?"

"Don't forget Rootpaw has the Sisters' blood," Alderheart pointed out. "And I saw Bramblestar's spirit at the medicine-cat meeting, as clear as I see you now."

"So did I," Jayfeather added. "At least, I heard his voice. It was Bramblestar."

Bristlefrost was dismayed to see that even with the backing of the medicine cats, some of the rebels still didn't believe Rootpaw, or were so confused they didn't know what to believe. *And these are the cats who are already resisting Bramblestar,* she thought. *If even they have trouble believing he's not really himself, how will the rest of the Clans react?*

"I haven't seen the spirit," she meowed. "But I know that

the cat who calls himself Bramblestar is nothing like our real leader."

"You're right, Bristlefrost!" Twigbranch exclaimed. "The real Bramblestar would never have treated me this way."

Twigbranch's support made Bristlefrost realize that it was time to share another fact about their so-called leader. *The resistance fighters should know the truth.* "There's something else you need to know," Bristlefrost went on, as the cats settled down again to listen. "On the night that Shadowsight disappeared, I saw Bramblestar returning to the camp with blood on his muzzle and his chest fur. And before that, I'm sure that some cat tried to kill Sparkpelt, too."

This time the yowls of shock and horror were even louder. Tigerstar and Dovewing were staring at each other, their eyes filled with identical expressions of anguish. Only for a moment—then Tigerstar wrenched his gaze away and leaped onto a nearby rock to seize control of the crowd.

"We must kill Bramblestar!" he announced.

Caterwauls of fervent agreement came from most of the ShadowClan cats, though Bristlefrost could hear protests, too. Eventually Tawnypelt managed to make herself heard.

"All of you know that Bramblestar is my brother," she meowed. "And I grieve at the thought of killing his body." She hesitated for a heartbeat, struggling to force the words out. "But whatever destructive spirit is inside him cannot be allowed to continue."

"No!" Bristlefrost raised her voice, her whole body quivering with outrage. "We just told you the real Bramblestar is still around! How can you suggest killing his body? What would happen to the real Bramblestar then?"

"Maybe he'd return," Lionblaze suggested hopefully. "Like when a leader loses a life in the normal way."

"And maybe he wouldn't," Twigbranch retorted. "Do we have the right to risk it?"

Once again the meeting erupted into chaos, every cat demanding to be heard, while no cat wanted to listen. Bristlefrost tried to make sense of the argument, finding a tiny shred of hope in the way that most of the ThunderClan cats were horrified at the thought of killing their leader's body.

"Bramblestar's dying is what got us into this mess," Crowfeather pointed out. "Would killing him even work?"

"We can't take that risk," Stemleaf insisted.

The young ShadowClan warrior Conefoot flicked his tail dismissively. "*Do* we know the real Bramblestar is still there to worry about?" he asked. "Rootpaw says he hasn't seen him since the medicine-cat meeting."

Squirrelflight pushed her way through the crowd and leaped up onto the rock beside Tigerstar. She waved her tail for silence, and the caterwauling died down to hostile hissing and muttering.

"Bramblestar isn't gone," Squirrelflight insisted, her green gaze compelling the attention of the crowd. "He wouldn't leave me like this, I'm sure of it." Turning to Tigerstar, she added fiercely, "If you won't give up on Shadowsight, you should understand that I won't give up on Bramblestar."

Tigerstar's voice was full of bitterness as he replied. "I'm sure Shadowsight is dead. If he were alive, he would never have left ShadowClan. If he were able, he would have come home."

"Maybe not." Dovewing was clearly trying to comfort her mate. "Remember, we once left the Clans without telling any cat—StarClan, how I regret that now!"

The argument broke out again, though more quietly this time. The cats must have been growing exhausted from shock and apprehension. Bristlefrost felt her muscles tense with fear as she realized that most of the cats in the clearing felt that they should kill, or at least drive out, the false Bramblestar.

"Just think what you're saying," Jayfeather challenged them. "Killing a leader—even if he's not the true leader—isn't like slapping your paw down on a mouse. Before we make a move, we have to think about what would happen next."

"That's right," Bristlefrost agreed, thankful for another argument against killing Bramblestar's body. "Berrynose is the ThunderClan deputy now. Does any cat think that he would make a good leader?"

The cats stood in a small pool of silence as each of them thought about that. Finally, Dovewing spoke. "But Squirrelflight, you're the *real* deputy, aren't you?"

"No, she's not," Jayfeather responded instantly. "However much we might like her to be. Her Clan leader banished her and appointed Berrynose, and how pleased do you think StarClan and every other cat would be if we didn't follow the usual succession? It's an outrageous idea!"

"Jayfeather's right," Crowfeather meowed, with a curt nod

in the direction of the blind medicine cat. "Besides, Harestar and WindClan will not accept ThunderClan murdering their leader and putting another cat in his place. We'd never get away with it."

"That's true," Violetshine agreed. "And Leafstar and Mistystar will probably feel the same way."

"But Leafstar said she would act to stop Bramblestar hurting other cats," Rootpaw pointed out. "Maybe if we told her about the time the impostor tried to kill Sparkpelt, SkyClan would turn against him."

Twigbranch shook her head. "There's not enough evidence. Bramblestar sent Sparkpelt to the place where she was attacked by dogs, and a trail of prey-scent led to that place, but there's no actual proof that the false Bramblestar was responsible for the attack. I know Leafstar well, from the time I spent in SkyClan. She won't even twitch a whisker until she's sure."

Lionblaze stepped forward, his voice rumbling deep within his chest. "Maybe killing Bramblestar is the right move," he growled. "He's controlling all five Clans now, not just ThunderClan, and he'll destroy everything if he isn't stopped. But we need to think it through first."

Squirrelflight stared down at him from her place on the rock, shock and disbelief in her eyes. "I can't believe I heard you say that!" she gasped. "I can't believe you would even consider killing Bramblestar. He's not just your Clan leader—he's been like a father to you."

Lionblaze opened his jaws to respond, then closed them again, shaking his head in confusion. He mumbled something that Bristlefrost couldn't catch.

Tigerstar took control of the meeting again, raising one paw in a commanding gesture. "One course of action is before us," he announced. "To kill Bramblestar's body." His gaze scorched across the assembled cats like flame through dry grass. "But Squirrelflight might be right that it's not time yet. We don't want to start a battle against RiverClan, WindClan, and ThunderClan, and right now they'd be allied against us, and we don't know what Leafstar would decide. *No cat* will harm Bramblestar until we have had time to think and make sure this is what we all want to do. Then we will come up with a plan." He gave a final wave of his tail. "For now, the meeting is over."

As she headed away from ShadowClan territory, Bristlefrost felt her legs shaking with every paw step. She had suspected that telling the others about seeing Bramblestar returning to camp covered in blood would put his life in danger, and she was right. She wasn't completely surprised that they were now suggesting killing Bramblestar's body, but she was certain that it would be a huge mistake.

If they succeeded, what then? she asked herself despairingly. With his body dead, they might never get the real Bramblestar back—and ThunderClan would be ripped apart for good.

CHAPTER 7

Shadowsight was floating in a dreamless haze when a voice cut through the fog and called his name. It seemed to be coming from an immense distance, and though it was vaguely familiar, Shadowsight couldn't quite place it. Slowly he opened his eyes, feeling as though he had been asleep for a long time. When he tried to stretch his limbs, the movement felt strange, as if he wasn't in control of his body.

All around him was gray mist; though he blinked several times, it didn't clear. Dark shapes that might have been large rocks loomed around him. All he could see were twin points of yellow light, piercing the gloom. Gradually a shape formed around them and became a cat: a skinny black tom with yellow eyes fixed intently on him. Shadowsight felt that he ought to recognize him, but he was so confused that the name wouldn't come to him.

Then the black tom spoke. "Greetings, Shadowsight."

The voice was the same one that had been calling to him, and with a gasp Shadowsight remembered. "Spiresight!" Warm gratitude filled him. "I can't believe it's you! I thought you went to StarClan. That's why my father gave you a warrior name."

Spiresight shook his head. "I chose not to go to StarClan, so that I could watch over you," he explained. "I haven't been around all the time, but I've checked on you regularly since I died. And I'm very proud of the cat you have become."

Shadowsight blinked, bewildered by everything he had to take in, but happy to be with the cat who had done so much for him and his kin. "I never saw you," he mewed. "How is it that I'm talking to you now?"

The black tom hesitated for a heartbeat before he replied. "Three nights ago, I saw a cat attack you, and when you were unconscious, he threw you into this ravine."

Horror coursed through Shadowsight, and he felt every hair on his pelt rise. Now he remembered the slash of sharp, curved claws and realized that his whole body should be throbbing with pain. *But I can't feel anything.* "Am I dead?" he asked. "Where am I?"

"You're not dead," Spiresight replied. "At first I was afraid you were, but then I realized that you were still breathing—just. But you must have been seriously injured, because until now I couldn't communicate with you at all—not even with your spirit."

Shadowsight took in a shaky breath. "Spirit?" he whispered. "Am I a *ghost*?"

Spiresight had just told him that he wasn't dead, but Shadowsight wasn't sure he could believe him. *Maybe I am, and*

I'll never see my kin again! Then he realized that if he was dead, he should be in StarClan, but this place was completely unfamiliar to him. For a moment he felt so confused that he just wanted to close his eyes again and forget everything.

Instead Shadowsight took a deep breath and forced himself to sit up. Looking around, he saw that the mist had dissipated and the ravine was gradually coming into focus around him. He and Spiresight were sitting on a flat rock jutting out of the steep wall, about halfway down. The narrow gully seemed to be about fifteen or twenty tail-lengths high, with a small stream running along the bottom. Outcrops of rock poked out from the thin, sandy soil, with thick bushes rooted among them. Shadowsight didn't recognize the place; he was sure it wasn't on ShadowClan territory.

I don't suppose many cats come here, he thought. *Scrambling among these rocks would be really hard.*

"I wanted to get help for you," Spiresight went on, "but I didn't want to leave you in case you woke up."

Shadowsight blinked affectionately at his old friend. "You were always a loyal cat," he murmured. "It makes sense that you would be a loyal ghost."

Spiresight ducked his head, embarrassment in his yellow eyes. "You must have begun to heal from your injuries," he meowed, "if I'm able to speak with you now. But you're still in great danger. You're hovering between life and death."

Angling his ears, he gestured to Shadowsight to turn and look into the ravine in the other direction. Shadowsight took in a rasping breath as he spotted his own body lying sprawled beside a twisted thorn tree a couple of tail-lengths farther down. He couldn't believe how battered he looked, his fur torn and matted and a dried trickle of blood spilling from his forehead and over his muzzle. At first he thought that he must be dead after all, until he spotted the faint rise and fall of his chest as he breathed.

"I'm *between* life and death?" he asked, echoing Spiresight's words. He remembered that after Leafpool's death Jayfeather had said something similar to the medicine cats, how Squirrelflight and Leafpool had been between two worlds. Jayfeather explained that Squirrelflight had come back, while Leafpool had moved on to StarClan, but Shadowsight had found it hard to imagine.

"Thank you for what you've done," he told Spiresight, not waiting for an answer. "But we need to tell a medicine cat about me. I need real treatment!"

Spiresight gave him a doubtful look. "I thought of that," he responded, "but I didn't know which cats I could trust . . . it must have been a Clan cat who did this to you."

"Really?" Shadowsight didn't want to believe what his friend had told him, but at the same time a terrible certainty washed over him, icy as a river in leaf-bare. Once more the brief memory of the attack flashed into his mind, this time bringing with it a strong scent of catmint.

The attacker masked his scent with herbs. Only a Clan cat would bother to do that.

"I'm sure of it," Spiresight assured him, his voice heavy with the knowledge. "I was so shocked, and so worried about you, and in the darkness I didn't get a good look at the cat. I only detected a Clan scent, mingled with catmint. We need to find out who attacked you, and it will be easier for you to do that as a ghost."

Shadowsight didn't think it would be easy at all. The problem seemed like a huge cliff that he didn't have the strength to climb. It was impossible to think about it, and his mind slid away to something else that was troubling him.

"I was on my way to a medicine-cat meeting," he meowed. "Do you know what happened there?"

Spiresight shook his head. "I'm not sure," he replied. "I do know cats have been looking for you." Spiresight's serious gaze fixed on him. "But I've heard . . . troubling mutterings from some of your Clanmates."

Cold claws seemed to grip Shadowsight's heart as he listened to Spiresight's words. He remembered how some of his Clanmates had reacted when he'd first begun to have visions. What he saw was so unusual that many of his own Clanmates had thought he was weird or dangerous, until he had finally been accepted by the other medicine cats. "I know some of them think I'm odd," he murmured. "But surely they would never . . ." His voice faded away as he looked down at his own battered body.

"Are you willing to bet your life on it?" Spiresight asked.

Shadowsight went on gazing at his body for a few heartbeats, then slowly shook his head.

"Good," Spiresight mewed with a brisk nod. "That's the right decision. I promise I'll keep you safe while you're in my care. Just resting will help you; that's what I would have suggested if a city cat had been hurt this way. It must be working already," he added, "because now you're strong enough to communicate with me as a spirit. If you get any worse, I will find help from a living cat. Meanwhile," he went on, "we can gather more information about what happened to you."

"How?" Shadowsight asked eagerly.

"By visiting the Clans in your spirit form. We'll have to be careful, though," Spiresight warned him. "It's dangerous for you to go too far from your body. If you leave it for too long, you might die, and then you would be a ghost forever. Mind you," he added, with a spark of mischief in his gaze, "being a ghost isn't all bad. You might even like it better than being alive and decide to—"

"I want to stay alive!" Shadowsight interrupted him abruptly. Then in a softer tone he added, "I'm sorry. I'm grateful to you for guiding me through this, but there's still so much I have to do, and I need to be alive to do it." He knew he didn't have to put what he was facing in words for Spiresight. They both knew the huge cliff wasn't going away—Shadowsight needed to know which cat was his enemy, and how the attack fit in to the troubles that beset the Clans. And beside that, if he was to recover from his injuries, he would need a cat to help him—one who wasn't a ghost—so he had to figure out which Clan cats he could trust, and there wasn't a moment to spare. "How do I start?" he asked.

As an answer, Spiresight pressed himself against Shadowsight's side. For a heartbeat everything blurred, and when his vision cleared, Shadowsight found himself standing in the shelter of a clump of ferns. Glancing around, he realized that he was at the edge of the old SkyClan camp, where they had stayed when they occupied part of ShadowClan's territory.

The center of the clearing was swarming with cats; their voices reached Shadowsight's ears as a confused noise, and at first he couldn't make out individuals among the mass of fur.

Gradually his confusion ebbed, and he began to make sense of what he was seeing. "There's Tigerstar!" he exclaimed. "And Dovewing—and that's Squirrelflight. Oh, and Rootpaw and Tree. Are there cats here from all the Clans?"

Spiresight nodded. "These are the rebel cats who oppose Bramblestar and his plans to exile the codebreakers," he replied. "Let's listen and see what we can learn."

With Spiresight's encouragement, Shadowsight slipped into the crowd of cats. An argument was raging about whether to kill Bramblestar, though Shadowsight found it hard to pay attention. All his mind was focused on the cats he cared for. His heart ached to see how desperate and exhausted his ShadowClan Clanmates looked, especially his mother and father. A powerful scent of grief wafted from them, making Shadowsight want to wail like an abandoned kit. He padded up to them and looked up into his father's face.

"Look, I'm here!" he meowed. "I'm not lost—I'm going to be fine."

But Tigerstar simply gazed through him, unaware that his son was standing less than a tail-length away. Urgency giving strength to his paws, Shadowsight sought out Tree and

Rootpaw, who were standing together at the edge of the crowd.

"Can you see me?" he asked. "Please—you must!"

But again there was no response. Finding Spiresight at his shoulder, Shadowsight turned to him and asked, "Why can't they see me? Tree sees dead cats all the time."

"I don't know," Spiresight replied. "It seems ghosts only appear to certain cats."

"But they should be able to see *me!*" Shadowsight flexed his claws in desperation.

"Not every cat with the Sisters' blood can see every ghost," Spiresight responded. "And I think it's time for you to go back to your body."

Shadowsight nodded, but almost at once he was distracted by his father's voice. "I'm sure Shadowsight is dead," Tigerstar began. "If he were alive, he would never have left ShadowClan. If he were able, he would have come home."

"Maybe not," Dovewing responded. "Remember, we once left the Clans without telling any cat—StarClan, how I regret that now!"

Tigerstar nodded, but there was no hope or belief in his eyes as he gazed at Dovewing. The anger and grief in his father's voice alarmed Shadowsight even more, and he surged forward once again through the crowd of cats.

"Tigerstar, I'm here!" he yowled. "I'm not dead!"

But just as before, Tigerstar stared straight through Shadowsight; he couldn't hear or see him. Shadowsight felt as helpless as a raindrop falling from the sky to be lost in a rushing stream.

As his distress overwhelmed him, Shadowsight's vision blurred. Sickness rose in his belly, and he felt every joint in his body giving way. He was conscious of Spiresight pressing against his side.

"You need to get back to your body right now!" the spirit cat meowed.

In the next breath, Shadowsight found himself back in the ravine. His legs wouldn't hold him up; he slumped down on the rock, staring at his own unconscious body. A terrible certainty grew in his mind that it was breathing more slowly.

How long do I have left?

CHAPTER 8

The sun was going down; scarlet light washed over the SkyClan camp, reaching even into the medicine cats' den. Rootpaw narrowed his eyes against the glare as he dabbed at Macgyver's tick with a ball of moss soaked in mouse bile. Macgyver kept shifting around, so Rootpaw found it hard to maneuver the moss ball into the right place.

"For StarClan's sake, keep still!" he hissed around the twig clamped in his jaws.

"That tick is really dug in," Fidgetflake commented cheerfully. "They can be tricky sometimes. Keep at it, Rootpaw—you'll get there in the end."

Rootpaw could barely keep from gagging at the stench and taste of the mouse bile. *This isn't fair,* he thought. *I had to do ticks when I was a warrior apprentice, and I still have to do them now. And I hate every last one of them!*

He dabbed again, and to his relief the tick finally dropped off. Rootpaw let go of the twig with the soaked moss ball, gasping for a breath of fresh air.

"Thanks, Rootpaw," Macgyver meowed, flexing his shoulders. "That feels much better." With a nod to Fidgetflake, he padded out into the camp.

Rootpaw barely had time to clean up his paws before he heard his name being called from the entrance to the den. He turned to see his father, Tree.

"Fidgetflake, can I borrow Rootpaw for a bit?" Tree meowed. "I need to talk to him."

With Fidgetflake's permission, Rootpaw followed his father outside. He was glad to get out of his den, even for a short time. It stank of mouse bile and would for some time.

"Has anything changed?" Tree asked, halting a couple of tail-lengths from the den. "Have you seen the real Bramble-star again, or had any kind of sign that he's still around?"

Rootpaw shook his head worriedly. "Not a whisker," he replied.

"Last night's meeting is still bothering me," Tree meowed. "There was so much debate about what to do with the impostor, but if we can't reach the real Bramblestar's spirit, it doesn't leave us with much choice. I'd have expected that if you haven't seen him, he would be near Squirrelflight," he added, for once sounding deeply serious.

"I thought the same thing," Rootpaw responded. "But yesterday, before the meeting, I talked to Squirrelflight and there was no sign of Bramblestar anywhere near her."

Tree twitched his whiskers thoughtfully. "Is it possible that Bramblestar has faded?" he murmured, half to himself. "We have no idea how it would affect a cat, to be out of his body for so long."

Rootpaw couldn't answer that question. "I wish there were

something we could *do*," he meowed.

"There may be." Tree's voice was hopeful again. "I've talked to Leafstar about an idea I had of a way to contact Bramblestar. She wasn't sure at first, but when I told her that the impostor might have tried to kill Sparkpelt, she agreed to give it a try. She said if she could see Bramblestar's ghost for herself, she might change her mind about going along with the false Bramblestar."

"What's the idea?" Rootpaw asked eagerly.

"Perform a summoning ritual. You know the group of cats I was born into, the Sisters? They used to call to their dead this way. Maybe if we do the ritual, we will be able to reach Bramblestar's spirit—if it's anywhere near the Clans. It would be a huge help if you would join in, Rootpaw."

Rootpaw fell silent for a moment as a rush of optimism flooded through him from ears to tail-tip. For so long, he'd been the only one who could communicate with Bramblestar's ghost, and his failure to find him had made Rootpaw feel helpless and alone. Having his whole Clan participate would take so much of the weight off his shoulders.

"Of course I will," he replied. It was wonderful to finally have something new to try. Maybe all hope wasn't lost after all.

"Great!" Tree purred. He bounded the couple of paces back to the medicine cats' den, stuck his head inside, and called, "Frecklewish, Fidgetflake, we need you!"

With the two medicine cats following him, exchanging bewildered glances, Tree raced across the camp to the

Tallstump and called for Leafstar.

The Clan leader emerged and leaped up onto the top of the stump. "Let all cats old enough to catch their own prey join here beneath the Tallstump for a Clan meeting!" she yowled.

Taken aback, Rootpaw padded up to his father as the rest of the Clan gathered around them. "Wait, we're doing this right now?" he whispered. He felt his optimism from a moment ago waver. Even though his powers had proven useful, he knew there were still cats in his Clan who thought of him and his father as weird. Calling on their Clanmates to join a ritual to summon the dead probably wouldn't help. "I didn't realize it was going to happen so fast," he mewed nervously. "I was hoping we could take some time to ease them into the idea. . . ."

"We don't *have* time," Tree told him. "It has to be at sunset."

"Tree is going to lead us in a ceremony from the Sisters," Leafstar announced when the Clan had assembled. "We hope it will bring the spirit of the true Bramblestar back to us."

Doubtful muttering arose from the Clan. "The Sisters?" Sandynose exclaimed. "Why are we bothering with that weird bunch?"

Just as I feared, Rootpaw thought, feeling embarrassed. If the Clan thought Rootpaw and Tree were weird, of course they'd think the same of their kin, the Sisters.

"Yeah," Sagenose agreed. "Those rogues don't know anything that the Clans don't know!"

"Like Bramblestar's ghost is real anyway," Sandynose added.

"Quiet!" Leafstar ordered, with a stern look at the two

toms. "This may not work, but at least we're going to try."

The sun was beginning to dip below the horizon as Tree and Rootpaw stepped into the center of the clearing, with their Clanmates in a circle around them. Though Fidgetflake nodded at him supportively, Rootpaw sensed the reluctance of the other gathered cats and felt more exposed than ever.

"Tonight we sing to guide the spirit of Bramblestar back to us," Tree announced, his voice ringing clearly across the camp. "We know he has much to tell us, and we will try to help him on his journey to regain his body. Bramblestar, come to us!"

Tree threw back his head and let out an eerie, high-pitched wailing. It was met by a stunned silence from the other cats, and Rootpaw spotted several of them exchanging skeptical looks.

Then Violetshine stepped forward and joined in the wailing, nervously at first, then more confidently as she matched her voice to her mate's. Her participation seemed to shift the mood of the circle. They might have thought Tree and Rootpaw were strange, but they respected Violetshine. If she took the ritual seriously, maybe they would too. Encouraged, Rootpaw joined his voice to his parents'. Then Hawkwing padded up to support them, followed by Needleclaw and Fidgetflake. Soon many others were wailing, their voices shivering upward as the stars began to appear.

Rootpaw felt that the sound was stretching out across all the lake territories, calling Bramblestar to them. *This is going to work*, Rootpaw thought, hope rising inside him. *It has to. If Bramblestar is anywhere nearby, he will come.*

Even as the last of the sunlight died, the song continued. Rootpaw gazed around while the rest of the cats went on with their wailing. He was sure that Bramblestar would come if he could, but there was no sign of him.

Tree fell silent, looking questioningly at Rootpaw, who could only shake his head sadly. But he wasn't ready to give up yet. At last Rootpaw broke out of the circle and searched more and more desperately for Bramblestar around the edges of the camp and inside the dens. *Please, Bramblestar, show yourself!* he urged silently, but the ThunderClan leader was nowhere to be found. The voices grew more ragged, then finally faded into silence. Full darkness had fallen, and Bramblestar had not come.

Rootpaw gazed around and saw deep disappointment on the faces of his Clanmates; Leafstar in particular sat with her shoulders drooping and her gaze fixed on her paws.

"I'm sorry!" Rootpaw's voice was shaking. He had let himself believe that this could work, and now he felt like even more of a failure than before. "I tried so hard, and it was no use."

"Don't blame yourself," Fidgetflake offered, casting a kind glance at Rootpaw.

Tree curled his tail around his son's shoulders. "Ghosts are unpredictable," he mewed comfortingly. "And Bramblestar's spirit is probably even more so, as his body is still alive. We can try again."

But Rootpaw felt heavy with dread. *If it didn't work this time, what's the point of trying again?*

"I have an idea," Frecklewish announced unexpectedly. The Clan was breaking up now, cats heading for their dens, leaving the medicine cats in the center of the clearing with Tree, Rootpaw, and Leafstar. "Why don't we try the ritual again, but this time at the Moonpool?"

"You know, that might just work." Tree gave her an intent look. "But don't the medicine cats go there at moonhigh? This ritual must be performed at sunset."

"Sunset didn't seem to work this time," Frecklewish pointed out gently. "So maybe moonhigh will."

Tree nodded. "I can't argue with that," he said. But he still seemed uncertain as he gazed around the clearing.

"The Moonpool is where we meet with the spirits of our warrior ancestors," Frecklewish continued. "It might be easier for Bramblestar to come to us there."

Leafstar nodded slowly. "That's definitely worth a try," she meowed. "Frecklewish, I know that only medicine cats are allowed at the Moonpool, but with your permission, Tree and I will come with you."

"Of course, Leafstar," Frecklewish replied immediately. "It's not like we haven't broken that rule over these past few moons. These are strange times, and until Star Clan returns"—Frecklewish glanced away sadly—"*if* they return, we must do whatever has a chance of working. You and Tree will be most welcome."

Buffeting winds scoured the moor as the five cats made their way to the Moonpool. Rootpaw's eyes watered and his fur was flattened to his sides as he struggled into the teeth of it. By the time he clambered up the final rocky slope to the top of the hollow, he felt fit for nothing except to curl up and sleep.

The Moonpool was dark as the SkyClan cats pushed through the bushes and began making their way down the spiral path. The stream cascading down from the rocks hardly seemed to disturb the surface. Here and there a glinting light reflected the stars and a claw-scratch of moon that appeared now and again through gaps in the racing clouds.

Rootpaw shivered. "Oh, StarClan, let it work this time!" he murmured.

Frecklewish ordered her Clanmates to find spaces for themselves around the edge of the pool. Then Tree threw his head back and sent up his eerie wailing to the silent sky. Rootpaw and the others joined in.

As the ritual song continued, Rootpaw gazed into the dark water, willing the spirit of Bramblestar to appear. *Come—come now! You have to!*

For a moment he thought that he saw something glimmering in the depths of the Moonpool, something more than the faint and fugitive stars. His heart lifted, everything within him reaching out to the light.

But at that moment Tree brought his song to a close, and the other cats dropped out, too, so that the wailing died away. The gleam of light faded too, as if it was sinking back into shadow.

"I saw something!" Rootpaw exclaimed, lashing his tail in

frustration. "A light there—in the pool."

Frecklewish padded to his side and peered downward. "I can't see anything," she mewed.

"It's gone now."

Frecklewish raised her head to meet Rootpaw's gaze. "Are you sure you saw it?"

"Yes!" Rootpaw replied. "At least . . . I think so."

"You probably imagined it," Frecklewish stated briskly. "It's easy to do, with the moon and starlight flickering like this. And it's easy to imagine seeing what you're really hoping for."

The other cats murmured agreement, and Rootpaw had to agree too. He couldn't put his paw on exactly what he had seen, and he couldn't bring himself to argue with cats who were all much more experienced than he was. He let out a sigh of discouragement.

His companions all seemed to share his mood, their tails and whiskers drooping at this second failure of the Sisters' ritual.

"It's my belief that Bramblestar's spirit is fading as he goes longer and longer without a body," Tree meowed. "I've never known it to happen to ghosts before, but Bramblestar's situation isn't what you could call normal."

Sadly Rootpaw decided that his father must be right. "Is it already too late to save him?" he asked anxiously.

Leafstar turned to Tree. "What do you think?"

"We know whoever is controlling Bramblestar's body *isn't* Bramblestar," Tree began slowly. "No matter how much time we have left, if we want to save the ThunderClan leader, we have to fight against whoever has stolen his body."

"You're right, Tree," Frecklewish agreed.

"Maybe that's true, but I'm still not ready to start a war with ThunderClan," Leafstar responded firmly. "Especially when two of the other Clans support them. I have to think of SkyClan first."

"But what about Bramblestar?" Rootpaw asked, dismayed by his leader's decision. "We *can't* just abandon him."

Tree gave his son an approving nod. "Leafstar, you have to realize that this . . . creature, whatever it is, inside Bramblestar's body, is going to destroy us all, sooner or later."

"Yes." Frecklewish's voice was harsh, quite different from her usual gentle demeanor. "He has already caused chaos in ShadowClan, and made two other Clans exile a deputy and a medicine cat. Where will it all end?"

"I understand what you're saying," Leafstar responded. "And I don't mean to do nothing. We will watch and wait. It's a terrible thing that I have to say, but I would rather sacrifice Bramblestar than SkyClan. No, Rootpaw," she continued, as the apprentice opened his jaws to object again. "For now, we will carry on as we have."

Rootpaw trailed a little way behind as he and his Clanmates set out for their own territory. He couldn't help thinking that Leafstar was making a terrible mistake.

If only I could explain exactly what I saw in the pool, he thought sadly, his gaze fixed on his paws. *Or if Tree hadn't ended the song just at that moment! Why does everything have to go wrong?*

His Clanmates were walking in near silence, and Rootpaw started in surprise at the sound of Leafstar's voice. He looked up to see Leafstar padding beside him, her amber gaze sympathetic.

"Try not to worry too much, Rootpaw," she mewed, her tone reassuring. "All is not lost—not yet. We'll see what happens, and when we're ready, we'll act."

Rootpaw nodded, though he guessed Leafstar could see he was finding her promises hard to accept.

"Frecklewish and Fidgetflake have praised how hard you've been working," his Clan leader went on. "But they also say you don't seem that enthusiastic about being a medicine cat." Leafstar halted and looked deeply into Rootpaw's eyes. "It's up to you, Rootpaw. Honestly, now, if you listen to your heart, do you really want your paws to follow the path of a medicine cat?"

Rootpaw thought about the tasks he had carried out in the medicine-cat den. He had felt pride in mastering something new, but none of the joy he experienced in making a good catch on a hunting patrol or sniffing the fresh dawn air in the forest as he set out to patrol the border. And a deep pang of loss pierced him at the thought of never having a mate and kits. He let out a deep sigh. "No, I don't," he admitted.

He had half expected that Leafstar would be angry, but instead she nodded in understanding. "I'm proud of you for considering so seriously where you belong," she told him. "Consider yourself a warrior apprentice again—but not for long. Tomorrow I'll talk to Dewspring about your warrior assessment."

For the rest of the way back to SkyClan territory, Rootpaw felt that his paws were carrying him on the wind.

CHAPTER 9

Bristlefrost arched her back in a good long stretch, while her jaws parted in a massive yawn. She felt chilly and stiff, her pelt still damp from rain that had fallen during the night. Above her head, she could just make out the trees at the top of the hollow, their tracery of branches outlined against a sky paling toward dawn.

"Thank StarClan it's morning!" she exclaimed to Rosepetal, who was sitting on the opposite side of the camp entrance.

Rosepetal nodded and raised one paw to lick it and scrub it over her face. "Now that Bramblestar has doubled the guards, we'll all be keeping watch twice as often," she complained. "He says he wants to keep the camp safe, but we were perfectly fine before."

"True." Bristlefrost blinked in an attempt to keep herself awake. "I can't wait until I can go for a nice piece of prey and a nap."

Rosepetal licked her paw again and gave her ears a wash. "I'm so looking forward to that!" she sighed. Then she glanced at Bristlefrost nervously. "I'm sure Bramblestar has a good reason for adding guards, though," she added.

Bristlefrost sighed. *I wish every cat didn't think I was going to run off to Bramblestar to report everything they say.*

Slow, uncertain paw steps sounded in the thorn tunnel, and both she-cats straightened up anxiously as Bramblestar appeared at the entrance. Bristlefrost remembered seeing him leave the camp just after sunset. *Where has he been all night?*

The false Clan leader appeared not to notice the two guards as he dragged himself into the camp. His head was hanging low, and his tail brushed the ground as if he was very tired. Bristlefrost noticed too how much weight he'd put on.

What can you expect when he takes first pick of the fresh-kill pile and doesn't hunt or patrol anymore? He's lost a lot of his energy.

"Greetings, Bramblestar," Rosepetal meowed, dipping her head respectfully, and Bristlefrost echoed her words. But Bramblestar looked at neither of them, replying only with a grunt. He headed across the camp, his dark pelt soon lost in the darkness that still lay over the stone hollow.

Bristlefrost and Rosepetal waited for a few more moments, hoping that the Clan leader had gone to his den. Then, as the dawn light strengthened, they followed him farther into the camp, their guard duty over with the approach of day.

Heading for the fresh-kill pile, Bristlefrost was just in time to see Bramblestar leave a half-eaten squirrel behind him and shamble off into the medicine cats' den. She exchanged a worried look with Rosepetal.

There's something off *about Bramblestar,* Bristlefrost thought. She knew that even the most loyal ThunderClan warriors could see it now, but still, she didn't dare to share the thought with Rosepetal. In grim silence the two warriors chose their prey; Bristlefrost devoured her mouse in a few hasty gulps, then headed for the warriors' den.

Bristlefrost could tell that it was raining again as she woke in her nest. The sloshing of busy cats tromping through the mud reached her through the branches of the den. Rosepetal had already left, and apart from Bristlefrost the den was empty.

Bristlefrost rose, shook scraps of moss and bracken from her pelt, and gave herself a quick grooming. Then she ventured out into the camp.

Instantly, drizzle matted her fur. Not far from the entrance of the den Bristlefrost spotted her brother, Flipclaw, in the middle of a group of younger warriors, and paused to listen to what they were saying.

"You'll never guess what a weird dream I had last night," Flipclaw was meowing. "I was hunting some birds, and suddenly they grew to three times their size. They were huge! They looked really fierce, and they turned around and started chasing *me*!"

"Wow, scary!" Plumstone commented.

"You better believe it. I was their prey, and they had this creepy sparkle in their eyes. I knew somehow they would get me! I was running and running, but they were flying faster . . ."

As Bristlefrost listened, amused at the outlandish story, she noticed that Bramblestar had appeared from somewhere and was also listening to Flipclaw, his eyes narrowed. Seeing that Bristlefrost had spotted him, he gave her a nod and shuffled off, back to the medicine cats' den.

Why is he spending so much time there? Bristlefrost wondered. *Is he sick?*

Just at the entrance to the den, Berrynose intercepted him. "Bramblestar, Sorrelstripe reported—"

The Clan leader cut him off with a dismissive wave of his tail. "Whatever it is, deal with it," he snapped. "Are you Clan deputy or aren't you?"

Bristlefrost's amusement at her brother's weird dream had faded; watching their leader's erratic behavior made her deeply uneasy. Her pads itched with curiosity, and when Bramblestar had disappeared into the den, she sneaked closer, crouching in the shelter of the brambles that screened the entrance.

At first, she could only hear murmuring, until Bramblestar raised his voice, his ill temper as obvious as if she had been able to see his face.

"I'm your Clan leader!" he snarled. "The warrior code makes it clear that you have to do what I tell you."

"But I can't find anything wrong with you," Alderheart responded, his voice calm and reasonable.

"And I'm telling you that I'm in pain!"

From the tone of Bramblestar's voice, Bristlefrost could believe him. She was surprised to feel an unexpected pang of pity for him.

"I'm sorry about that," Alderheart continued. "But I can't give you any more poppy seeds. It's not safe."

Bristlefrost blinked in sudden understanding. Poppy seeds were strong. If Bramblestar had been taking them regularly, it would explain why he had become so lethargic.

Bramblestar let out a growl of anger and pushed his way out of the den. Bristlefrost had just enough time to leap backward and pretend to be dislodging a piece of grit from between her claws. She watched as the impostor stormed into the middle of the clearing.

"Let all cats old enough to catch their own prey come here and listen to me!" he yowled.

Bristlefrost joined her Clanmates as they gathered around their leader. She could sense their uneasiness in their twitching tails and whiskers, and their shared glances of apprehension. Once again, they were gathering in the rain for a speech from their leader. It was as though all the cats were asking themselves, *What now?*

Alderheart had appeared from his den and remained standing at the entrance, his gaze fixed on Bramblestar with a deeply disturbed look that made Bristlefrost shiver.

Bramblestar gazed around the Clan as they settled around him. "ThunderClan is very lucky indeed," he announced in that honeyed voice that Bristlefrost instinctively mistrusted, her pelt prickling at the sound. "Now that Jayfeather has been exposed as a codebreaker and sent into exile, we have been gifted with another medicine cat."

Bristlefrost could see her own confusion reflected in the eyes of her Clanmates. *Another medicine cat? Why has Alderheart said nothing about this?* She knew that medicine-cat apprentices were recognized when they had a vision or some kind of communication with StarClan. *But StarClan isn't communicating with any cat right now. So what is Bramblestar meowing about?*

She felt even more confused a heartbeat later as Bramblestar went on. "Flipclaw will become our new medicine-cat apprentice!"

"Flipclaw?" their mother, Ivypool, exclaimed in disbelief, at the same moment as Flipclaw blurted out, "Me? No way!"

Bramblestar turned his amber gaze on Flipclaw. "Do you doubt yourself?" he asked. "Just now, I heard you talking about a prophetic dream you had."

"Prophetic?" Flipclaw blinked in bewilderment, while confused muttering came from the other assembled cats. "I'm not sure the dream was *prophetic*. At least, I hope it wasn't! It was just weird. . . ."

Bramblestar padded forward until he stood close to Flipclaw, staring straight into the younger cat's eyes. "Are you sure about that?" he purred. "You recalled being preyed on by *birds*. Birds that live in the sky, with a strange sparkle in their eyes. Come on, Flipclaw! What else sparkles and lives in the sky?"

For a moment Flipclaw stared blankly at the Clan leader. "Stars . . . *StarClan*?" he choked out at last.

Bristlefrost spotted movement at the corner of her eye and turned her head to see Alderheart padding forward from the medicine-cat den. His eyes were wide with surprise.

"That doesn't sound like any vision I've ever heard of," he meowed as he crossed the camp to join the false Bramblestar. "Even what Shadowsight saw was clearer than that!"

Bramblestar let out a hiss of exasperation, his tail-tip twitching to and fro. "In case you hadn't noticed, Alderheart," he snapped, "StarClan isn't sharing traditional visions with us. We have to look harder for guidance! Flipclaw's dream makes perfect sense to me."

"Enlighten us, then," Alderheart murmured.

"The birds are StarClan," Bramblestar responded. "For seasons they have fed us, nourished us with their wisdom. But now things have changed. They have become angry, vengeful. Until we do as StarClan has demanded, the Clans will suffer. We will be their prey!"

Bristlefrost felt every hair on her pelt prickle with horror at the interpretation the impostor was placing on what had clearly been a silly dream. Alderheart opened his jaws to comment, then shut them again with a snap.

Flipclaw, too, obviously shared Bristlefrost's feelings, his eyes wide with dismay.

"But Bramblestar . . . I don't feel any pull to be a medicine cat," he mewed nervously. "Isn't that something StarClan has to call a cat to be?"

Bramblestar curved his tail forward to rest it on Flipclaw's shoulder. "As StarClan isn't speaking to the Clans," he began, "the only link we have to what they want is through me, the leader they approved for ThunderClan. And I want you, Flipclaw, to be the new medicine-cat apprentice. After all, we need one," he continued, raising his head to address the rest of the Clan. "What if something happens to Alderheart?"

Gazing at Alderheart's sudden wary expression, Bristlefrost

could see that the medicine cat recognized the impostor's words for the threat they were. *Once Flipclaw is able to treat sick cats, Bramblestar can get rid of Alderheart anytime he wants.*

"This is ridiculous!" Alderheart meowed, his voice full of bitterness. "Bramblestar, how is this in keeping with the code that you've been enforcing so fiercely?"

Bramblestar turned toward him, his muscular body looming over the slighter medicine cat. "I am the leader!" he snarled. "I make the decisions!"

His tail bushing out with fury, he stormed off toward the tumbled rocks, heading for his den. But before he reached it, he halted, glancing back over his shoulder. "Bristlefrost, follow me!" he snapped.

Bristlefrost's heart began thumping hard with alarm. *Does he know that I was listening to him and Alderheart in the medicine cats' den? Am I in trouble?*

But her only choice was to obey the false leader. She was aware of her Clanmates staring at her as she climbed the tumbled rocks in his paw steps and reached the entrance to his den.

"Come in, come in," Bramblestar mewed testily. "I need to talk to you."

Though she looked forward to getting out of the rain, Bristlefrost needed to take one last breath of fresh air before she could force herself into the stench of the den. She stepped inside warily, trying not to let her nose wrinkle at the stink of stale prey and soiled bedding. Dipping her head respectfully, she padded forward to within a tail-length of where

Bramblestar sprawled in his nest.

"I've been in the Twolegplace, searching for Squirrelflight," he told her. "But I haven't caught the least hint of her scent. I was there all night, but it was no use. I don't have the faintest idea where she is."

Apprehension began to gnaw at Bristlefrost's belly. "Why are you looking for her?" she asked. "Squirrelflight left Clan territory, just as you ordered. Surely you don't think she deserves more punishment?"

Bramblestar shook his head sadly. "To tell the truth . . . I expected Squirrelflight to come home and ask to be taken back into ThunderClan," he admitted. "But she hasn't. I must have really angered her," he continued, gazing up at the den wall as if he could see his former deputy standing there. "I know she must still love me, deep down. If I could only talk to her again . . ." His voice choked and he closed his eyes, resting his nose on his paws.

Bristlefrost was growing steadily more alarmed. An irrational Clan leader, sending Clan members into exile for supposedly breaking the warrior code, was one thing. But this befuddled creature, driveling on about how much Squirrelflight must love him, was far worse.

He couldn't lead a kit out of the nursery, much less a whole Clan!

While Bristlefrost was wondering what she could possibly say, Bramblestar's head snapped up again.

"I have a new task for you," he rasped. "You have to search for Squirrelflight. You *must* find her. And when you do, you must tell her that her exile is revoked. You must get her to come back to ThunderClan."

"But what will the rest of the Clan think about that?" Bristlefrost asked. "You exiled all the codebreakers. How can you let just one come back? Wouldn't that encourage other cats to start doubting your leadership?"

"Oh, Bristlefrost . . ." Bramblestar blinked at her with a look of amused affection that made her feel cold right down to her claw-tips. "When you're older and more experienced, you'll realize that there is such a thing as forgiveness, even from StarClan. I'm their representative in the Clan, now that the medicine cats can't speak to them, and I've decided that Squirrelflight can be forgiven, if she changes her ways. Squirrelflight is . . . special."

"Then I'll go and look for her right away," Bristlefrost mewed, not knowing what else she could say. *What will he do if I don't come back with Squirrelflight?* she wondered nervously. But maybe Squirrelflight *would* agree to come back. That would be so wonderful! If she did, Bristlefrost wouldn't have to carry this burden of pretending to agree with Bramblestar alone any longer. And if the impostor made Squirrelflight deputy again, she might be able to influence his behavior and protect their Clan. Bristlefrost dipped her head and backed out of the den, her belly trembling with relief once she was away from the impostor's baleful eyes.

Down on the floor of the camp, her Clanmates were huddling into groups, clearly discussing Bramblestar's latest edict. Near the medicine cats' den, Flipclaw seemed to be arguing with Alderheart. As she passed the groups of whispering cats, they fell silent, watching her warily.

Bristlefrost didn't wait to speak with any cat, only bounded across the camp and straight out into the forest. To begin with, she headed in the direction of the Twolegplace, in case any cat might be watching her, or—a horrific thought—Bramblestar himself decided to follow her. Once she was sure she was alone, she veered along the top border of SkyClan territory, then crossed into ShadowClan and made for the exiles' camp.

As Bristlefrost approached the camp entrance, Squirrelflight appeared out of a bank of ferns, followed by Twigbranch and Dovewing. All of them were carrying prey; it had been a successful hunt.

"Squirrelflight, I have to talk to you!" Bristlefrost called out, bounding toward her.

Squirrelflight's eyes widened in surprise. "Okay, come into camp," she mumbled around the vole in her jaws.

Bristlefrost followed the hunting patrol through the fern tunnel and waited while Squirrelflight deposited her prey on the fresh-kill pile.

"Would you like to eat with us?" Squirrelflight asked.

Bristlefrost shook her head; her belly was roiling, and she felt that she couldn't have swallowed a single mouthful.

"I can see something's bothering you," Squirrelflight meowed, resting her tail-tip briefly on Bristlefrost's shoulder. "What has Bramblestar done now?" She led Bristlefrost to one of the flat rocks beside the stream, where they could settle down in the sun. "It is Bramblestar, I suppose?"

"Or the thing inside him," Bristlefrost responded. "He's

changed more than ever," she continued, "and he seems to have lost all control. Now he's calling himself StarClan's only representative, and he says that StarClan has forgiven you. He wants you to come back. Oh, Squirrelflight, I wish you would!"

A gleam of longing lit in Squirrelflight's green eyes, and Bristlefrost realized how much she wanted to be part of her Clan again. Then, reluctantly, she shook her head. "I can't, Bristlefrost. I'm still loyal to ThunderClan, but there are ThunderClan cats here among the exiles. I'm still protecting my Clan. They need me here."

"Then what am I supposed to do?" Bristlefrost asked, struggling with deep disappointment. "Bramblestar isn't going to let this go. He's going to keep searching for you. What if he finds out about this camp?"

Squirrelflight sat silent for a few moments, her head bowed. Bristlefrost watched her in an agony of impatience, but she knew better than to interrupt the former deputy's thoughts.

At last Squirrelflight looked up. "I know what we must do," she meowed. "You must tell Bramblestar that I'm dead."

Bristlefrost stared at her. She had never told such a massive lie before, and she guessed she never would again. *And will Bramblestar believe it?* she asked herself. *I can't imagine it will work. . . .* "I told you," she mewed at last, "Bramblestar won't let this go. He'll need proof."

"Then we must give him some," Squirrelflight responded calmly.

While Bristlefrost wondered what she meant, Squirrelflight

rose to her paws and padded over to the medicine cats' den, which Jayfeather now shared with Mothwing. Halting at the entrance, she called out, "Jayfeather!"

The blind medicine cat padded out into the open, the scent of tansy clinging to his pelt. "Oh, it's you, Bristlefrost," he muttered. "What has that mange-ridden furball done now?"

Quickly Squirrelflight told Jayfeather how Bramblestar had forgiven her and wanted her to go back to ThunderClan. "I'm not going, of course, so what we need to do is convince Bramblestar that I'm dead," she explained. "Tell me, Jayfeather, can you wound me in a way that would cause a lot of bleeding but heal easily and safely?"

Bristlefrost suppressed a gasp of shock, staring at Squirrelflight. *That's so risky . . . and would Bramblestar even accept it?*

Meanwhile Jayfeather was gaping at Squirrelflight. "*Wound* you? Have you got bees in your brain?"

"No, I haven't!" Squirrelflight retorted. "But these are desperate times. If you can think of a better idea, tell me what it is."

Jayfeather let out a snort. "I'm not going to injure you on purpose," he insisted, his voice rising in anger. "I'm a medicine cat, not a weasel!"

As he was speaking, Mothwing stuck her head out of the den. "What's going on?" she asked. "What's all the meowing about?"

"Squirrelflight has lost whatever wits she possessed," Jayfeather replied with a disgusted lash of his tail. "She wants me to wound her."

"Bristlefrost and I need to create proof that I'm dead," Squirrelflight explained. "It's the only way to stop Bramble-star from looking for me. Jayfeather doesn't like the idea of blood."

"No, I don't. The whole idea is ridiculous!" Jayfeather hissed. "It's gone too far when a cat asks a medicine cat to wound her and—"

Squirrelflight looked at Mothwing pleadingly. "I know that Bramblestar won't let this go," she said. "If he's determined to bring me back to camp, he'll keep looking for me and sending patrols to look for me. Some cat would be bound to eventually figure out where I am, and that would expose all of us."

"I'll do it," Mothwing interrupted. "Wounding a cat is a lot easier than healing one. But are you sure that's the only way? Seems pretty brutal."

"I'm sure," Squirrelflight mewed. "Bristlefrost has told me how relentless he's been about searching for me. It's clear that he won't let me go until he has to."

Mothwing nodded, considering Squirrelflight's words. "Good enough for me," she said. "Besides, if we don't do some-thing now, he might come searching again, and we can't risk him finding us here. He'd start a war with ShadowClan. And Jayfeather, if you don't believe that you and I together can't let a little blood from a cat and heal her afterward, you're the one who has lost your wits."

Jayfeather glared at her from sightless blue eyes. "I don't want anything to do with this!" he snarled, and whipped around to disappear into the den.

"He'll come around," Mothwing mewed, entirely unimpressed by Jayfeather's exhibition of temper.

I wonder how those two are getting along, Bristlefrost wondered, briefly amused in spite of the tension around her. *I'd like to be a fly on the wall of that den!*

"We'll both look after you when it's done, Squirrelflight," Mothwing continued. "There's no need to worry."

"I'm not," Squirrelflight responded. "I'm just so grateful to you, Mothwing. Can you get what you need right now? And then we'll head for the Twolegplace."

I sure hope this works, Bristlefrost thought. *Or things will be even worse than they are now!*

"It's this way," Bristlefrost meowed.

Sunhigh was long past, and the rain had ended when Bristlefrost led Bramblestar to the spot near the Twolegplace where she and Mothwing had helped Squirrelflight arrange the evidence of her "death" one day earlier. Emerging from the trees, she halted beside a Thunderpath. Clumps of grass near the edge were soaked with blood, while strewn on the hard, black surface were several tufts of Squirrelflight's fur and a single claw. The stench of blood filled the air. She realized now that the blood might smell too fresh, the fur seem too carefully arranged. But there was nothing she could do about it now. She didn't dare put him off any longer, so they'd had to hurry to set the scene. But she knew if he caught on to the truth, it would mean her life.

Oh, StarClan, let him believe me! Bristlefrost prayed, fighting to hide her fear as the false Bramblestar padded up to join her.

His amber eyes widened as he saw the blood and fur, and then, to Bristlefrost's astonishment, his face contorted in what looked like real grief. Hunching his shoulders, he bowed his head and flattened his ears. For a few heartbeats he seemed unable to speak.

"She's dead . . . and I killed her," he choked out at last.

CHAPTER 10
♣

"It just set in overnight," Spiresight explained.

Shadowsight shuddered as he crouched in spirit form once again, looking down at his broken body still sprawled in the ravine. Where his fur was torn away he could see that his wounds were red and swollen. In his next breath he took in the sweetish smell of infection, almost gagging as it hit him in the throat. Yet he couldn't feel a thing. Normally, that would be a blessing, but right then, being able to feel pain might have helped him figure out what was wrong and how to fix it.

"My Clan thinks I'm dead," he murmured. "And soon they may be right." He knew that he would never heal on his own now that his wounds were festering.

Since he first awoke and saw Spiresight, Shadowsight had spent some time observing the other Clans, trying to find some kind of clue as to who had attacked him. It had been interesting to visit other camps, especially ThunderClan's, where the tension was so thick, he could almost see it. But although it had been fun at first to eavesdrop on private conversations and see cats that he cared about, it soon grew frustrating that he couldn't communicate with any of them. He didn't know how Spiresight had done it for so long. Maybe the pull toward the living was not as strong when a cat was truly dead. But if the yearning was even half as strong as what he felt now, he wanted no part of it.

Plus, being a ghost had its limitations. He couldn't taste scents on the air or feel the breeze rustling through his pelt. It was disorienting. And for all his efforts, and Spiresight's, they hadn't learned anything.

"We can't just go on investigating," he told Spiresight. "I need my wounds cleaned, and poultices of the right herbs, and the bleeding stopped with cobwebs. Even that might not be enough to cure the infection—but it's certainly more than a ghost can handle!"

"But who can we tell?" Spiresight asked. He was standing beside Shadowsight, his eyes filled with anguish as he gazed down at his friend's unmoving body. "We don't know which cat we can trust."

"Maybe not, but I know that no cat in ShadowClan would ever hurt me. And I need a medicine cat's help if I'm going to survive. We need to get Puddleshine."

Spiresight looked skeptical. "Isn't Puddleshine one of the cats who was with you the night you were attacked?" Spiresight asked.

Shadowsight nodded.

"He didn't keep up with you when you searched for the injured cat," the ghost cat continued. "That gave your attacker time to strike. And Puddleshine chose to stop searching for you and head on to the Moonpool."

"What are you trying to say?" Shadowsight asked, afraid that he already knew the answer.

"Are you *sure* Puddleshine wasn't involved?"

"Of course I am!" Shadowsight retorted. "Puddleshine was my mentor, and he's one of the most dedicated medicine cats I know. He would never cause harm to any cat, let alone me."

Spiresight took a step toward Shadowsight, his expression sympathetic but grim. "I know that's what you believe. Yet until this happened to you, I'm sure you would have sworn that no cat in *any* of the Clans would have hurt you, but clearly one of them did. So don't be naive. Think—really think—about who had the opportunity to do this to you. Was Puddleshine there, and did he leave you behind?"

Shadowsight stared at him. "Yes, but I—" He broke off. He couldn't imagine Puddleshine hurting any cat, but he had to admit that he *had* been there on the night of the attack, and they had gotten separated. *But I can't believe he was part of a plot to kill me!* ShadowClan had had its share of conflict and trouble, but nothing would make him lose faith in his Clanmates, or his mentor. He felt guilty for even entertaining the thought. "Puddleshine would never hurt me," Shadowsight repeated, and this time his tone left no room for doubt.

Spiresight sighed. "Fine. I'll have to take your word for it. But there is still a problem."

"What's that?" asked Shadowsight.

"There are only certain Clan cats I can communicate with," Spiresight replied. "And that means we don't have many choices. There's a young SkyClan cat who seems to see me.

I've never spoken to him, but it's worth a try. His name is—"

"Rootpaw?" A warm feeling spread through Shadowsight at the thought of the young tom. He didn't know Rootpaw well, but he had always been kind. And he had shown great courage and good sense in the way he'd responded to seeing Bramblestar's ghost. *He seems like a trustworthy cat.*

"Yes," he mewed to Spiresight. "Rootpaw is definitely the cat we need. Let's go."

"You're not going anywhere," Spiresight responded brusquely. At Shadowsight's stricken look, he went on, "Getting a living cat—even one who is sensitive to spirits—to see me may take some time. Time that you may not have. You've already been separated from your body for too long."

"But—" Shadowsight started to argue.

"Trust me. I'll go now, and when I return, it will be with a cat who can help." Spiresight seemed to concentrate for a moment, then vanished.

Shadowsight stared at the spot where he had been. Even though he wanted to be back in his body again, he reflected that there were advantages to being a ghost. *But I'm not ready to become one just yet,* he thought. *You'd better hurry, Spiresight.*

CHAPTER 11

Rootpaw crept between two boulders, keeping his claws sheathed so they wouldn't scrape on the hard surface. He could just make out the gray fur of the cat in front of him, who seemed unaware of his presence. Drawing his hind legs up beneath him, Rootpaw plunged forward in a pounce; at the same moment he let out a blood-curdling yowl.

He landed squarely on the back of the gray cat, who slid to one side, trying to shake him off. But Rootpaw's claws were too securely embedded in his fur. Finally, he spoke.

"Okay, you can let go now." When Rootpaw didn't move, he added, "Let me get up, you daft furball!"

Rootpaw sprang to his paws, every hair on his pelt glowing with triumph. His mentor, Dewspring, scrambled up and shook debris from his fur. He gave Rootpaw an approving nod. "Not bad."

Not bad? It was brilliant! Rootpaw couldn't believe how good it felt to be a warrior apprentice again. In his hunt with Dewspring that morning he had caught two voles, and now his battle moves were better than ever. *This beats learning the difference between tansy and comfrey!*

"Okay," Dewspring continued. "You've done well so far, but I did hear you creeping up. You breathe like a badger! This time, I want you to sneak up on me without me hearing a thing."

He padded off for several paces and sat down with his back to Rootpaw, pretending to be very busy cleaning dirt out of his claws. Rootpaw examined the ground between them; it was littered with dead leaves, dry twigs, and odd-shaped pebbles. He knew that if he laid a paw on any of them, they would give him away by rustling or snapping or rolling over the earth.

I need to be clever.

Glancing around, he spotted a fallen tree that had lodged against the hillside at a steep angle. He realized that if he could reach the tree he could pad quietly to the other end and surprise Dewspring from above.

Rootpaw raised his head so that his whiskers could test the wind, and he was satisfied to find that it was blowing away from his mentor, who wouldn't be able to scent him until it was too late. All he needed to do was to land on the tree trunk without making a sound.

I'll only have one chance; I can't miss when I make the leap.

Focusing every muscle on the jump, Rootpaw crouched low, coiling himself into a ball, then launched himself at the tree. Springing upward, he had time to arrange his paws in the air so that he could land as silently as a falling snowflake.

Wow, it worked! he thought triumphantly after he touched down on the tree bark. Then he padded cautiously along the trunk until he reached a spot where he could look down at his mentor. *And this time I'm not breathing like a badger!*

Dewspring seemed to have forgotten that he was only pretending to clean his claws. He was engrossed in dislodging a tiny splinter of twig from between his pads. Seeing his chance, Rootpaw leaped from his perch and landed with a thump on Dewspring's shoulders, forcing him to the ground.

His mentor let out a gasp as he rolled away from Rootpaw. "Very good!" he meowed. "I didn't hear you coming at all. How did you do that?"

Rootpaw waved his tail toward the fallen tree. "I came along there," he explained. "I knew I'd be bound to make a noise if I tried creeping over all those dead leaves and stuff."

Dewspring nodded, clearly impressed. "You were always a good apprentice," he told Rootpaw, "but ever since you came back from the medicine cats' den, your skills seem even sharper."

Pleased at his praise, Rootpaw reflected that he might have improved because now he didn't have an anxious ghost following him around and relentlessly demanding his attention.

It's amazing what I can accomplish when I'm not distracted by a restless spirit!

But following the thought, Rootpaw immediately felt guilty. He knew that Bramblestar's ghost hadn't been following him just to annoy him or interfere with his training. He really needed help. But Rootpaw had no idea what he could do to help him—or bring him back. *So there's no point in ruining my chance to become a great warrior.*

"As you know, Rootpaw," Dewspring began, "Leafstar and

I had decided that you would have your warrior assessment soon."

Rootpaw felt his heart begin to pound harder, and his pads prickled with anticipation. *It's like Dewspring could hear my thoughts!* "Yes . . . ," he said, not sure what to expect. Sudden dread sent a shiver down his spine. They hadn't changed their minds, had they?

"Well," Dewspring continued, "you've impressed me with your skills today, and I see no reason to put off your assessment any longer. I'll confirm it with Leafstar when we get back to camp, but I think we'll do it tomorrow."

"Tomorrow? Really?" Rootpaw gasped in excitement.

Dewspring grinned. "Really. There's no sense in waiting when you're clearly ready."

Rootpaw let out a joyful yowl, springing straight up in the air. A few moments before, he had focused all his energy on being quiet. Now, as he and Dewspring headed to collect the voles he had caught earlier, he romped boisterously through the fallen leaves and grass.

"You're making enough noise to drive all the prey deep underground," Dewspring commented, though his tone was humorous and Rootpaw could tell he wasn't angry at all.

By the time he and his mentor arrived back in camp, Rootpaw had managed to calm down a little, though excitement still thrilled through him. Once he had deposited his voles on top of the fresh-kill pile, he bounded over to Tree and Violetshine, who were sharing a squirrel a few tail-lengths away.

"I'm going to be a warrior!" he announced. "Dewspring

says I can do my assessment tomorrow."

"That's excellent news," his mother purred, leaning over to give Rootpaw's ear a lick.

Tree's eyes gleamed with approval, too, though he seemed slightly concerned as his gaze traveled over his son. "Are you absolutely sure this is what you want?" he asked.

Rootpaw could see the reservation in his father's eyes. It wasn't so long ago that Tree had argued against staying in the Clans at all. When Rootpaw finally became a full warrior, it would tie him to the Clan in a way that would be hard to walk away from.

"Yes, *absolutely*," Rootpaw assured him eagerly. "All I've ever wanted is to be a warrior for my Clan."

Tree nodded. "Good. In that case, I'm very happy for you."

To Rootpaw's relief, he could see that his father was being genuine. Perhaps the issue of whether to stay or leave the Clans was finally closed, once and for all.

"Congratulations!" Rootpaw turned to see his sister, Needleclaw, dashing toward him. "Dewspring just told me. I wonder what your warrior name will be."

She plopped down beside Rootpaw and nuzzled his shoulder; Tree and Violetshine joined in too. Rootpaw thought it wasn't possible to be any happier.

Curling up that night in his nest in the apprentices' den, Rootpaw felt better than he had in a long time. Even though he could hear the wind howling outside, and his worries about Bramblestar still nagged at the back of his mind, all he could really think about was his assessment and how he had to make sure he did his best.

When at last he went to sleep, he fell instantly into a dream where he and Dewspring were in the middle of the forest. Dewspring was calling out battle moves for him. "Backward leap! Strike with forepaws! Underbelly dive!" Rootpaw performed them all perfectly.

But then Dewspring began yowling at Rootpaw to wake up. Rootpaw couldn't understand him, because he was awake already. He was staring right at Dewspring.

"I don't understand," he meowed. "Is this another sort of test?"

But Dewspring didn't explain. He just kept on calling Rootpaw's name as he drew closer, and his gray pelt began to give off a silver glow. As Rootpaw gaped in astonishment, the light grew brighter and brighter until it was so dazzling that it blinded him. He let out a choking cry of terror and found himself startling awake in his den.

His chest heaving from the memory of the dream, Rootpaw needed a few heartbeats to be sure he wasn't still in the woods. Wrenpaw was curled up asleep close by, and above his head Rootpaw could make out the arching ferns that formed the roof of the den. The wind had calmed, and dawn was creeping into the sky, but Rootpaw realized that wasn't the only light. A warm glow was coming from behind him, casting his shadow forward. He turned around and saw that something was standing there.

No, not something . . . Some cat.

As the glow began to fade, Rootpaw was able to make out the cat's features. He was a small, skinny tom with sleek black fur and intense yellow eyes. Rootpaw had the strange sense he had glimpsed him before, and he was sure of one thing. *This cat is dead.*

"Who are you?" Rootpaw asked.

"There's no time to explain," the ghost cat responded. "You have to come with me—now."

"What?" Rootpaw yowled so loud that he was afraid he had woken Wrenpaw, but the younger apprentice never stirred. "I can't! I have my warrior assessment at sunrise. I can't miss it for anything."

The ghost cat was already heading toward the mouth of the den. Glancing back over his shoulder to look at Rootpaw, he asked, "Not even to save your friend's life?"

His words brought Rootpaw upright, out of the den, and across the camp into the forest, as if he were being pulled along by an invisible tendril. *I have no idea who this is,* he thought, *but could he be talking about Shadowsight? Is it possible that Shadowsight is still alive?*

The dawn light was strengthening as the ghost cat led Rootpaw to the border with ThunderClan, and straight across it, ignoring the scent markers. Gulping nervously, Rootpaw followed.

I really hope we don't meet the ThunderClan dawn patrol.

When he sniffed the air, all the ThunderClan scents were stale, but Rootpaw still kept his senses alert as he padded through the rival Clan's territory, ready to leap up into the nearest tree if he caught even the faintest trace of an approaching ThunderClan cat.

Is this ghost really leading me to Shadowsight? Rootpaw asked himself. *And is the ghost cat right, that his life is in danger?* He had never heard of any cat daring to miss their warrior assessment. *Oh, I hope it's true, or I'll be in so much trouble, and all for nothing!*

Eventually the sun came up, casting long golden rays across the forest floor. Rootpaw felt a tightening in his chest, knowing that at that very moment Dewspring would be heading to his den to tell him it was time. *But he'll find my nest empty.* Rootpaw's only hope was that when he returned to camp and explained what happened, Dewspring would forgive him and give him another chance.

"Is it much farther?" Rootpaw called to the cat in front of him. His paws were beginning to ache.

"No, we're almost there," the spirit replied, not turning to look at him.

A few heartbeats later, Rootpaw began to pick up the scent of something bad, like prey that had been left out too long in the sun. "What's that?" he muttered to himself, wrinkling his nose.

At the same moment, the ghost cat halted at the edge of a narrow ravine. Rootpaw padded up to join him and immediately spotted why he had been brought there. His belly clenched as he saw Shadowsight's body, sprawled out beside a thornbush near the bank of the small stream that ran along the bottom of the ravine.

Rootpaw realized that the bad smell was coming from

Shadowsight, but he couldn't detect the scent of death. Shadowsight appeared to be unconscious; deep, swollen scars marred his pelt, which was matted with dried blood. He looked terribly frail, as if he hadn't eaten in days.

Rootpaw padded along the edge of the ravine, desperately searching for a way to reach his friend. Eventually he spotted a ledge that led downward, though it looked too narrow for his paws.

I have to give it a try.

Nervously, Rootpaw ventured onto the ledge, pressing up against the rock face and trying not to think of the sheer drop on the other side. After he had followed it for a few paw steps, it began to grow even narrower, until it vanished altogether.

Now what do I do? I can't even turn around safely. StarClan, don't let me be stuck like this!

Just below Rootpaw an elder bush jutted out of the side of the ravine. Its branches looked too thin to support his weight, but Rootpaw didn't think he had any choice. Bunching his muscles, he launched himself onto it; the branch swayed wildly, but from there Rootpaw could leap to an outcrop of rock and then to a twisted root just above the stream.

Finally Rootpaw jumped down the last tail-length and rushed over to Shadowsight, pressing his ear to his friend's body. Relief flooded over him as he detected a faint heartbeat and saw Shadowsight's chest rising and falling with each shallow breath.

"He's alive!" he cried out happily.

The ghost cat, who had appeared beside him, let out a

scornful huff. "Of course he's alive. Why do you think I brought you here? But you can probably smell that his wounds are infected, and it's getting worse."

"I'll fetch help," Rootpaw promised. "I'll be back before you know it. Hang in there, Shadowsight!"

Rootpaw scrambled back to the top of the ravine with far less caution than he had used coming down, and raced through the forest back to the SkyClan camp. *I'll find Fidgetflake. He'll know what to do.*

But before he could reach the medicine cats' den, Dewspring loomed up in front of him. Intent on his mission, Rootpaw hadn't noticed him, and had to skid to a halt to stop himself colliding with his mentor.

"There you are!" Dewspring yowled. "I've been looking for you all morning. I thought you wanted to be a warrior."

"I do!" Rootpaw panted. "But—"

"Skipping your assessment is a funny way of showing it," Dewspring snapped, his eyes narrowed with fury. "Has all your training been a big waste of time?"

"I'm sorry," Rootpaw meowed. "I know how angry you must be. But I had a good reason—really I did. I've found Shadowsight, and he's hurt!"

Dewspring's anger gave way to confusion. "Shadowsight?" he asked. "What is he doing on SkyClan territory?"

"He's not," Rootpaw explained. "He's in the forest just over the ThunderClan border."

Dewspring gave Rootpaw a hard stare. "And what were you doing all the way over there, on ThunderClan territory?

"I'll explain later!" he meowed, realizing that thanks to this delay, he probably didn't even have time to go find Fidgetflake now. "Shadowsight is seriously wounded. We have to bring him back to camp right away!"

Dewspring hesitated for a moment, then gave Rootpaw a brisk nod. "Show me where Shadowsight is. If he's as badly hurt as you say, there's no time to spare!"

Rootpaw bounded through the forest, following his own scent trail back to the ravine, with Dewspring hard on his paws. He showed Dewspring the way down he had taken to reach Shadowsight, and his mentor scrambled down after him. There was no sign of the ghost cat; Rootpaw guessed he had only appeared long enough to call for help.

In the time it had taken Rootpaw to fetch Dewspring, Shadowsight seemed to have grown even weaker. His breath was coming in thin wheezes and rattles, his chest convulsing as if it was taking him a massive effort to breathe at all.

"How will we ever get him out of here?" Dewspring asked, gazing up at the top of the ravine. "There's no way we can carry him the same way we came down."

"We have to figure it out," Rootpaw responded. "Stay with him; I'll go look for another path."

He set off up the ravine, in the opposite direction from the way he had come on his first visit. But both sides rose up like almost-sheer cliffs; there were enough paw holds for a cat on his own, but not for one who had to carry Shadowsight.

Rootpaw was almost ready to give up and try the other direction again when he spotted a place where a few larger boulders had rolled down into the ravine, creating a path stretching almost to the top.

Hope rising inside him, Rootpaw dashed back to Dewspring. "I've found a way," he panted. "Can you carry Shadowsight on your back?"

Dewspring nodded. Crouching down beside Shadowsight, he nudged his head under the injured cat's limp body. Rootpaw hauled Shadowsight upward until he lay sprawled on Dewspring's back, with his forepaws dangling over Dewspring's shoulders. Now that he was so close, the terrible stench of Shadowsight's wounds was almost too much to bear.

Slowly and carefully Dewspring stood up, managing not to dislodge Shadowsight. "Okay, let's go," he mewed. "Walk beside me and keep him steady."

Transporting Shadowsight was easy until they came to the fallen boulders. Dewspring looked up, blinking. "Oh, StarClan . . . ," he murmured, then added to Rootpaw, "Keep a grip on him so we don't drop him. We don't want to hurt him worse."

He began to clamber up the rocks, trying to keep his back as level as he could. Rootpaw snagged Shadowsight's fur in the claws of one forepaw, ready to support him if he started to slip. In one steep place Dewspring almost lost his balance, and the three cats tottered together at the edge of the rock. Rootpaw had a horrific picture of them falling and bouncing down the slope until they reached the stream again.

With poor Shadowsight squashed underneath us . . .

Then Dewspring heaved himself up, Rootpaw settled

Shadowsight securely on his back again, and the climb continued.

The path made by the fallen boulders ended about a fox-length from the top of the ravine. A sheer stretch of rock separated them from level ground. "Now what?" Rootpaw asked gloomily.

"Can you leap up there?" Dewspring asked.

"I'm a SkyClan cat," Rootpaw responded. "Of course I can leap!"

"Then do it."

Rootpaw crouched down, gathering himself and bunching his muscles for the leap. Then he drove himself upward; his claws scrabbled in the loose soil at the top of the ravine, and he managed to heave himself over the edge.

"What now?" he asked, gazing down at Dewspring.

Dewspring stretched upward so that he was holding Shadowsight as close to Rootpaw as he could. "Reach down and grab him by the scruff," he directed. "Don't try to pull him up, just hold him. I'll be with you in a heartbeat."

Rootpaw wasn't sure that would work, but he didn't try to argue. Leaning down, he craned his neck until he could fasten his teeth in Shadowsight's scruff. "Got him," he grunted.

Dewspring slipped out from underneath Shadowsight. Even though Shadowsight was so small and frail, when Rootpaw took his weight he thought it would tip him over the edge and back down into the ravine. He dug all his claws into the loose earth and focused on holding on.

Then Dewspring was beside him, leaning over to get his

own grip on the injured cat. "Pull!" he mewed around his mouthful of fur.

Together Rootpaw and his mentor edged backward, drawing Shadowsight with them until his limp body lay safely at the top of the ravine. Anxiously Rootpaw checked him over. "He's still breathing, thank StarClan!"

"Great!" Dewspring huffed out a long breath. "Give me a moment to rest, and we'll head back."

And this would be just the right time for a ThunderClan patrol to appear, Rootpaw thought, warily scanning the surrounding trees. Then he realized that any ThunderClan cats would be so shocked to see Shadowsight that they might not think to ask what two SkyClan cats were doing trespassing on their territory.

But no patrol appeared. Dewspring took Shadowsight on his back again; after their struggle in the ravine, the journey home seemed to take no time at all.

As soon as they emerged into their camp, they were spotted by Plumwillow, who was on guard. She sprang to her paws, her eyes wide with shock. "Who's that on your back?" she asked.

"It's Shadowsight, that missing ShadowClan cat," Dewspring explained. "We need to get him to the medicine cats."

But as he and Rootpaw headed to find Frecklewish, more of the SkyClan cats ran across from the fresh-kill pile or emerged from their dens, gathering around and asking what had happened.

"Let us through!" Rootpaw yowled, but no cat was paying attention to him.

At last, to his relief, he spotted Fidgetflake shouldering his way through the crowd. "Shift your paws!" the medicine cat hissed at the crowd of warriors. "We have an injured cat here." Beckoning Rootpaw and Dewspring with his tail, he added, "Bring him to our den right away."

Violetshine bounded over to join them as Fidgetflake led the way back to his den. She padded alongside Dewspring on the opposite side from Rootpaw, helping to support Shadowsight's limp body.

"Rootpaw, are you okay?" she asked. "I was so worried when you missed your assessment. I thought something must have happened to you. And you're covered in blood!"

Rootpaw glanced down at himself, to where Shadowsight's blood was smeared over his pelt. "It's not mine," he reassured his mother. "I'm not hurt."

Inside the medicine cats' den, Fidgetflake clawed together a nest of moss and fern. Dewspring gently lowered Shadowsight into it, letting out a huff of satisfaction and flexing his shoulders as he was relieved of the young cat's weight.

"Some cat should go right away to fetch Tigerstar and Dovewing," Fidgetflake meowed. "They'll want to be with their son . . . whatever happens."

Rootpaw felt his belly heaving at the ominous suggestion in the medicine cat's words. *Shadowsight* can't *die! Not after we went to all that trouble to find him.* "I'll go," he offered immediately.

"You're still an apprentice," Dewspring pointed out. "You can't go wandering into another Clan's territory by yourself."

But that's just what I did! Rootpaw thought, though he had the sense to keep his jaws shut.

"I'll go with him," Violetshine mewed. "Shadowsight should be with his kin."

As Rootpaw left the medicine cats' den, with his mother padding beside him, Leafstar came bounding across the camp from beside the fresh-kill pile.

"What's going on?" she asked.

Hurriedly Rootpaw told her how he and Dewspring had brought Shadowsight back from where he lay in the ravine on ThunderClan territory. "He didn't run away," he finished. "Some cat tried to kill him." Daringly he added, "*Now* do you think challenging Bramblestar is worth the risk?"

Leafstar's eyes widened; clearly she was too stunned to ask Rootpaw what he had been doing on ThunderClan territory, or to object to an apprentice telling her what to do. She stood staring after Rootpaw and Violetshine as the two cats headed out of the camp.

CHAPTER 12

Bristlefrost stood in the entrance to the Clan leader's den on the Highledge, gazing down at the listless figure of the false Bramblestar where he lay in his nest. The sun was well above the trees at the top of the stone hollow, and yet the impostor had barely moved since dawn.

"Maybe you should get up now," Bristlefrost suggested. "There's a hunting patrol waiting for your orders, and a few warriors want to speak to you about border marking. And—"

Bramblestar gazed at her with confusion in his face. "What are you meowing about?" he grumbled. Then he lifted a weary paw and waved her away. "Let Berrynose deal with them," he murmured. "I don't care about any of it. How can I? Squirrelflight is dead, and it's my fault. If I hadn't exiled her . . ."

A tiny spark of hope woke inside Bristlefrost, and she wondered if the intruder might possibly change his mind. "If you're having second thoughts about the exiles," she began tentatively, "it's probably not too late to find the others."

Bramblestar just moaned and looked away, closing his eyes as his whiskers drooped in pain. Bristlefrost wasn't even sure that he had heard her. Then with a pitiful whine he buried his face in the bracken fronds of his nest.

He looked so miserable that Bristlefrost couldn't suppress a pang of sympathy. For a moment she was tempted to tell him the truth, that Squirrelflight wasn't dead at all; she just didn't want to be found. *But that would undo all our hard work. It would put Squirrelflight and the rest of the exiles in danger,* she reflected. *And me, too, because it would prove that I lied to him.* She thrust the temptation away and remained silent.

For a few heartbeats she stood still, looking down at the wretched creature who was supposed to be her Clan leader. Then an idea crept into her mind.

"Maybe instead of seeing Squirrelflight's death as a punishment," she suggested to Bramblestar, "you should make sure she didn't die in vain."

Bramblestar raised his head and gave her a wary glance. "What does *that* mean?" he rasped.

"You know that Squirrelflight was a good cat," Bristlefrost told him. "Even if she was named as a codebreaker. It's not too late to turn things around, to make things right. In Squirrelflight's memory, you could rededicate yourself to making ThunderClan the strongest and most prosperous Clan. That means trusting your loyal warriors."

Bramblestar's gaze narrowed. "My *loyal* warriors," he repeated. Bristlefrost thought that a glow began to kindle in the depths of his amber eyes. Her heart lurched, and for a moment she could hardly get her breath, in fear that he would punish her for her boldness. *It's not my place to advise a Clan leader!*

But before Bramblestar could say any more, the sound

of paw steps came from the Highledge, and Alderheart slid inside the den. Bristlefrost shivered, thankful that her sense of menace had evaporated at the medicine cat's appearance.

"You wanted to see me?" Alderheart asked, casting a curious glance between Bramblestar and Bristlefrost.

"You took your time," Bramblestar grumbled. "Where have you been?"

"I was out collecting herbs," Alderheart explained, dipping his head respectfully. "I only just got your message. Are you hurt?"

"Of course I'm hurt!" Bramblestar snapped. "Why else would I have called you here?"

Alderheart seemed unworried by the Clan leader's irritable tone. "Then tell me what the problem is," he mewed calmly.

"My chest hurts, and my fur itches."

Padding across the den, Alderheart ran his paws carefully over Bramblestar's body. He gave his pelt a good sniff, parting the strands of fur, and sniffed again around the Clan leader's muzzle, his eyes and ears.

"I still can't find anything wrong with you," he pronounced at last.

Bramblestar convulsed in his nest, half sitting up. "That's because you're useless!" he hissed. "Just a second-rate medicine cat! Maybe I should have sent you away instead of Jayfeather. Even a blind cat could see something's wrong with me." Drawing his lips back in a snarl, he added, "Go get something to help me, or you can join Jayfeather in exile!"

Turning his head away, Bramblestar buried himself deeper

in the moss and bracken of his nest.

With a slight twitch of her ears, Bristlefrost signaled to Alderheart to follow her out of the den. When they reached the Highledge, the medicine cat halted and faced her.

"I can't help Bramblestar when there's nothing wrong with him," he complained, his tail-tip flicking to and fro in exasperation.

"I know," Bristlefrost murmured. "But maybe you could bring him something to make him sleep. He might get back to normal if he could rest."

"I hope so," Alderheart agreed. "I don't know how much more of this I can take. Some of the Clanmates who mean the most to me are gone, and the cats who remain are miserable." It was clear to Bristlefrost that Alderheart was really referring to himself. His eyes were full of pain, reminding her that the real Bramblestar was Alderheart's father as well as his Clan leader. This ordeal had been hard for all for them, but Alderheart had obviously been suffering more than most and keeping it to himself.

"I think he's grieving for Squirrelflight," she murmured, hoping at least a bit of explanation might help to ease Alderheart's mind.

Alderheart nodded; Bristlefrost had told him about the former deputy's deception. "He has some feelings, then," he responded. "But I'm still convinced that something dark and terrible has taken over Bramblestar's body." His tail-tip twitched in frustration. "I'd join the exiles without a backward glance, but I can't leave the Clan when I'm the only medicine cat left."

"Oh, please don't do that!" Bristlefrost exclaimed, alarm throbbing in her chest. "Don't leave us to Flipclaw!"

Alderheart rolled his eyes. "Flipclaw!" he snarled. "StarClan help us all!"

He cast one final glance back into the den, then hurried off down the tumbled rocks.

Bristlefrost remained on the Highledge, looking out across the stone hollow. After a moment, she noticed Spotfur standing at the edge of the camp. Their gazes locked; then Spotfur angled her ears toward the thorn tunnel, clearly beckoning Bristlefrost to follow her out.

There must be another meeting of the rebel cats, Bristlefrost realized, her pelt tingling with a mixture of fear and excitement. *I need to go.*

She turned and craned her neck to look inside the den. Bramblestar was curled up in his nest, letting out a miserable whine. Bristlefrost knew that soon Alderheart would be back with herbs to help him sleep; this could be her best chance of slipping away unnoticed.

Bristlefrost padded quietly down into the camp, then followed Spotfur through the tunnel and into the forest. The spotted tabby she-cat led her through the undergrowth until they came upon Stemleaf waiting in the shelter of a holly bush. He rose to his paws and joined them as Spotfur turned and headed toward the lake.

None of the three cats spoke a word until they emerged from the trees and padded down a grassy bank to reach the strip of pebbles that bordered the lake. For the first time, Bristlefrost became confident that no cat was pursuing them.

"What's going on?" she asked.

"You'll see," Spotfur responded, and refused to say more.

She set a brisk pace along the edge of the lake and across SkyClan territory. When they reached the ShadowClan border, Spotfur veered away from the water and led the way into the pine forest. The wind had risen again; branches creaked and thrashed above their heads, and Bristlefrost could hardly hear her own paw steps as she padded over the thick layer of needles that covered the ground.

At last she began to make out movement ahead, and she picked up the mingled scent of many cats. All the same, as she followed Spotfur, whisking around a sprawling bramble thicket, she was amazed to see the crowd of cats that met her gaze.

Bramblestar had exiled many cats, and had encouraged other Clans to exile theirs. Bristlefrost's eyes flicked between Jayfeather, Squirrelflight, Crowfeather, Lionblaze, and Mothwing, along with most of ShadowClan. Now that they were allied with the rebels, there were almost enough of them to form a Clan of their own.

But that's not *what we want to do,* she thought uneasily.

Noticing Twigbranch sitting by herself at the edge of the crowd, Bristlefrost padded over to her. "Greetings," she mewed, sitting beside her. "Are you okay?"

Twigbranch shrugged uneasily. "I suppose . . . ," she mewed. "To be honest, Bristlefrost, I don't feel like I belong here. I can't wait for the half-moon to be up so that I can go home."

Bristlefrost stared at her in surprise. "You really want to do that—knowing the truth about Bramblestar?"

"Bramblestar isn't the only cat in ThunderClan," Twigbranch responded. "I love my Clan, and I think of myself as a ThunderClan cat. I'm going back as soon as I can."

"But you can be a real help to us here," Bristlefrost pointed out.

"I can be a real help there, too," Twigbranch meowed. "I can't turn my back on ThunderClan, but what I can do is resist the false Bramblestar from within. After all, Bristlefrost, isn't that what you're doing?"

Okay, I stuck my paw in my mouth there, Bristlefrost thought regretfully. But maybe Twigbranch was right. They weren't so different, and it would help to have another cat on the inside, keeping a close eye on Bramblestar and helping to limit the damage he tried to do.

While she and Twigbranch had been talking, Harelight and Icewing, warriors of RiverClan, had slipped out of the undergrowth to join the group. Clearly the rebels had been waiting for them to arrive. Every cat settled down in the shade cast by the thicket; Tigerstar ordered a couple of the younger ShadowClan warriors to remain standing on watch. Bristlefrost padded over to sit beside Stemleaf and Spotfur, anticipation fluttering in her belly.

Squirrelflight was the first to speak, stepping forward into the center of the group. "There's something I need to tell every cat," she began. "Mothwing and Bristlefrost and I have convinced the false Bramblestar that I am dead. It was the only way to stop him looking for me."

Bristlefrost saw the rebel cats flick up their ears in surprise. "How did you do that?" Conefoot called out.

"Never mind," Squirrelflight responded. "That's not important. The point is, for StarClan's sake, if you meet the impostor, don't give me away. If he discovers I'm alive, it will cause no end of trouble."

Bristlefrost suppressed a shiver and felt Stemleaf rest his tail-tip briefly on her shoulder. *I don't even want to think about what Bramblestar would do to me if he found out I lied to him.*

"I'm not sure I like the idea of lying to a Clan leader," Crowfeather meowed thoughtfully. "Especially your own," he went on, with a glance at the ThunderClan cats.

"We can lie to him, no problem," Spotfur retorted.

"Yeah, because he's *not* our leader," Stemleaf added.

Crowfeather shrugged. "Good point."

"Then are we agreed?" Tigerstar asked, his gaze traveling over the assembled cats as he rose to stand beside Squirrel-flight. "No cat will even *mention* Squirrelflight to Bramblestar, and if he should ask you, she's dead, okay?"

Murmurs of assent rose from the crowd of cats. Squirrel-flight dipped her head. "Thank you," she mewed, and stepped back to sit down again.

"And now we have more news," Tigerstar went on; to Bristlefrost's surprise she saw a gleam of happiness in his eyes.

"Frecklewish, I think this is for you to tell."

The SkyClan medicine cat rose to her paws. "Yes, I have news," she announced. "And for once, it's good. Shadowsight has been found. He's alive, but unconscious, in the SkyClan medicine-cat den. Fidgetflake is taking care of him."

Gasps of astonishment and soft purrs of pleasure greeted the medicine cat's news. "Thank StarClan," some cat mewed softly.

Jayfeather's harsher tones cut across the sounds. "How did a ShadowClan cat end up in the SkyClan medicine cat den?" he asked.

Bristlefrost noticed that Rootpaw was glancing around awkwardly as if he expected some older cat to tell the story. But no cat spoke.

Eventually Frecklewish meowed, "Come on, Rootpaw. Spit it out."

"I was the one who found him," Rootpaw explained, still looking faintly embarrassed to be addressing the whole group. "It's a long story—I can't tell it all now—but I could see that another cat had attacked him and he'd been terribly wounded."

"Who attacked him?" Jayfeather asked. "Was it Bramble-star?"

Rootpaw shrugged. "I don't know. He's been unconscious since I found him, so he hasn't been able to tell us anything. But whoever did it nearly killed him."

"If Rootpaw hadn't found him when he did," Freckle-wish added, giving the SkyClan apprentice an approving nod, "Shadowsight would probably be dead by now."

Tree rose to his paws and took a pace forward to stand beside his son. "And now SkyClan is uncertain what to do about Bramblestar," he meowed.

"What do you mean by that?" Bristlefrost asked.

"At best, Bramblestar lied about Shadowsight just running off," the yellow tom told her. "Not that any cat believed him, anyway. At worst, he had something to do with the attack." He paused, letting his gaze travel around the group of cats. "Until Rootpaw found Shadowsight, Leafstar resisted doing anything to support the rebels. But now . . . she's seriously thinking about it."

Bristlefrost shuddered. Despite the blood she'd seen coating Bramblestar's chest that night, she wanted to reject with every hair on her pelt the idea that Bramblestar—or whoever he really was—could do something so wicked. Attacking Sparkpelt was bad enough, but it was far worse for any cat to attack a medicine cat. And why would he want to? *But I have to admit it's probably true.*

For a few moments the assembled cats broke up into little groups, anxiously discussing what they had just heard.

"Bramblestar would never attack another Clan cat!"

"No—but the thing inside him obviously would."

Then Crowfeather's voice rose above the rest. "Things have gone too far," he stated, his dark gray fur bristling. "I don't like it, but it's clear what we need to do: kill Bramblestar."

Protests arose from the cats around him, mingled with murmurs of agreement.

"I never thought it would come to this," one of the

RiverClan cats mewed sadly. "Every cat admired Bramblestar so much."

"But whatever is inside him isn't Bramblestar," Breezepelt argued. "And it looks like there's only one way to get rid of him."

A jolt passed through Bristlefrost's chest. She felt like she had been racing through the forest and the ground had suddenly given way beneath her paws.

"There must be another way!" she objected. "We want the Clans back the way we were, but we're not cold-blooded murderers. If we do that, are we any better than he is?"

"But he obviously tried to kill Shadowsight!" Kitescratch argued, giving Bristlefrost a hostile glare. "We need to kill him before he can hurt any other cat. And if you want to prove you're really with us now, you'll go along with it."

For a few heartbeats Bristlefrost didn't know how to reply. She glanced around at the gathered cats and saw vague uncertainty in their eyes. It was unnerving how easily the notion that she was working for the impostor could take hold, but she doubted any of them still truly believed that. She knew that Kitescratch had only brought it up as a way to quiet her protests. But he didn't need to. She couldn't deny that there was a lot of sense in what Crowfeather and Kitescratch said, and she could see that many cats agreed with them. Even Stemleaf and Spotfur were nodding assent, although they both looked unsure.

In the end it was Squirrelflight who broke the silence. "You're all forgetting something," she meowed loudly. "We haven't been in touch with StarClan in moons. The truth is, not even the medicine cats know what would happen if any leader were to die now."

Rootpaw blinked in shock as he shifted his gaze to Jay-feather. "Is that true?"

The medicine cat shook his head. "There's no way to know. But I suspect that with StarClan gone, they might not go on to their next life."

Squirrelflight was staring at the blind medicine cat, her green gaze filled with horror at the thought of losing her mate. "This means we have to wait," she pleaded. "At least until we find out for sure what happened to Shadowsight. Surely we can delay until he regains consciousness and we can find out what he knows. There are too many unanswered questions for us to act now."

"You're right, Squirrelflight," Stemleaf mewed, though Bristlefrost thought he sounded reluctant to admit it. "We should wait until Shadowsight wakes up before we do any-thing."

But in spite of his words, Bristlefrost could tell from Stemleaf's hesitant voice and his unwillingness to meet Squirrelflight's gaze that he didn't really want to do that at all.

She could hear more arguing among the younger Shadow-Clan warriors.

"I'd kill him now! I'd rip his throat out!"

"For StarClan's sake, haven't you listened to a word Squirrelflight said?"

It was clear that the assembly was splitting between cats

who were willing to wait, and those who wanted to kill Bramblestar—right now.

Bristlefrost wasn't sure what she wanted. She knew how dangerous the false Bramblestar was, and how much safer every cat would be if he was gone for good.

But what about the real Bramblestar? If we're ever to bring him back, he'll need a body to come home to. I admired him so much, she added sadly to herself. *I wanted to impress him. And now . . . Who will lead ThunderClan, if not Bramblestar?*

"So are we agreed?" Tigerstar demanded, taking control of the meeting. "We will do nothing until we have talked to Shadowsight." His amber gaze raked the assembly. "Do you promise to stick to this plan?"

Slowly each cat in turn gave their promise, though Bristlefrost could still see angry or bitter looks coming from many of the cats. *I hope this doesn't cause a split among the rebels,* she thought.

"Why is it that Tigerstar gets to decide?" she heard Breezepelt whisper. "He's a leader, but he's not my leader."

"Doesn't seem right to me," Kitescratch agreed.

Crowfeather flicked his tail. "First Tigerstar wanted us to wait until we were all in agreement; now we're waiting for Shadowsight to wake up. We're never going to make a plan at this rate."

Bristlefrost's pads prickled with apprehension. *Bramblestar might need protection.*

"I may be blind, but I'm not deaf," Jayfeather grumbled, clearly having picked up the whispering. "If any cat has something to say, you should speak up so we can all hear it."

The whispering stopped, and for a few heartbeats no cat said anything. Eventually Breezepelt rose and gave his pelt an irritable shake.

"The only reason we aren't killing the impostor," he snapped, "is because the real Bramblestar might need his body one day. But his ghost hasn't been seen in nearly half a moon. And that means," he added with an apologetic glance at Squirrelflight, "that his spirit might be gone. In that case, what are we waiting for?"

Tigerstar turned to Rootpaw. "Do you have any news?" he asked the apprentice.

Reluctantly, Rootpaw shook his head. "I haven't seen Bramblestar's ghost for a long time," he replied. "But that doesn't mean he's gone for good."

"He *isn't* gone," Squirrelflight insisted, with an angry lash of her tail. "I can still feel his presence. And any cat who tries to kill my mate's body will have me to answer to."

Seeing Squirrelflight's claws out and her eyes blazing, Bristlefrost thought she would be a formidable opponent for any cat. Breezepelt and the others clearly thought so too. For a few heartbeats they looked as if they might say more; then Breezepelt backed off, muttering something into his chest fur.

"There's one more thing we can do," Frecklewish announced as the tension began to die away. "Kestrelflight and Willow-shine aren't here. We should speak to them and see if they're prepared to join us."

"That won't be easy," Crowfeather responded. "Harestar

and Mistystar, at least, are convinced that StarClan is punishing us with this heavy rain and wind, and that Bramblestar is the only cat who knows how to appease StarClan. And the medicine cats won't want to act against their leaders' wishes. At least not without good reason. If we move against Bramblestar without them, we'll be fighting WindClan and RiverClan as well."

"Then you'll have to give them that good reason. Tell them what Bramblestar tried to do to Shadowsight," Stemleaf told Frecklewish. "Surely they wouldn't take the advice of a murderer?"

"We haven't proved that he *is* a murderer yet," Tree pointed out, though no cat took much notice of him.

Frecklewish let out a long sigh. "I hope Kestrelflight will listen," she replied. "As a medicine cat, Shadowsight has a connection to at least one cat in each of the Clans. This attack on him should be enough to push them to do something."

At Frecklewish's words, the meeting began to break up. Bristlefrost was about to follow her Clanmates back to their own territory when Squirrelflight halted her, resting her tail on her shoulder and drawing her to one side.

"Please, Bristlefrost, watch over Bramblestar," she begged. "I know it's a lot to ask. After all, the impostor could be dangerous. But you're one of the few cats he trusts, and you'll know which cats to look out for," she finished, with a sharp glance at Breezepelt and some of the other cats who were pressing for action.

"Don't worry," Bristlefrost assured her. "I won't let anything happen to Bramblestar."

Not if I can help it, she added to herself. *But I hope I won't have to battle cats I know, just to protect this stranger.*

CHAPTER 13

Shadowsight stood at the side of the SkyClan medicine cats' den, watching his mother, Dovewing, bending over his motionless body. "Please wake up . . . please," she whispered, gently stroking his fur with one forepaw.

Shadowsight could hardly bear to see Dovewing's grief and anxiety. He longed to feel his mother's comforting touch; he wanted to wake up, if only for her sake, but he wasn't ready to rejoin his body just yet. *I'll come back soon, Dovewing,* he thought, *but only after I figure out who attacked me.* He knew that finding the culprit was the only way to protect himself and his Clan, and to do that, he'd have to stay a spirit a little longer.

Meanwhile his father, Tigerstar, was pacing back and forth across the den, his amber eyes smoldering and his pelt alive with anger. "I know Bramblestar is behind this!" he snarled. "He didn't like the way Shadowsight was contradicting him, so he did his best to shut him up."

Fidgetflake shook his head. "We have no proof that Bramblestar is behind the attack," he pointed out.

Tigerstar whipped around to face him, fixing him with a

glare. "But you know it was a cat, right?" he challenged the medicine cat.

"Yes . . . I know that much," Fidgetflake admitted. "The size and depth of his wounds show that a cat attacked him—one who knew how to inflict serious harm."

"Then that settles it," Tigerstar snapped.

Dovewing looked up from her place beside Shadowsight's body. "Things aren't always what they seem," she told her mate. "Remember when we suspected some other Clan of poisoning our fresh-kill pile, but it turned out to be Juniper-claw? We can't go accusing a cat—especially a Clan leader—of something so serious, without proof."

Tigerstar lashed his tail. "Look at the way Bramblestar has been acting!" he exclaimed. "How much more proof do you need? Besides, how are we supposed to get real proof? You were going to spy on ThunderClan when you were pretend-ing to atone, but it turned out to be much harder than we expected." He began his impatient pacing again. "Bramble-star, or whoever he really is," he continued, "is so demented that I fear for the life of any cat who is caught spying."

Dovewing nodded agreement. "I'm not sure how we can get proof," she mewed, "but the truth always has a way of com-ing out."

"Fine," Tigerstar snorted. "But meanwhile, if Bramblestar so much as raises a paw against my kin again, he will die. I'll take care of him myself."

Shadowsight could understand his father's frustration. But for once, he could do something about it. As a spirit, he could visit ThunderClan and eavesdrop, just as he was doing now, and as he had done before his body was brought back to Sky-Clan.

Shadowsight padded out of the medicine cats' den and across the camp, heading in the direction of ThunderClan territory. As soon as he began to imagine what he would dis-cover in their camp, he found himself there, balancing on a narrow ledge halfway up the side of the stone hollow.

Another benefit of being a ghost, he thought with satisfaction.

Gazing out across the camp, Shadowsight spotted a couple of apprentices hauling a mass of soiled bedding toward the thorn tunnel. They passed Leafshade at the head of a hunt-ing patrol on its way in, each cat laden with prey, which they dropped onto the fresh-kill pile. Daisy was sunning herself at the entrance to the nursery, while Alderheart appeared from his den with a bunch of leaves in his jaws and headed toward the elders.

It all looks so peaceful, Shadowsight thought. But there was a tension in the air that wasn't usual for any Clan, and he knew exactly which cat was to blame. *Bramblestar . . . I need to find out what he's doing.*

As Shadowsight watched, Stormcloud emerged from the elders' den, swiftly glanced from side to side, then bounded over to the fresh-kill pile. He picked up a vole and headed back the way he had come. But before he had taken more than a couple of paw steps, Bramblestar slipped out from behind the warriors' den and stood blocking his path.

"Have I chosen the prey I want to eat yet?" he demanded.

Stormcloud's eyes widened in alarm and he dropped the vole at his paws. "No," he replied, "but Brackenfur said he was hungry, and I just thought I would bring him—"

"You know the rules," Bramblestar interrupted. "The leader eats first, no exceptions!"

Stormcloud cast a glance full of regret toward the elders' den, then reluctantly picked up the vole and carried it back to the fresh-kill pile. "Sorry," he muttered as he dropped it; Shadowsight thought he didn't sound sorry at all.

"If you like prey so much," Bramblestar continued, narrowing his eyes, "you can go out into the forest and sleep with it tonight. Don't come back until you're ready to uphold the code like a real warrior should."

Stormcloud stared at the Clan leader for a moment and then whipped around, heading for the thorn tunnel with his head and his tail held high. Bramblestar followed him with a baleful gaze until he disappeared.

For the first time Shadowsight noticed that a small tortoiseshell she-cat—obviously an apprentice—had been close enough to see what had just happened, and had begun to back away, her nervous gaze fixed on her Clan leader. But she was not quick or quiet enough to escape.

"You!" Bramblestar snarled, turning and looming over the apprentice. "Go and fetch some mouse bile, and pick the ticks off the elders. All of them."

"But I didn't steal prey!" the apprentice protested.

"Maybe not." Bramblestar's growl came from deep within his chest. "But you stood by and let it happen. Go!"

The apprentice scurried off. Watching her and the other cats out in the stone hollow, Shadowsight realized how miserable they seemed. Every cat had a wary look—the same one they had when they expected a fox to leap out at them from a patch of shadow. No cat wanted to draw Bramblestar's attention as he stalked past on his way back to his den.

My father was right, Shadowsight thought. *This is the cat who attacked me. I just need to hear him say it.*

He began to look for a way down from his ledge, but the rock wall below seemed sheer. His paw slipped as he tried to force it into a crack, and he bit back a yowl of terror as he imagined plummeting to the floor of the camp. Instead he found himself standing a tail-length from the rock, his paws firmly planted on the air.

Wow! he thought. *I didn't expect that!*

Shadowsight let himself drop as gently as a falling leaf and began to follow Bramblestar, realizing it was no effort at all to keep quiet. He was not even sure that his paws were touching the ground; certainly he couldn't feel any sharp edges as he climbed the tumbled rocks to the Highledge.

"Ungrateful cats!" Bramblestar was grumbling as he entered his den. Shadowsight slipped in behind him. "They need discipline. They need to be taught not to steal, not to question their leader, not to trespass . . ." He glanced back over his shoulder. "Wouldn't you agree, Shadowsight?"

Shadowsight's jaw dropped, and he stood gaping, utterly astonished. The false Bramblestar was staring straight at him. Panic surged through him, and it took all his courage not to flee back to his body in the SkyClan camp.

The ThunderClan leader bared his teeth in a grin. "That's right . . . I can see you," he meowed. "I knew you were trespassing in our territory the minute you appeared in the camp."

Shadowsight struggled to find words. "But how?" he asked eventually.

Bramblestar shrugged. "Maybe it's because I've been to StarClan and come back more powerful than you can imagine. Maybe it's because I have a connection to those I've killed."

Shadowsight let out a gasp. *He's confessed! He's the one who attacked me!*

"Or maybe," Bramblestar continued, his face still set in the same chilling grin, "it's because spirits can always recognize other spirits."

As Shadowsight stared at him with a mixture of fear and disbelief, he thought he saw the edges of Bramblestar's body begin to blur, as though mist were seeping out of his pelt. A heartbeat later another cat slid out like smoke from a burning fire and stood in front of Shadowsight, while the body he had left slumped to the floor of the den.

A glow pulsed around the cat's pelt; Shadowsight found it hard to make out the color of his fur. But his eyes were dark blue, so different from Bramblestar's warm amber ones. His gaze was fixed on Shadowsight with a menacing gleam.

Shadowsight felt horror turn his blood to ice and freeze his paws to the ground. *I don't know who this cat is, but I know it isn't Bramblestar.*

"What have you done to Bramblestar?" he asked, his voice

shaking in spite of all his efforts to keep it steady.

The glowing presence glanced over at Bramblestar's limp form, which lay stretched out as if he were sleeping. "All I did was take advantage of an opportunity," he meowed in a voice that Shadowsight felt was strangely familiar. "You would think Bramblestar would be grateful. I'm living his life so much better than he ever could." He flicked his tail dismissively. "But all he could do was moan about wanting his body back."

Shadowsight could hardly believe what he was hearing. "Do you mean you've seen Bramblestar?" he asked. "Have you spoken to him?"

The impostor let out a contemptuous huff. "I don't want to give myself away by letting the Clan cats know I can speak to the dead," he replied. "So I just ignore Bramblestar and all his bitter muttering." He paused, then added, "Well, I used to. Before Bramblestar . . ."

His words gave way to a drawn-out *mrrow* of laughter. Shadowsight thought he had never heard anything so evil; all the fur on his back stood on end at the sound.

"What did you do to him?" he demanded. "Where is Bramblestar?"

A moment before, Shadowsight had thought the stranger's laugh was frightening, but now he found that the grim, determined look in his cold blue eyes was so much worse. He forced himself not to back away as the impostor slowly drew closer, stretching one long paw out in front of him.

"You shouldn't ask what became of Bramblestar," he responded in a husky voice. "Not unless you want the same thing to happen to you. That cat won't ruin my plans again . . . and neither will you."

Shadowsight couldn't tear his gaze away from that blue, malignant stare. He summoned all his courage, desperate not to let the stranger, whoever he might be, intimidate him. "You can't just take over his life," he insisted. "There's only one Bramblestar!"

The spirit cat nodded slowly. "You're right," he mewed. "And it's me. If Bramblestar wants his body back, he'll have to fight me for it."

The stranger let out a loud hiss, raising himself onto his hind paws. Shadowsight braced himself, expecting that the false Bramblestar would pounce on him. Instead he dropped back to the ground, arched his glowing back, and gave his pelt a shake. His breathing slowed, and a heartbeat later he spoke again.

"I knew you weren't faithful enough as a medicine cat to pass on the codebreaker vision properly. You *are* a codebreaker, just like the rest!"

With a shock as if he had just plunged into an icy pool, Shadowsight realized where he had heard this cat's voice before. The memory overwhelmed him. "It was you!" he yowled. "You're the voice I heard at the Moonpool, telling me about the codebreakers! It was never StarClan that spoke to me—it was you. And you've been possessing Bramblestar ever since the night he died on that hill."

The strange cat nodded, looking almost pleased to have his clever deception recognized.

"You stole Bramblestar's body," Shadowsight accused him. "You deceived me and tried to kill me. Is there no end to your evil?"

For response, the stranger merely licked one forepaw and drew it over his ear.

"How did you do all this?" Shadowsight continued. "If you're a spirit—like me—and you know the Clans . . . then you should be in StarClan. Or the Dark Forest."

Light glinted from the impostor's bared teeth. "There are ways to move between those worlds, if one is clever enough," he replied.

With a fresh flood of horror, Shadowsight understood that without knowing it, he had been this cat's accomplice. If he hadn't followed the orders he had believed came from StarClan, Bramblestar might have survived instead of being left to die on the snow-swept hill. He shuddered, overwhelmed by racking guilt. *I was right to doubt my visions. They were all a lie.*

Summoning every scrap of his courage, Shadowsight took a pace forward to confront the impostor. "What's happened to the real Bramblestar's spirit?" he demanded. "Have you destroyed it altogether?"

The glowing cat let out a *mrrow* of amusement. *He's enjoying this,* thought Shadowsight. But as he waited for the impostor's response, he felt a tug in his gut, stronger and more insistent than before, pulling him back to SkyClan.

My body . . . How long have I been gone? He realized that he had no idea, except that it was too long. He wanted to finish this encounter with the false Bramblestar, but if he didn't leave right away, he might be lost forever.

"This isn't over," he told the intruder, then raced out of the den into the night, focusing all his thoughts on the body he had abandoned.

A heartbeat later, Shadowsight found himself back in the SkyClan medicine cats' den, where his mother was curled up asleep beside his unconscious form.

Spiresight stood beside them, shaking his head as he saw Shadowsight. "You're cutting it close," he mewed. "Where have you been? Who were you with?"

Shadowsight realized that he had no idea how to answer that question.

CHAPTER 14

Gusts of wind swept across the SkyClan camp, carrying a spatter of rain and ruffling Rootpaw's pelt. He ignored the chilly drops as he stood with his head held high, staring at the group of SkyClan cats around him. His parents, Violetshine and Tree, were standing nearby; he felt warmed as he met their proud gaze. Dewspring was there, too, and Rootpaw's sister, Needleclaw, had pattered up, so close that their pelts were brushing.

A little farther away, Frecklewish and several of the SkyClan warriors were joining the circle. Even Tigerstar had appeared, peering out of the medicine cats' den where he and Dovewing were visiting Shadowsight. He was shifting from paw to paw, showing Rootpaw how anxious he was to get back inside, where his son still lay unconscious. It would be dangerous to move Shadowsight, Rootpaw knew, so he would remain in the SkyClan den until he woke, or until . . .

No, Rootpaw told himself firmly. I won't think about that.

Tigerstar was present now out of respect, but his mind was clearly elsewhere, his head turning as if he was compelled to look back toward his son. Rootpaw couldn't blame him. No cat *seems to be fully present. . . . How could they be?*

Leafstar, who had been sitting on the Tallstump as her Clan assembled, leaped lightly down and padded into the center of the circle. "We are here for one of the most important moments in the life of a Clan," she announced. "The making of a new warrior."

"This is weird," Rootpaw whispered to Needleclaw. "I haven't even had my warrior assessment."

"You've done better than that," his sister whispered back. "Now shut up and listen."

"Rootpaw saved Shadowsight," Leafstar continued, "the young medicine cat who had been missing for some time. And in doing that, he created a strong bond between SkyClan and ShadowClan. While we've had conflicts in the past, Rootpaw has given us a way to heal those divisions. He demonstrated bravery, strength, and clearheadedness in a time of great peril. Not only that, he showed wisdom in seeking help when he needed it. Because of this, I don't think it's necessary to give him a formal assessment. His actions speak for themselves. Does any cat object?"

Flooded with embarrassment at his leader's praise, Rootpaw was staring at his paws. Now his pelt prickled with apprehension as he wondered if any of his Clanmates would protest.

But the only cat who spoke was his mentor, Dewspring. "Just get on with it, Leafstar," he said, amused.

Rootpaw looked up to see Leafstar beckoning to him with her tail. He padded out into the circle to stand in front of her. His heart was pounding as he waited for the words that would make him a warrior.

"I, Leafstar, leader of SkyClan, call upon my warrior ancestors to look down on this apprentice," the Clan leader began. "He has trained hard to understand the ways of your noble code, and I commend him to you as a warrior in his turn." Bending her head to gaze at Rootpaw, she continued, "Rootpaw, do you promise to uphold the warrior code and to protect and defend this Clan, even at the cost of your life?"

Rootpaw knew what a heavy commitment he was making—even heavier, in this confused time of accusations of codebreaking. "I do," he responded firmly.

"Then by the powers of StarClan," Leafstar announced, "I give you your warrior name. Rootpaw, from this moment you will be known as Rootspring. StarClan honors your strength and resilience, and we welcome you as a full warrior of Sky-Clan."

Leafstar stepped forward and bent to rest her muzzle on the top of Rootspring's head. In response Rootspring licked her shoulder, then stepped back.

"Rootspring! Rootspring!" the cats of SkyClan acclaimed him.

Warm pride swept through Rootspring as he listened to his Clanmates' congratulations, and his chest swelled even more as he caught a nod of approval from the deputy, Hawkwing, and several of the senior warriors.

As he waited for the clamor to die down, Rootspring tried out his new name in his mind. He was a warrior at last. For so long, he had worried that his ability to see ghosts would separate him from his Clan. He'd been embarrassed by his difference from other warriors. But that difference had let him save Shadowsight, and had made him a warrior.

Rootspring accepted that he *did* see spirits, and he wanted to believe that what Leafstar had said was true: that his own spirit was strong and resilient. He wasn't sure; he wished he felt that strong inside, but the whole episode with Shadowsight had shaken him. He hadn't told any cat about the ghostly presence that had led him to Shadowsight's body. That cat was still hanging around the camp; Rootspring had seen him several times.

What is he doing here? Rootspring asked himself. *Is he waiting for Shadowsight to die?* Then he shook his head. *No! I won't believe that. Shadowsight has to survive.*

By now the circle of cats was breaking up into smaller groups, some of them heading for their dens or the fresh-kill pile, while others left the camp on patrol.

Needleclaw gave Rootspring a nudge. "Come on, I'll find you a big, juicy piece of prey," she urged him. "You deserve it."

Rootspring was tempted, water flooding his jaws at the thought of a fat vole or a squirrel. But he shook his head. "I'll join you later," he responded. "There's something I want to do first."

"Okay." Needleclaw flicked his ear with her tail. "I'll save you something tasty."

As she bounded off toward the fresh-kill pile, Rootspring saw that Leafstar and Tree were heading for the medicine cats' den, where they joined Tigerstar. As all three cats vanished inside, Rootspring followed them.

Inside the den Fidgetflake was sorting herbs for Shadowsight, while Dovewing was crouched beside her son, cleaning his damp fur with long strokes of her tongue. "Come back to us," she whispered lovingly into his ear. "We all need you."

When Rootspring entered with the other cats, Dovewing looked up, warm welcome flooding into her eyes. "It's good to see you again, Rootpaw," she mewed.

"It's Rootspring now," Leafstar corrected her gently.

Dovewing let out a gasp. "I'm so sorry!" she exclaimed. "I'd forgotten that your warrior ceremony was today. Congratulations, Rootspring."

Rootspring dipped his head humbly. "Thank you."

Meanwhile, Tigerstar had approached Fidgetflake. "Has there been any change?" he asked, his voice taut with anxiety.

"His wounds are clean now," Fidgetflake replied, "and they seem to be improving. That's good." In spite of his encouraging words, his face was somber as he glanced across at Shadowsight, and he shook his head a little. "I can't tell you when he'll wake. You'll have to be patient and wait."

Rootspring found himself a spot to sit close to Shadowsight's head, relieved that every cat was too worried about the young medicine cat to ask him any more questions. He understood their fear, but he knew he would have a hard time explaining how he'd found Shadowsight.

I'd just make myself sound mouse-brained. At this point, they would have no trouble believing that a dead cat helped him find Shadowsight, but they would definitely question the wisdom of following a cat he didn't even know without telling anyone where he was going. Rootspring suppressed a snort. *Probably not the smartest thing I've ever done.*

A few heartbeats later he was distracted from his thoughts when he saw Shadowsight's ears twitch. Then he stirred, and his eyes slowly eased open.

"Look!" Dovewing exclaimed, the worry in her eyes giving way to joy. "He's waking up!"

Tigerstar bent over his son; he said nothing, but he was purring so hard Rootspring thought his chest might burst open.

At first, Shadowsight looked dazed, peering from Rootspring to his parents and back again, his eyes clouded with confusion. "Have I returned?" he asked, his voice hoarse with disuse. "Am I really back?"

Rootspring wasn't sure what his friend meant by that. "Back?" he echoed. "You've been here the whole time, ever since I found you."

Shadowsight shook his head feebly, struggling to get to his paws but finding his legs unable to support his weight. He sank back into the nest. "No, you don't understand. I wasn't here. Well, I was, but I was other places too, and no one could see me—"

"Shhh," Dovewing said, trying to soothe him. She looked helplessly at Fidgetflake. "Are you sure he isn't feverish? He isn't making any sense."

Fidgetflake came forward, extending his paw to feel

Shadowsight's pelt, but Shadowsight pushed Fidgetflake's paw away with his own.

"Please, listen to me!" Shadowsight urged. He took a long deep breath and closed his eyes. When he opened them again, there was a focus and urgency there that demanded attention. "I've been out of my body," he explained. "And I've just been in the ThunderClan camp."

"What were you doing there?" asked Rootspring.

Shadowsight exhaled in what seemed like relief that some cat was finally listening. "I spoke to Bramblestar . . . ," he began haltingly. "He confessed that he was the cat who attacked me."

Rootspring listened with growing horror as Shadowsight told how a strange cat spirit had emerged from Bramblestar's body, gloating over how he had driven out the real Bramblestar and intended to go on living his life.

By the time Shadowsight had finished, he was exhausted, shivering and gasping for breath. Dovewing reached out a paw to touch his shoulder. "You're still too weak for this," she mewed. "Rest now."

"No." In spite of his weariness Shadowsight sounded determined. "I'm afraid that the cat inside Bramblestar has done something to the real Bramblestar's spirit. We have to try to find him! If we don't, Bramblestar may never be able to come back to his body."

"Are you sure it isn't too late?" Tigerstar asked.

"I'm sure," Shadowsight asserted. "And I can prove it. Rootpaw, can you try to reach Bramblestar's spirit? I know you did it once before."

Rootspring knew that this was no time to explain his warrior name to Shadowsight. Every cat in the den turned their gaze toward Rootspring; he felt his belly flutter nervously under their intent stares.

"I don't know," he replied. "We've tried everything to find him, but nothing has worked. If he is still around, he's not responding to me."

Shadowsight's expression never changed. His evident faith in Rootspring, despite his failures, was touching. "Will you try one last time?" he asked earnestly. "I have a feeling that if anyone can reach Bramblestar, it's you."

Rootspring sighed deeply. How could he say no when Shadowsight seemed to have such confidence in him? "I'll try," he meowed softly. He closed his eyes and concentrated on reaching out to Bramblestar with his mind. For a single heartbeat he felt something like a rushing wind, and his fur prickled as if he had been struck by lightning. He opened his eyes to see a soft glow lighting up the den, but it flickered out almost at once like a small flame in a breeze. Rootspring let out a long, disappointed sigh. "I'm sorry," he murmured.

"Don't be," Tree meowed. "You definitely connected with something there. I could feel it." Turning to Leafstar, he asked, "How much more proof do you need? Shadowsight and Rootspring are not liars. If they say that some spirit has taken over Bramblestar's body, and that the impostor tried to kill Shadowsight—well, that's what is true. No question."

Leafstar was silent for a few heartbeats, looking as if she didn't know what to believe. "Shadowsight has just woken up," she pointed out at last. "He's been seriously wounded, and what he's said sounds . . . well, unbelievable." She glanced at Tigerstar. "I'm not calling him a liar, but what if what he's describing is a fever dream, not something he actually experienced? I can't spread wild rumors about another Clan's leader when they might be the result of a bad infection."

To Rootspring's surprise, Tigerstar shook his head. "I know how it sounds," he responded. "But look at him—his eyes are clear, and he knows the difference between a dream and reality. Rootspring has convinced me. And I don't think that you really believe Shadowsight was dreaming, either."

"It doesn't matter what I believe," Leafstar retorted. "What matters is, I don't want to depose another Clan's leader based on nothing more than a flash of light and a puff of wind. But that doesn't mean we should do nothing," she continued, as Tigerstar opened his jaws to protest. "I know what's at stake. We're not just talking about Bramblestar. We're talking about the fate of our Clans as well."

Tigerstar nodded and sat back on his haunches, apparently satisfied that the SkyClan leader understood the gravity of their situation. Leafstar continued, "I want to work through ThunderClan's warriors. Frecklewish told me there's a secret meeting tonight, and several of them will be there, as well as their medicine cats. Together we'll decide what to do about Bramblestar."

Tigerstar gave a reluctant nod. "All the same," he growled, "I'm going to prepare my warriors for battle. If I'm right, the moment we confront Bramblestar—or the impostor—with what we know, it's going to lead to fighting. He still has warriors loyal to him, and they'll protect him at all costs."

Dovewing looked up at him, concern clouding her eyes. "Surely it won't come to that?" she asked.

"I hope not," Tigerstar responded grimly. "But if it does, we need to be ready."

As Tigerstar finished speaking, Fidgetflake stepped forward and set a dandelion leaf down in front of Shadowsight. "Eat that," he meowed. "It will help you sleep and bring your fever down. As for you," he added with a glance at Leafstar, Tree, and Rootspring, "it's time you left. Shadowsight has already tried his strength too far. He needs to rest now."

At once Leafstar dipped her head to Fidgetflake and slipped out of the den. Tree curled his tail around Rootspring's shoulders. "Let's go."

Rootspring glanced back over his shoulder as they left, to see Shadowsight lapping up the herb while Tigerstar and Dovewing settled down at his side. Relief swept over him. *At least Shadowsight is going to be okay.*

Tree padded off to find Violetshine, but before Rootspring could join Needleclaw by the fresh-kill pile, he found himself surrounded by some of his Clanmates.

"That was awesome!" Turtlecrawl exclaimed. "Do you think Shadowsight's spirit really did go to ThunderClan?"

"Have you been eavesdropping?" Rootspring demanded. "It's a good thing Leafstar didn't catch you at it!"

Turtlecrawl just shrugged. "Who cares? Anyway, Leafstar is wrong. We need to do something!"

"Yeah, we believe you and Shadowsight," Kitescratch asserted. "We think we should go to ThunderClan tonight and get some proof about Bramblestar!"

Turtlecrawl and the others—Gravelnose and Pigeonfoot— let out yowls of agreement.

"What about it, Rootspring?" Kitescratch asked. "Are you with us?"

Rootspring looked around at their eager faces and gleaming eyes. Part of him wanted to agree, if only to prove that he wasn't a coward, but the more sensible part of his mind told him what a bad idea it was.

"I'm not going anywhere tonight," he meowed. "Have you forgotten? I've just been made a warrior. I have to sit vigil. And you shouldn't go either," he added. "What do you think you could do, against the whole of ThunderClan?"

His friends exchanged sheepish glances, their excitement dying away. Rootspring hoped he'd said enough to discourage them.

He was thankful for the excuse of sitting vigil, but he realized that wasn't the only reason he wanted nothing to do with the plan. At last he was truly a SkyClan warrior, and his whole being tingled with a fierce loyalty to his Clan and his leader. If Leafstar decided that SkyClan would follow ThunderClan's lead, then Rootspring would trust that was the right thing to do.

I only hope that Bramblestar can wait that long. . . .

CHAPTER 15

Raised voices from outside in the camp woke Bristlefrost from her
nap in the warriors' den. Still heavy with sleep, she stumbled
to her paws and poked her head out of the entrance to see what
was going on. The wind of earlier in the day had dropped, but
a thin drizzle was falling; Bristlefrost flicked her ears at its
chilly touch.

A moment later her eyes widened and she forgot all about
the rain. Rosepetal and Bumblestripe, the border patrol, had
returned to the camp, and between them, limping and weary
but with her head held high, came Twigbranch.

Several of her Clanmates were rushing across the camp
to greet her, letting out yowls of welcome. Bristlefrost joined
them, delighted to see the gray she-cat returning from her
atonement.

Twigbranch's eyes were bright and determined, though she
looked skinny, and her pelt could do with a good grooming.
Bristlefrost guessed that her scruffy appearance was at least
partly faked, in case any cat should ask awkward questions
about where she had been staying.

Dipping her head in response to her Clanmates, Twigbranch

drew to a halt as Berrynose shouldered his way through the crowd around her and looked her over, wrinkling his nose as if he were faced with a piece of crow-food.

"Greetings," he meowed, his tone disdainful.

Twigbranch gave him a brisk nod but otherwise ignored him. "I need to see Bramblestar," she announced, her tail-tip twitching with impatience.

Berrynose swiveled around until his gaze fell on Bristlefrost. "Go get him," he ordered.

Bristlefrost bounded across the camp and climbed the tumbled rocks to the Highledge. Peering into Bramblestar's den, she saw the false leader curled up asleep in his nest.

"Like he does anything else these days," she muttered to herself.

Padding forward into the den, trying not to gag at the smell of stale prey scattered on the floor, Bristlefrost shook the impostor by the shoulder. "Wake up," she mewed. "Twigbranch has come back."

Bramblestar gazed up at her, blinking and bleary-eyed. "What?" he mumbled.

With an effort, Bristlefrost stopped her neck fur bushing up at his evident confusion. "Twigbranch has come back," she repeated. "Remember, you sent her to atone for half a moon, and said she couldn't come back unless she brought twenty pieces of prey."

For a moment Bramblestar gaped in surprise, then jumped to his paws and strode out of his den. His confusion had vanished; he was focused and purposeful.

In the center of the camp Bramblestar threw his head back and let out a yowl. "Let all cats old enough to catch their own prey join here around me for a Clan meeting!"

The summons was hardly necessary, because so many of the cats were already out in the open, welcoming Twigbranch back home. The last few stragglers bounded up, while Twig-branch stepped forward to face the Clan leader, giving him a respectful dip of her head.

"Well?" Bramblestar asked. "Have you carried out the task I gave you?"

Twigbranch's eyes shone with pride. "I have," she replied. "And I need some cat to help me carry my prey into camp. It's hidden under a bush just outside."

Bramblestar twitched his ears toward the nearest warriors. "Finleap, Thriftear, go and help her."

Bristlefrost watched as Twigbranch led the way out of the camp; moments later the three cats returned, laden with prey, and set it down at Bramblestar's paws. They had to go back a second time before they had brought it all: a row of mice, voles, squirrels, and a few birds, neatly set out in front of the Clan leader.

Wow! Bristlefrost thought. She knew the exiles had helped, but Twigbranch had insisted on catching most of the prey her-self. *She's a brilliant hunter!*

Bramblestar strolled along the line of prey, sniffing each piece as he counted it. When he reached the end he turned back to Twigbranch and gave her a nod. "So, Twigbranch," he meowed. "What have you learned in the course of your atone-ment?"

Twigbranch straightened herself, exchanging a swift glance with Bristlefrost. She seemed eager to get this over with.

"I learned the importance of my Clan," she replied, "and how wrong I was to doubt that I'm a ThunderClan cat. But I know now—I'm ThunderClan through and through!" Lowering her head in the deepest respect, she added, "In the hearing of every cat, I pledge my allegiance to ThunderClan, and to you, Bramblestar, as my leader."

"And you will never question my authority?" Bramblestar demanded.

"I never will, I promise," Twigbranch responded; her whiskers twitched, but she didn't utter a word of complaint.

"Hmm . . ." Bramblestar began pacing back and forth in front of the line of prey. "Now every cat can see how important it is to be true to your Clan," he began. "That is such a crucial part of the warrior code, even though so many cats seem to forget it these days."

What is he rambling on about? Bristlefrost wondered, flicking raindrops from her ears. *Why can't he just welcome Twigbranch back and let us all get back someplace dry?* She guessed that Twigbranch was just waiting to settle down and get some rest, and Finleap, his eyes shining as he gazed at his mate, clearly couldn't wait for the chance to share tongues with her and hear all about her adventures.

"So, among you all," Bramblestar continued, "I imagine no

cat has had her allegiance tested as much as Twigbranch."

The gray she-cat nodded agreement, seeming to relax a little.

Bramblestar halted in his pacing and fixed her with a cold, unforgiving gaze. "That's why it's such a pity that I can't allow you back into ThunderClan."

"What?" Several warriors let out yowls of shock. Finleap didn't speak, but Bristlefrost was shaken at his look of stunned disappointment as he glanced from his mate to Bramblestar and back again. Twigbranch simply stared at the Clan leader, her disbelief at what she was hearing obvious.

"You can atone all you want, Twigbranch," Bramblestar went on, "but that can't undo the fact that you are a code-breaker, one of those so named in Shadowsight's vision. I can't possibly let you back into the Clan. Given what happened to Squirrelflight"—he paused, a pained look flashing in his eyes—"and Flipclaw's prophetic dream, I'm more sure than ever that leniency for the codebreakers is not what StarClan wants."

"But—but I atoned!" Twigbranch stammered, casting a confused glance at Flipclaw. "If you were just going to kick me out anyway, why did you let me atone?"

"*You* insisted on atoning," Bramblestar sneered. "I never said it would make a difference one way or the other."

Even before he had finished speaking, Twigbranch's Clanmates began to let out furious protests in her defense.

"That's not fair!"

"You *did* promise her!"

"Twigbranch is a loyal warrior!"

Bramblestar raked the assembled cats with a hard glare, his shoulder fur bristling. "Do you like living in safety?" he demanded. "Having plenty of prey to hunt and a warm camp to return to at night? Then you should *want* me to exile Twigbranch! We've seen how StarClan has punished us with wind and rain this newleaf. So far, ThunderClan has been spared the struggles some other Clans have faced . . . don't you wonder *why*?"

Bristlefrost looked around at her Clanmates' faces. *Do they believe that?* Newleaf was often windy and rainy, and it was ThunderClan's location in the forest that kept them well fed and protected. But of course Bramblestar would try to take credit.

It seemed to be working. The warriors' protests died into an indignant muttering, but soon Finleap's voice rose above them all. "If Twigbranch is leaving, then so am I," he meowed, pressing himself against his mate's side.

Bramblestar let out a snort of amused contempt. "You won't be missed," he mocked. "I want loyal warriors only—warriors who will serve without question! Not cats who just followed their mate from one Clan to another."

For a few heartbeats the Clan seemed frozen between anger at the way Bramblestar was treating Twigbranch, and fear of what might happen if she was allowed to stay. Then a quiet voice spoke up from the direction of the medicine cats' den, and Alderheart padded up to stand beside Twigbranch and Finleap. Bristlefrost was stunned by the suppressed fury in the gentle medicine cat's voice and in his eyes as he faced Bramblestar.

"In all the times I have shared dreams with StarClan," Alderheart began, "our warrior ancestors have never asked any cat to serve a leader without question. Sometimes it's right to question! How much more devastation would Darktail have caused if none of his followers had questioned him?"

Bristlefrost suppressed a shudder as she remembered the stories the older warriors told about the cat who had brought a band of rogues into the lake territory and almost destroyed the Clans before he was killed and his followers scattered. *Alderheart is right! No leader should be obeyed without question.*

Bramblestar thrust out his head toward Alderheart. It was still a shock to see so much hostility from their leader toward his son—but she reminded herself that this cat was not the real Bramblestar, and he was not Alderheart's father.

"The code says you will obey your leader!" Bramblestar hissed. "But since you've made it clear you can't do that, you can leave too. ThunderClan has no use for a faithless medicine cat!"

Alderheart faced the Clan leader without flinching. His ears were flattened and his tail-tip flicked to and fro. He was clearly at the end of his patience. "What about a faithless leader?" he retorted.

For answer, Bramblestar drew his lips back in a snarl. "Get out!"

A rumble of protest came from the assembled cats, their concern clear in their wide, anxious eyes and bristling fur. *This can't be happening!* Bristlefrost thought, every hair on her pelt tingling with apprehension. *But it looks like Alderheart has taken all he can.*

It was her mother, Ivypool, who voiced what every cat was thinking. "If Alderheart leaves," she pointed out, "then ThunderClan will have no medicine cat. Surely that can't be what you want, Bramblestar?"

The Clan leader angled his ears toward Flipclaw, who was standing at the front of the crowd, gaping with horror as he realized where this was leading.

"We do have an apprentice," Bramblestar meowed. "Flipclaw had that prophetic dream, and he has been studying herbs with Alderheart long enough to know what to do. What more does a Clan need?"

Every cat's gaze shifted to Flipclaw, doubt and worry in their eyes, and Flipclaw bowed his head miserably, staring at his own paws.

"I'm sorry, Flipclaw." Alderheart cast a sympathetic glance at the younger cat. "You don't deserve to be put in this position. But I can't stay to watch ThunderClan become a mockery of itself."

With a sweep of his tail he signaled to Finleap and a stunned Twigbranch, and led the way out of the camp. Bristlefrost watched as they disappeared into the thorn tunnel, wondering if somehow this could all be a hideous dream. She bit her lip, and the pain assured her that it was really happening.

At least Twigbranch knows about the exiles' camp on ShadowClan territory, she reflected. *And Alderheart can be reunited with his mother. . . .*

With the departure of the three exiles, the meeting was at an end, and the crowd of cats split up into small groups, their heads together as they whispered their disbelief. Bristlefrost exchanged a glance with her mother, Ivypool, and wondered whether she should tell her the truth—about the rebel cats, about everything.

Maybe Bramblestar is beyond control now, she thought despairingly. *Maybe it's time I took my family and escaped to the exiles' camp. . . .*

Bristlefrost took a hesitant step toward her mother, only to be intercepted by Bramblestar, who came bounding up to her. "I want to talk to you, Bristlefrost," he announced. "You're the only one I can trust. Follow me."

He headed for the thorn tunnel, and Bristlefrost had no choice but to obey him, warily treading in his paw steps as they entered the forest. Bramblestar seemed on edge, casting nervous glances in all directions and sometimes whipping around as if he was facing some imaginary threat.

"I've heard rumors some cats are working against me," he told Bristlefrost, leading her into the shelter of a hazel thicket. "I want to know what you think, Bristlefrost."

A chill crept through Bristlefrost from ears to tail-tip. *Does he know the truth,* she asked herself, *that I'm one of those cats?* These days Bramblestar seemed so erratic that she wouldn't be surprised if he suspected every cat, whether he had evidence or not.

Her chill deepened as she realized that she had followed him into a dark part of the forest. If he wanted to make her disappear, like Shadowsight, this would be a good place.

"I have my doubts about Berrynose," Bramblestar went on. "Surely all that loyalty must be an act—don't you think so?"

At his words, Bristlefrost became a little reassured. She realized that Bramblestar truly had no idea what was going on, and was genuinely anxious for her opinion.

"Well," she began, "I don't really know—"

She broke off with a gasp of horror as a group of cats slipped out of the undergrowth, creeping toward Bramblestar as quietly as if they were stalking a mouse. Death glinted in their eyes and on their outstretched claws.

Stemleaf and Spotfur . . . oh, and Conefoot, Kitescratch, and Dappletuft! What are they doing? They promised Tigerstar they wouldn't kill Bramblestar!

Her gasp alerted Bramblestar, who spun around before the rebel cats could reach him, and let out a yowl as he leaped at his attackers. They sprang forward, letting out earsplitting shrieks and swarming closer in a circle of teeth and claws.

For a moment, Bristlefrost stood frozen, staring at the whirling group of cats. She caught Stemleaf's gaze, knowing he would expect her to fight at his side, but at the same moment Bramblestar screeched out her name.

"Bristlefrost—get help! There must be a patrol nearby!"

Her heart pounding, Bristlefrost fled through the trees, back toward the camp. *Who should I be helping?* she asked herself. She didn't want Bramblestar killed; there would be no chance of getting the real Bramblestar back if his body was destroyed. *And I promised Squirrelflight I would protect him.* But at the same time she didn't want Stemleaf and the other rebels to be wounded in a fight. *There's no way to win!*

Too shocked and fearful to listen or taste the air for signs of a patrol, Bristlefrost had almost reached the camp when she spotted Berrynose, bounding out of the thorn tunnel and looking around with alarm in his eyes.

"Did you hear anything?" he asked Bristlefrost as she raced up to him. "I thought I heard Bramblestar yowl."

Bristlefrost was suddenly sure of what she should do. "Yes, some cats attacked Bramblestar," she replied. "And there may be more attackers coming. We have to help Bramblestar and get him out of there before we're overwhelmed."

Maybe I can get Berrynose to focus on saving Bramblestar—and his body—not fighting against the rebels.

Berrynose paused for a heartbeat, staring at Bristlefrost in consternation, then spun around and raced back through the thorn tunnel. Bristlefrost heard his voice raised in a yowl to summon more warriors.

Moments later Berrynose was back, with Dewnose, Sorrelstripe, and Snaptooth hard on his paws. "Lead the way!" Berrynose snapped at Bristlefrost.

As Bristlefrost pelted through the forest, the screeches and snarls of battle grew louder in her ears. As she burst out into the open, she saw that Shellfur and Leafshade had appeared and were fighting shoulder to shoulder with Bramblestar.

They must be the patrol Bramblestar told me to find.

She noticed too that there were fewer of the rebels than she had thought at first. As soon as she appeared with Berrynose and the others, Spotfur and Kitescratch backed away, staring at them in dismay, then spun around and fled.

Bramblestar turned toward his rescuers, his chest heaving and his muzzle covered with blood. While Berrynose and the rest of his warriors surrounded him, Bristlefrost noticed the blood streaking the grass and pooling in the hollows; the reek of it caught her in the throat. And she saw the three limp bundles of fur lying motionless in the middle of it.

Conefoot . . . Dappletuft . . . and—oh, no, it's Stemleaf!

Bristlefrost bounded over to the white-and-orange tom, stretching out a paw to rouse him. But she halted before she could touch him, staring down into his open, lifeless eyes. "No . . . ," she whispered.

She remembered her time as an apprentice, when she had filled her mind with pictures of what her life would be like with Stemleaf as her mate. Everything would have been so different if he could have loved her back, and if Bramblestar had never died and come back as whoever or whatever he was now. . . .

Dimly Bristlefrost became aware that Bramblestar was speaking to her, but all she could hear was a whirring in her head, as if she had thrust herself into an enormous nest of bees. Her legs wouldn't support her anymore; she felt herself falling, and a soft surge of darkness enfolded her.

"Oh, thank StarClan you're awake!"

Bristlefrost blinked, and the familiar outlines of the medicine-cat den swam into focus around her. Flipclaw was bending over her, his eyes full of relief.

"I'm *pretty* sure those were thyme leaves I gave you, and not daisy," he chattered on. "I'm always mixing those up. But you're awake now, and getting over the shock, so I must have gotten it right. Anyway, even if it was daisy leaves, they would just make sure your joints don't ache, so it's not like they would *harm* you. . . ."

As he finished speaking, Brightheart stepped forward from the shadows. "Don't worry, Bristlefrost," she mewed, her one good eye shining with sympathy. "And Flipclaw, don't forget that I checked the leaves, too. Bristlefrost will be fine."

Bristlefrost gazed up at her, confused. "I never knew you were a medicine cat."

"I'm not," Brightheart explained. "But way back, Cinderpelt taught me the basics of healing, and I won't let Flipclaw hurt any cat."

"Thank StarClan," Bristlefrost murmured feebly. "And thank you, Brightheart." Reaching out to put a paw over Flipclaw's, she added, "What happened?"

Brightheart's eye darkened and she backed away, while Flipclaw's expression grew suddenly somber. "How much do you remember?" he asked his sister.

Bristlefrost struggled with the fog in her mind, thinking back until the picture of the battle's aftermath grew bright and horrific in her memory. Her belly convulsed and she retched, vomit rising into her throat. "I think . . . I think Stemleaf is dead," she whispered when she could speak again.

Flipclaw nodded sadly. "Yes, he is. Conefoot of Shadow-Clan and Dappletuft from RiverClan are dead too. And—"

He broke off as Bramblestar thrust his way past the bramble screen and into the den. "Good, you're finally awake," he began. "I have to speak to you—alone."

Bristlefrost saw that apart from a scratch on his muzzle and a few missing clumps of fur, the impostor seemed to be uninjured. *Whoever he is, he's a formidable fighter,* she thought.

"Flipclaw, you're doing a great job," Bramblestar continued. "You're going to be a terrific medicine cat."

Flipclaw looked doubtful but said nothing, merely giving his leader a nod and ducking out of the den.

As he departed, Bramblestar spotted Brightheart in the shadows by the herb store at the back of the den. "What are you doing here?" he demanded, giving her a startled look.

"I've just come to help Flipclaw," Brightheart explained.

The false Bramblestar's shoulder fur began to bristle, and he shook his head. "No, that won't do," he snapped. "You're an elder, not a medicine cat! Sometimes the elders want special treatment, and sometimes they want to take over the duties of younger cats! I'm your leader, and I'm telling you to get out! How will Flipclaw ever learn if you're here?"

"But how will he learn if there's no cat to teach him?" Brightheart protested. "I only know a little, but—"

"Are you arguing with me?" Bramblestar growled. "I told you to go, so go!"

Brightheart let out a sigh, casting a regretful look at Bristlefrost, then brushed past the bramble screen and out into the camp.

Once she was gone, Bramblestar padded up to Bristlefrost,

his shoulder fur lying flat again. "What a brave and loyal warrior you are!" he meowed. "I admit," he continued with an uneasy twitch of his whiskers, "that I doubted your loyalty in the past. A smart leader must have some doubts about all his followers, even the best of them. But now you've proven yourself as my strongest ally in ThunderClan."

Uncomfortable with his praise, Bristlefrost opened her jaws to protest, but the false Bramblestar swept on, disregarding her.

"I knew cats were working against me, and my suspicions have been proven right. Now we must travel to the other Clans and let them know about the traitors in their ranks. With you as my deputy, we can—"

"Wait—what?" Bristlefrost exclaimed, scrambling to sit upright. She was sure she couldn't have heard what she thought Bramblestar had just said. "What happened to Berrynose? He's a very good deputy. Without him, you might not be alive now!"

Bramblestar loomed over her, a purr rumbling in his chest. "You're generous to say so, Bristlefrost, but I know the truth. Berrynose was too slow to bring help. He should have been there faster than the patrol. He should have fought to kill, instead of letting cats get away!"

"But Berrynose did his best," Bristlefrost began to argue. "He ran as fast—"

"Calm down, Bristlefrost," Bramblestar meowed. "I know who I can trust now, and that's what's important. That's why I'm exiling Berrynose and making you my new deputy."

He did *say what I thought he said!*

"But I haven't had an apprentice yet," Bristlefrost pointed out, "so I can't be deputy. It goes against the warrior code!"

The false Bramblestar seemed untroubled by the implication that he himself might be codebreaking. "You won't remember this," he meowed, "because it happened long before you were born, but I myself was made deputy before I had an apprentice. StarClan sent a vision to Leafpool that I was the right cat. And now I feel the same certainty about you."

But StarClan hasn't sent you *a vision—have they?* Bristlefrost thought doubtfully. Every hair on her pelt was prickling with horror at the thought of trying to take authority over warriors who were so much more experienced than she was.

"Now that you're awake, we'll announce your new position to the whole Clan," Bramblestar told her, his eyes gleaming with satisfaction.

Bristlefrost stared at him in disbelief. "But I—"

"No buts!" the impostor insisted. "Remember that the new deputy must be appointed before moonhigh. Get up; we'll tell them all now."

There was no way for Bristlefrost to refuse. Slowly she rose to her paws, feeling her legs shaking as she padded after Bramblestar. Her head swam, and she felt as though this must all be a hideous dream.

Outside in the camp the rain had stopped, but the air was still raw and damp. Bristlefrost shivered as the chill penetrated her pelt. Clouds covered the sky, and the daylight was fading; she guessed she had lain unconscious in the medicine cats' den for a long time.

"Let all cats old enough to catch their own prey join me here for a Clan meeting!" Bramblestar yowled.

The warriors began to gather, most of them exchanging confused glances as they formed a circle around their Clan leader. Bristlefrost heard Thornclaw mutter to Mousewhisker, "For StarClan's sake, what now?"

Flipclaw reappeared to stand outside his den, and Cloud-tail led the elders over to stand at the back of the crowd. Even Daisy emerged from the nursery to see what was going on.

"My life was in danger today," Bramblestar began when all the Clan was assembled. "Some of my warriors rose to the occasion—and others didn't. Berrynose, come here."

The cream-colored tom stepped forward eagerly, his head raised with pride as he stood beside his leader. Bristlefrost couldn't help feeling sorry for him; he had worked hard as Bramblestar's deputy, and he clearly had no idea of what was coming.

"You failed me today." Bramblestar's voice was harsh. "I can't trust you any longer. From this moment you are no longer deputy of ThunderClan."

Berrynose stared at him, his jaw dropping and his eyes wide with dismay. "But—but Bramblestar," he stammered. "I did my best—"

The impostor cut through his excuses. "Then your best wasn't good enough. You are no longer deputy, or a member of this Clan. Leave now."

For a moment longer Berrynose stared at his leader.

Bristlefrost heard a low wail from a cat in the crowd, and realized it came from Berrynose's mate, Poppyfrost. He turned his head to give her a long look, then headed for the thorn tunnel, his tail trailing in the mud.

Shocked murmurs were rising from the crowd of cats as they watched the exiled deputy leave. Berrynose had never been a popular cat, but he had been an efficient deputy, and Bristlefrost could see how his Clanmates thought his banishment was unfair.

"So, now I must appoint a new deputy," Bramblestar announced proudly when Berrynose had vanished. "I say these words before StarClan, that the spirits of our ancestors may hear and approve my choice. Bristlefrost will be the new deputy of ThunderClan."

Bristlefrost cringed as the Clan erupted in yowls of protest and concern. Several of her Clanmates were glaring at her, their fur bristling. She wished that she could vanish like a mouse into a gap beneath a tree root. But she had to stay and listen to the warriors arguing over their leader's decision.

"Bristlefrost?"

"But she's barely even a warrior!"

"She hasn't had an apprentice!"

"Enough!" Bramblestar cut off the objections with a furious lash of his tail. "Who is leader?" he demanded. "What is the only thing standing between you and StarClan's wrath? Remember that StarClan already killed Squirrelflight—or have you forgotten already?"

The warriors grew silent, staring at their leader with open

mouths. Bristlefrost's pelt prickled with anger: So Bramblestar had already gone from blaming himself for Squirrelflight's supposed death to implying that it was a punishment from StarClan. Was there any situation he wouldn't twist to his own ends?

After several moments, Molewhisker spoke up hesitantly. "We're loyal to you, Bramblestar. It's just . . . well, if we're being so careful to follow the code, isn't it against the code to choose a cat as deputy when she hasn't had an apprentice?"

Bristlefrost expected Bramblestar to unleash his fury. Instead he seemed to grow calmer. He glared at Molewhisker, his eyes flickering; as Bristlefrost watched him, her pads tingled with a mixture of fear and confusion.

For a heartbeat there, I thought his eyes looked blue.

Then Bramblestar spoke, his voice quiet, but full of menace. "I am your leader. My word is the code."

CHAPTER 16

Shadowsight *woke to see the pale* light of dawn creeping into the SkyClan medicine cats' den. He stretched his jaws in a massive yawn and glanced around. Frecklewish and Fidgetflake were beginning to stir toward the back of the den, and in a nest beside Shadowsight's, Kitescratch was still deeply asleep.

The young SkyClan warrior had returned to camp the previous day bearing the marks of claws, including one deep wound all along his flank. He had told the medicine cats that he had been injured fighting an owl, though Shadowsight had his doubts.

Kitescratch is too big for an owl to attack, and he must have bees in his brain if he tried to take one as prey.

Shadowsight was distracted from puzzling over Kitescratch's wounds by the sound of paw steps and voices outside the den. It sounded as though some cat was visiting, though it was very early for a patrol to have arrived from another Clan.

Then Shadowsight relaxed as he recognized his father's voice. He knew how worried Tigerstar was about him, so it made sense that he would come visit as soon as there was enough light to see by.

"Greetings, Tigerstar." Leafstar's voice came from the direction of her den. "You and your warriors are welcome. How can I help you?"

"You've helped us enough," Tigerstar responded warmly. "And I'm grateful for it, but I want my son with me in Shadow-Clan. I've come to take Shadowsight home."

At that, Shadowsight struggled to his paws and stumbled toward the entrance to the den. His father was standing just outside, flanked by Tawnypelt and Strikestone. Shadowsight gave them a respectful nod.

Tigerstar's eyes grew warm at the sight of his son. "Greetings, Shadowsight. It's time to come home."

"Of course that's your decision, Tigerstar," Leafstar meowed. "But I must check with my medicine cats. Fidgetflake?" When the black-and-white tom appeared at the entrance to the den, she asked, "Is Shadowsight ready to travel?"

Fidgetflake's gaze flicked over Shadowsight; then he nodded. "He's still a little weak, but he's getting stronger every day. With help, there's no reason why he can't make the trip back to ShadowClan's camp. But take it slowly," he added to Tigerstar, "and stop for a rest at least once."

"It's true that Shadowsight's health is improving," Frecklewish added, emerging from the den to approach her leader. Her expression was somber. "But he'll be in danger if any cat outside SkyClan realizes that he's alive. Some cat—possibly Bramblestar—tried to kill him. If they realize they didn't succeed, they'll try again."

Shadowsight remembered his last vision as a spirit, before he returned to his body, and the shock he had felt when Bramblestar saw him. *He didn't even try to hide that he was the cat who attacked me! Will he come after me, if he finds out that I'm alive?* Then Shadowsight shook his head firmly. *It doesn't matter if he does. I'll find some way to defeat him.*

Frecklewish was still speaking as Shadowsight struggled with his thoughts. "With that in mind, Tigerstar, don't you want to let your son stay here for a bit longer?" she asked. "I promise we're treating him with all the concern and care we would give to a SkyClan cat."

"I know that," Tigerstar told her. "And there aren't words to tell you how much I appreciate what you did to save his life. I'll always be in your debt. But I'm sure that Shadowsight will be safe on ShadowClan territory, because I'm already preparing my cats for battle."

"You think it's come to that?" Leafstar asked, anxiety in her voice.

"I do. Bramblestar cannot be allowed to give orders to all five Clans in the way that he has. And I'm sure he had some paw in hurting Shadowsight."

Except it wasn't really Bramblestar, Shadowsight thought with a glance at his father.

"But still, to go into battle . . . ," Leafstar began, reluctance in her eyes and the set of her whiskers.

"Peace has reigned in the five Clans for moons," Tigerstar interrupted. "But that peace is coming to an end soon. We are living in a den of twigs, and Bramblestar—or whoever that truly is—is about to send it crashing down. Now that some foolishly brave cats have made an attack on Bramblestar's life, the end will come even faster."

Leafstar stared at him, as if she was finding it hard to accept the bleak future he was prophesying. "I understand how upset you are over Shadowsight's injuries," she mewed, "but I hope you're wrong. Bramblestar would never attack a medicine cat, would he?"

Tigerstar brushed past her, flicking his tail to summon Tawnypelt and Strikestone. "Help Shadowsight, and follow me," he instructed. He took a pace toward the camp entrance, then turned back to Leafstar. "*Bramblestar* wouldn't," he added. "Thank you for your kindness, Leafstar, Fidgetflake, Frecklewish."

Shadowsight scarcely had time to say good-bye before he had to follow his father out of camp.

By the time he reached the bushes that surrounded the ShadowClan camp, Shadowsight felt weak and exhausted. His legs were wobbling, and it was all he could do to push his way through the barrier and stumble down into the hollow.

On the way home, his father had told him how a group of the rebels had attacked Bramblestar. "They were brave but stupid," Tigerstar had meowed. "It was too early to strike, and now we have to deal with the consequences. Surviving the attack will make Bramblestar all the bolder."

Now Shadowsight's Clanmates bounded up to him and crowded around him, letting out yowls of greeting and brushing against his pelt to welcome him home. Shadow-sight's heart lifted to realize how glad they were to see him. *I missed them, and my camp, so much. It's good to be home!*

His mother, Dovewing, appeared from her den and raced across the camp to nuzzle him close. "I'm so, so relieved that you're okay," she purred. "Come on, let's get you to Puddle-shine."

As soon as Shadowsight set paw in the medicine cats' den, Puddleshine was there to greet him.

"I've never been so glad to see any cat!" his former mentor exclaimed, ruffling up Shadowsight's nest with his forepaws. "Come and lie down; I've put extra moss in here for you."

Shadowsight let out a sigh of gratitude as he sank into the deep, soft bedding. "That feels so good," he murmured. "I'm glad to be home."

Puddleshine stood over him, his whiskers drooping and a look of distress in his eyes. "I'm so sorry, Shadowsight," he meowed. "I should have looked harder for you. If I'd known you were alive, suffering somewhere . . ."

Shadowsight realized that he had been crazy to ever sus-pect that Puddleshine might have been involved in his attack. The medicine cat was clearly full of remorse.

"If you had found me, I might not have discovered what I did about Bramblestar," he pointed out.

"What was that?" Puddleshine asked.

Tigerstar, who had supported his son as far as the den and still stood in the entrance, let out a growl. "You might find it hard to believe. I did—but I do believe it now."

Shadowsight explained how he had visited the Thunder-Clan camp as a spirit, and how the spirit of another cat had emerged from Bramblestar's body. "It was his voice I heard, warning the Clans about codebreakers," he finished, "and not StarClan's at all."

Puddleshine listened to the story with wide, horrified eyes. "This is terrible!" he breathed out. "Rootspring showed us Bramblestar's ghost, but to realize that whoever is controlling his body is so vicious, and has been plotting this for so long?"

"And planning to control all of us," Tigerstar snarled. "It leaves us with no option but to go into battle. We can't wait any longer for the other Clans to join us. The only way to solve this is to kill whatever is living inside Bramblestar."

Shadowsight half started up; every hair on his pelt tingled with fear at his father's determination. "No!" he protested. "Please, you have to listen to me! You can't attack Bramble-star—not until I can find out what has happened to the real Bramblestar's ghost!"

CHAPTER 17

Rootspring crouched beside the stream in the exiles' camp on Shadow-Clan territory. Thick clouds covered the sky, hiding the moon and stars, and scarcely a glint of light touched the dark water beside him. He could hear the quiet gurgle of the current and the soft paw steps of cats as they brushed through the grass and ferns to gather for the meeting. Rootspring caught glimpses of their shining eyes as they settled down, and he picked up the mingled scents of all the Clans, but as yet there was no sign of Tigerstar.

A familiar voice spoke behind him. "Greetings, Rootspring."

The young tom swung around to see Squirrelflight, with Spotfur at her shoulder, and a pace farther back another cat whose pale pelt glimmered in the uncertain light.

"Greetings, Squirrelflight, Spotfur." Rootspring peered harder at the third cat. "And—great StarClan, is that Berrynose?"

The cream-colored tom ducked his head awkwardly. "Greetings," he muttered.

Before Rootspring could get over his surprise, another cat

strode up: Tigerstar, who halted face-to-face with Berrynose. Anger and mistrust were rolling off him like the scent of fox.

"What do you want here?" he demanded. "Aren't you Bramblestar's deputy?"

"Not anymore," Squirrelflight explained, resting a calming tail-tip on Tigerstar's shoulder. "Crowfeather found him wandering in the forest earlier today. It seems Bramblestar exiled him for not being quick enough in his defense when the young warriors attacked."

"Not being quick enough!" Tigerstar repeated with a lash of his tail. "We've just finished burying Conefoot. It seems like Bramblestar's defenders were *quite* effective."

"You don't have to convince me," Squirrelflight responded calmly. "But clearly Bramblestar sees it differently. He's made Bristlefrost deputy."

Rootspring couldn't suppress a gasp of shock.

"Bristlefrost!" Tigerstar's voice was raised in a yowl. "That very young cat who's been coming to the rebel meetings? I didn't think she'd even had an apprentice."

"She hasn't," Squirrelflight told him. "She's a good cat, but yes, she's very young."

"She shouldn't be deputy," Berrynose hissed, clearly furious at being supplanted. "It's against the code!"

"True," Squirrelflight agreed. "It's just another sign that Bramblestar is losing touch with reality."

"Bristlefrost warned Bramblestar of the attack," Spotfur added, "and she brought him help. It would seem that she's a traitor."

Rootspring felt as though a badger had clawed his chest open and ripped out his heart. *Bristlefrost couldn't be a traitor, could she?* But he couldn't explain why she would warn Bramblestar, when she knew what he was—and what he wasn't.

More cats were gathering to listen, and their shocked, fearful comments rose up around Rootspring. Squirrelflight's voice cut through all of them.

"Bristlefrost isn't a traitor," she meowed. "I asked her to protect Bramblestar's body, in case the real Bramblestar needs it someday."

Rootspring caught her gaze falling on him, and he looked down at his own paws, embarrassed at the relief he must be showing. *Bristlefrost is a good warrior. She would do her best to obey an order from her former deputy.*

Spotfur's response was a contemptuous grunt. "You can't know why she did it. Would Bristlefrost value Bramblestar's life over Stemleaf's, and the other rebels'? I doubt it, not if she's loyal to us. And don't forget, if Bristlefrost is loyal to Bramblestar, she knows all our secrets. We have to assume from now on that Bramblestar knows we're working against him. That's our only safe option, to make sure we're not . . . surprised, by anything he does now."

Rootspring stared at the ThunderClan cat, not wanting to believe her words, but finding it hard to dismiss them. *Bristlefrost wouldn't! Would she?* he asked himself again.

"What do you think about all this?" Tigerstar asked, turning to Berrynose. "Can you tell us anything about Bramblestar that would help defeat him?"

Berrynose's eyes widened in consternation. "No—I—" he stammered. "I'm sure this is all a misunderstanding. Bramblestar is a good cat. I would *never*—"

"So we can't count on your support in the battle," Tigerstar sneered.

Berrynose glanced from Tigerstar to Squirrelflight and back again. "I don't know," he mewed despairingly. "I don't know what I believe. But I can't imagine fighting with you against Bramblestar. He's my leader, for StarClan's sake!"

"Get out, then!" Tigerstar snarled. "I won't shelter cats loyal to Bramblestar on my territory."

Berrynose stared at him, stunned; before he could move to obey the order, Squirrelflight stretched out a warning paw to Tigerstar.

"Don't be shortsighted," she advised him. "If we let Berrynose go, he could run right back to Bramblestar and tell him everything. Let me keep him here in the exiles' camp as a prisoner, until he decides where his loyalties lie." She looked at Berrynose. "You're right that a good warrior supports his leader. But that *isn't* Bramblestar. If we tell you more, maybe we can convince you of the truth."

Tigerstar grunted, clearly unimpressed with the idea, then gave a reluctant nod.

"Thank StarClan you've made a decision," Spotfur snapped, her voice full of bitterness. "Like Berrynose is the most important cat in the forest! He's not. In case you've forgotten, we lost strong allies in that fight; Stemleaf, Conefoot, and Dappletuft are all dead."

At her words, the cats around them stirred, and began to repeat the names of the fallen in soft and loving voices. "Stemleaf . . . Conefoot . . . Dappletuft . . ." Rootspring and the others stood with bowed heads until the voices died away.

"We will never forget them," Tigerstar meowed at last. "But they acted expressly against orders. We'd all agreed *not* to kill Bramblestar yet."

"Then what are we waiting for?" Spotfur demanded angrily. "Bramblestar—or whatever cat is living inside him—is turning the Clans against one another at this very moment. How far will you let him go?"

"Spotfur . . ." Squirrelflight touched her nose gently to the younger she-cat's ear, but Spotfur shook her off with a jerk of her head.

"I'm sick of all the arguing!" she snarled. "I don't want Stemleaf to have died for nothing!"

Pain clawed at Rootspring's heart at the raw grief in Spotfur's voice, but he realized that the loss of her mate hadn't overwhelmed her. She was as strong as ever, and determined to seek vengeance.

"Some cat is going to pay for what has happened," she vowed. "And I want that cat to be whoever is inside Bramblestar."

At that moment, Rootspring caught a glimmer in the corner of his eye and turned his head to see Stemleaf's ghost staring at Spotfur, his gaze full of love and sadness. He stood close to her for a heartbeat, then turned away and was lost among the ferns.

"You're right, Spotfur," Tigerstar mewed. "And now we have *proof* that the cat who now leads ThunderClan is not the real Bramblestar."

Rootspring listened with renewed apprehension as Tigerstar told the rest of the cats about how Shadowsight had visited Bramblestar as a spirit and had seen another spirit cat emerge from within the Clan leader. By the time Tigerstar had finished, a horrified silence had fallen over the rebel group.

Lionblaze was the first cat to break it. "That's what I've feared all along," he stated. "But now that we're sure it's true—how does that help us decide what to do about it?"

"We have to defeat whoever is inside Bramblestar's body," Squirrelflight responded.

Lionblaze twitched his ears. "But how?"

"That depends on who the cat is," Squirrelflight told him. "Who—or *what*—has stolen Bramblestar's life?"

"You would be best placed to know," Tigerstar pointed out. "He's your mate; you know the *real* Bramblestar better than any cat."

Squirrelflight blinked thoughtfully; a few moments passed before she spoke again. "Whoever is inside him now is lazy," she replied at last. "He wants the glory of leading the Clan, but he doesn't want to do the work. And he clearly wants to disrupt the peace between the five Clans."

"Tigerstar?" Lionblaze asked, then shot a guilty look at the ShadowClan leader. "I mean the first Tigerstar," he added hastily. Tigerstar gave him an awkward nod.

"Tigerstar was many things," Crowfeather meowed, "but

not *lazy*. Besides, the cats who were defeated in the battle with the Dark Forest are gone for good—those of us who fought saw them destroyed."

"I believe that's true," Squirrelflight agreed. "When Leafpool and I spent time in StarClan, we were told that the Dark Forest was nearly empty."

"Then what about Darktail?" Mothwing asked. "He certainly wanted to disrupt the peace when he was alive. Disrupting the peace was what he was *good* at!"

A shudder passed through Squirrelflight from ears to tailtip, every hair on her pelt rising. "The time I spent with the false Bramblestar didn't fit with what I remember of Darktail," she responded. "Darktail was hungry for power—but he seemed to have strict control of his Kin, too. Half the time, this Bramblestar was almost indifferent to the rest of ThunderClan."

Rootspring was becoming more despondent with every word spoken by the senior warriors. His hopes had been so high when he joined the rebel group, but now everything was going wrong. Tigerstar seemed angry . . . and cats were *dying*! And even worse—*no, not exactly worse,* Rootspring had to admit—it was possible that Bristlefrost was a traitor, in league with whatever ghostly presence was inside Bramblestar.

How could this be?

Glancing around at the trees, Rootspring spotted a ghost emerging from the darkness again. Once more it was Stemleaf; Rootspring nodded at him, and Stemleaf nodded in response before passing close to Spotfur, brushing against her side.

And I'm seeing ghosts again, Rootspring thought, *but not the one I really want to see.* Bramblestar's spirit was still missing.

Tree, who was standing beside Rootspring, touched his nose to his son's shoulder, then angled his ears toward Stemleaf as the dead ThunderClan tom melted back into the shadows.

So he can see him, too.

Meanwhile, the meeting had broken down into an argument.

"Be quiet and listen!" Squirrelflight's challenging yowl cut through the commotion. "Every cat needs to admit that we have a problem worse than all the others: If Bristlefrost has betrayed us, we have been exposed. I still believe that she was only doing what I asked of her, but we can't take that chance."

"You're right." Lionblaze straightened, gazing around with the commanding air of a leader. "We have to put aside our disagreements and come together now, if we're to have any hope of survival."

"Then how long are we going to let this go on?" Tigerstar asked. "I've heard rumors that Bramblestar is sending his so-called deputy from Clan to Clan now, demanding that they exile any cats involved in the attack."

Breezepelt nodded. "Harestar has listened, and he wants to encourage other leaders to do the same. He truly believes this will bring StarClan back, and bring prey back to the moor."

"Bramblestar has already exiled all the codebreakers in ThunderClan, not to mention any cat who's annoyed him," Spotfur added. "He's thrown out both his medicine cats. Are we going to let this false Bramblestar remake all the Clans? Who knows what he wants?"

"To figure that out," Squirrelflight responded, "we have to find out who he is. And to do that, we need a cat close to him on our side."

"Bristlefrost?" Tigerstar suggested.

Spotfur shook her head. "Bristlefrost can't be trusted now."

No! Rootspring thought, anguished. *If Bristlefrost could betray us, then I never really understood her.* The thought made his heart ache.

"But I think Flipclaw is getting fed up with being stuck as a medicine cat," Spotfur continued. "He might be prepared to pass on information."

"Speaking of Flipclaw," Puddleshine meowed, "we'll all need to discuss Shadowsight's return at the next half-moon meeting. I'm sure the others won't be happy about Alderheart's exile, or the way that Flipclaw was forced to take his place with scarcely any training. Of everything the false Bramblestar has done to break the warrior code, this might be the worst! The life of the whole Clan is in danger with an untrained medicine cat working alone."

"That's all well and good," Lionblaze commented, "but the last I heard, Kestrelflight and Willowshine still hadn't even shared the information about Bramblestar's ghost with their leaders."

Several voices spoke up from the WindClan and River-Clan cats. "That's true."

"If the leaders knew that," Crowfeather added, "not to

mention the new information about what Shadowsight saw, surely they would back any effort to get rid of this impostor."

"That's far from certain," Tigerstar argued. "Mistystar and Harestar have hung their hopes for reconnecting with StarClan on Bramblestar and his so-called leadership. This news might not be enough to change their minds."

"But we have to try," Frecklewish insisted.

Tigerstar took control again, gathering the cats around them with a commanding glance. "Then we will wait and see what the medicine cats decide," he announced. "If Mistystar and Harestar can be convinced that Bramblestar is not a true leader, that will make it much easier to get rid of him."

Murmurs of agreement rose from the assembled cats, though Rootspring thought that some of them sounded reluctant. But after the death of the rebels who had attacked the false Bramblestar, he guessed that no cat wanted to risk another disaster.

Following Tree and Frecklewish back to the SkyClan camp, Rootspring wondered what the future held for all the Clans. But he couldn't help his thoughts flying especially to ThunderClan. The idea that Bristlefrost might be a traitor to the rebels had struck him as hard as if a falling tree had slammed down on his body and crushed out his life.

I know I was stupid to like her the way I did. But was I completely wrong about her?

CHAPTER 18

Wind was buffeting the trees and whipping the surface of the lake into white-tipped waves as Bristlefrost followed Bramblestar and the other ThunderClan warriors chosen to attend the Gathering. The full moon floated in the sky like a drifting leaf as clouds raced and jostled across its shining circle.

Bristlefrost's paws felt heavy as she padded along the water's edge. Usually she looked forward to meeting the cats of other Clans, but on this particular night she would rather have been anywhere else than on the Gathering island.

Preoccupied with her forebodings, she didn't notice her sister, Thriftear, until she collided with her as she swerved around a boulder. Thriftear jumped backward and dipped her head with exaggerated respect.

"Oh, I'm *so* sorry!" she exclaimed. "I should know better than to get in the *deputy's* way. Of course, you *must* go first," she finished with a sweep of her tail.

Bristlefrost wanted to say that it had been her fault, and she didn't want to go first, but before she could speak she looked up and noticed that Bramblestar had glanced back over his shoulder and was watching her. Instead of speaking to

Thriftear, she gave her a dignified nod and padded on ahead.

I'd better get used to cats hating me, she thought, *even my own lit-termate. No cat at the Gathering is going to be happy about the news that I'm the new deputy.*

Even in ThunderClan, Bristlefrost knew that she didn't command a scrap of the respect that her Clanmates had given to Squirrelflight, or even to Berrynose.

The moment Bristlefrost had dreaded came when she and her Clanmates pushed their way through the bushes that encircled the Gathering space and found places for them-selves around the Great Oak. As ThunderClan deputy, she had to pad across the clearing and take her place on the tree roots with the other deputies, cringing inwardly at their con-temptuous looks. Hawkwing's greeting was a curt nod, while Cloverfoot of ShadowClan turned away and whispered some-thing into the ear of RiverClan's deputy, Reedwhisker.

Shocked and scornful comments arose from the warriors assembled in the clearing.

"*That's* a deputy?"

"What's *she* doing there? Where's Berrynose?"

"ThunderClan must be really short of cats!"

Bristlefrost sat and stared at her paws as the five leaders leaped up into the branches of the Great Oak, and Bramble-star stepped forward to begin the meeting.

"Cats of all Clans," he announced, "I am brave even to show up here tonight, because just a few days ago I was the victim of a savage attack. Stemleaf, Spotfur, Conefoot, and Dappletuft surprised and attacked me on my own territory, aiming to kill me. Yes, even cats from my own Clan! If it weren't for the quick thinking and protection of my loyal warrior Bristlefrost, I would be dead!"

"What about Berrynose?" Tigerstar asked.

Bristlefrost noticed that Tigerstar was behaving as if he didn't know what had happened to the former deputy. *I wonder if Berrynose made it to the exiles' camp—I hope so.* Even though Berrynose was the most annoying cat in the forest, he didn't deserve to fend for himself as an outcast.

"Berrynose failed me," Bramblestar replied. "He is no longer my deputy, or a ThunderClan warrior. I have exiled him. Bristlefrost is now ThunderClan's deputy."

Bristlefrost cringed. Normally when a new deputy was announced at a Gathering, all the Clans would acclaim them by calling their name. But now there was only silence; she couldn't meet the hostile glares of the cats around her.

"You exiled Berrynose?" Tigerstar repeated, sounding astonished. His claws dug hard into the branch where he stood. "But he was never a codebreaker. Mind you, neither was Alderheart, and I hear you've exiled him, too. At this rate, there'll be more ThunderClan cats wandering the forest than in your camp."

Bramblestar fixed the ShadowClan leader with a baleful amber glare. "ThunderClan business is ThunderClan business," he snapped. "Alderheart has been replaced by a new apprentice, Flipclaw, who is doing a fine job, dedicated to serving his Clan and StarClan—just as we all should be. And he has received at least one prophetic dream, the only contact a cat of any Clan has had from StarClan"

Tigerstar let out a snort of amusement. "Do tell!"

"I will keep the details within ThunderClan," Bramblestar retorted. "But the dream was *very* clear."

As he was speaking, Bristlefrost noticed that some of her Clanmates were exchanging dubious glances. She shared their doubts. Nothing would convince her that her brother had received a single message from StarClan, or that he had the talent to become a medicine cat.

"In any case," Bramblestar continued, "*I* am Thunder-Clan's leader, chosen by StarClan, and I run my Clan as I see fit. Remember that killing another Clan's leader is a serious offense to StarClan!" he added with a glance around the clearing. "And so I must ask all the Clans to exile any of my surviving attackers."

Mistystar looked down from where she sat in a fork of the Great Oak, her blue eyes gleaming with sorrow in the fitful moonlight. "Dappletuft died in the attack," she mewed, "but I was stunned and dismayed to hear how she dishonored her Clan. No cat who offended StarClan in such a way can be part of RiverClan. We did not sit vigil for her, and we buried her as we would have buried a rogue, with no words spoken over her."

Bristlefrost could see Dappletuft's kin huddled together at the back of the crowd; every one of them looked ashamed and miserable. Her heart ached for them. *Dappletuft must have known what she was risking, but to be exiled from your Clan in death . . .*

Leafstar was shifting uncomfortably, working her claws

into the bark of the branch where she sat. "I wonder why those young warriors risked so much to attack you, Bramblestar," she meowed, a challenge in her tone.

Bramblestar seemed unmoved by the challenge. "A leader who upholds the warrior code as strongly as I do is bound to make enemies," he responded smoothly. "After all, it can be difficult and painful to do what's right. But StarClan has advised and watched over the Clans for seasons upon seasons. Surely the right course is whatever brings them back?"

Leafstar opened her jaws to reply, but Bramblestar cut her off.

"That brings me to my next point," he continued. "My former mate and deputy, Squirrelflight"—he broke off for a heartbeat, then choked out the rest—"is dead." His voice was thick with emotion; Bristlefrost realized that he was still grieving. "She was killed by a monster near the Twolegplace."

Murmurs of surprise and dismay rose from the assembled cats. Bristlefrost noticed that Tigerstar looked particularly shocked. *He knows exactly what happened—but he's very good at pretending!*

"Of course, I was devastated at first," Bramblestar went on. "I loved Squirrelflight. I still love her. But then I realized: Not even the cats we love can escape punishment for breaking the code. StarClan will enforce the code regardless. And so we must brush aside our pain and put all our energies toward serving StarClan!"

His voice rang out clearly across the crowd of cats below, who responded with yowls and caterwauls of agreement.

Bristlefrost noticed that only Tigerstar, the rebels, and a few other warriors were looking doubtful.

"Now I ask my fellow leaders," Bramblestar continued, "whether I can count on their help in strictly following the code and serving StarClan in any way we can."

Silence followed the impostor's words for a few heartbeats. Then Mistystar dipped her head in agreement. "You have my support, Bramblestar, and the support of RiverClan," she mewed. "You're right that exiling the codebreakers has been painful at times." Bristlefrost detected a flicker of guilt in her eyes. *She must be thinking of Mothwing,* she thought. "But RiverClan is still suffering as a result of these rains. I hope that doing as StarClan has commanded will bring back their favor."

"I hope so, too," Harestar added. "I have lost a prized warrior and deputy, but we still struggle to feed our Clan. I believe our suffering will be rewarded when StarClan appears to us again, ready to help us through our difficult times. I've always respected you, Bramblestar, and I'll do as you say."

Silence fell again, as if the remaining two leaders were unwilling to speak. Bramblestar turned his head and fixed Leafstar with a hard stare.

"SkyClan has always served StarClan, and has always followed the code," she responded, meeting the impostor's gaze confidently. "We will not stop now."

With a curt nod, Bramblestar turned to Tigerstar, who crouched on his branch, fixing the ThunderClan leader with a menacing glare.

"ShadowClan follows the warrior code, and always will," he snapped. "I don't need you to watch over me."

"ShadowClan follows the code?" Bramblestar sneered. "When you haven't even exiled the codebreaker in your Clan? How can you—"

"Dovewing atoned!" Tigerstar interrupted, raising his voice to a yowl. "And I will not be told how to handle discipline within my own Clan. ShadowClan will enforce the code." His last few words were spat out. "Okay? Is that what you want to hear?"

"This isn't about words." The false Bramblestar was unsettlingly calm. "It's about actions. Maybe the attack on me was only the first of many. This will be a long battle, and in enforcing the code we will make enemies. But the Clans must agree that we're all in this together."

Murmurs of agreement and support came from the other leaders and the assembled warriors. But as Bristlefrost gazed around at the crowd, all she could see was how many beloved, valued cats were missing.

Squirrelflight, Crowfeather, Mothwing, both ThunderClan medicine cats. But they'll be back, Bristlefrost promised herself. *The rebels may have lost the first battle . . . but I have to believe that they'll win the war. Will I even be part of it, though? What if they think I betrayed them?* Since being named deputy, Bristlefrost hadn't had a chance to slip away and speak to the rebels, but she was afraid they must be blaming her for protecting Bramblestar.

As these thoughts passed through her mind, Bristlefrost spotted Rootspring across the clearing. For a moment their gazes locked. Rootspring looked completely shattered; he blinked once, then turned his head away.

Does he think I'm a traitor? Bristlefrost wondered, her throat clenching. *Do they all?*

On the day after the Gathering, Bristlefrost was dropping a blackbird on the fresh-kill pile when she was startled by a yowl of pain coming from the medicine cat's den. She whirled around, then raced across the camp and brushed past the bramble screen into the den.

Inside, Flipclaw was struggling to bind a poultice onto Shellfur's paw, but Shellfur was pulling away, scattering leaves and cobwebs over the den floor.

"I'm sorry! I'm sorry!" Flipclaw mewed frantically. "If you'd just keep still—"

"You don't even know what you're doing!" Shellfur screeched in despair. "It's just getting worse!"

Flipclaw turned away, and Bristlefrost could tell from his desperate expression that her brother knew Shellfur was right.

Paw steps sounded behind Bristlefrost, who turned to see Sparkpelt pushing the brambles aside as she entered. "What in StarClan's name is going on?" the orange tabby she-cat demanded.

Bristlefrost's pelt tingled with apprehension. *It would have to be Sparkpelt who walked in,* she thought. *I know she's grieving for Squirrelflight, but she doesn't have to claw every cat's ears off!*

"Shellfur's paw was wounded when he was defending Bramblestar," Flipclaw explained. "And now it's infected.

I keep applying cobwebs and a poultice made of dried oak leaves, but it's not getting better! Shellfur has a fever now."

"Oak leaves?" Sparkpelt asked. "Isn't that for *preventing* infection? I remember Alderheart treating my wound with oak leaves once, but when infection set in, he switched to marigold."

Flipclaw stared at her, stunned. "I didn't know about marigold," he murmured. "I thought oak leaves were used to *treat* infections."

Sparkpelt's tail lashed, and her fur bushed up until she looked twice her size. "You weren't even *trained!*" she snarled, glaring at Flipclaw. "How are you supposed to save cats' lives when you can't even treat an infected wound?"

Bristlefrost cringed in sympathy with her brother, especially when Flipclaw didn't try to defend himself. He bowed his head, giving his chest fur a couple of miserable licks.

"That's not fair!" Bristlefrost protested, her whiskers bristling with indignation. "Flipclaw didn't ask for this. It's not his fault he isn't trained."

"I'm sorry," Sparkpelt sighed, letting her fur lie flat again. "You're right, Bristlefrost. It's not his fault." Glancing past the bramble screen into the camp, she added, "It's not your fault at all, Flipclaw. Come with me."

Flipclaw followed her as she strode out into the open and came to a halt below the Highledge. "Bramblestar!" she yowled. "Come down here! I need a word with you."

Bristlefrost padded out and stood a few tail-lengths away, her pelt tingling with apprehension at how Bramblestar might

react. Flipclaw looked completely terrified at Sparkpelt's dis-
respectful tone.

But the impostor looked almost amused as he leaped lazily
down the tumbled rocks and strolled up to face Sparkpelt.
"Yes?" he rumbled.

"We can't go on like this, Bramblestar," Sparkpelt meowed.
"Whatever strange dreams Flipclaw had, he isn't trained, and
a Clan can't function without a trained medicine cat. Do you
realize that Shellfur has an infection raging out of control
from a simple wound in his paw? Poor Flipclaw's inexperience
is threatening cats' lives!"

In response, Bramblestar just blinked at her; Bristlefrost
guessed that he hadn't known, but he didn't much care, either.

"I know you had disagreements with Alderheart and Jayfeather," Sparkpelt went on. "But surely you can understand
that we need a real medicine cat, for the good of the Clan? At
the very least, let Brightheart help him until he gets the hang
of it! You've always been a caring leader," she added, her voice
softening. "Please, won't you reconsider? I'm asking you not as
a warrior, but as your daughter."

But you're not his daughter, Bristlefrost thought, suppressing a
shiver.

"You make an interesting point," Bramblestar replied; he
sounded quite detached, unaffected by Sparkpelt's appeal to
their kinship. "Bristlefrost, what do you think?"

Reluctantly Bristlefrost padded forward. By this time more
warriors were gathering around, wanting to know what the
fuss was about, and she felt they might be testing her, waiting

for her to put a paw wrong as deputy.

"I understand what Sparkpelt means," she replied to Bramblestar. "Would you like me to look for Alderheart or Jayfeather?"

"Not just yet," Bramblestar told her, with a lash of his tail. "True, a good medicine cat is one component of a strong Clan, but there's another, far more important one: loyalty."

Bristlefrost cringed inwardly, because she knew where the impostor's words came from. She remembered what she had told him when he was grieving for Squirrelflight: that he'd need to depend on *loyal* warriors.

I meant the exiled ones. But clearly, he took it differently.

Bramblestar turned back to Sparkpelt, who was watching him warily, seemingly realizing that her appeal had done more harm than good. "A cat who respects the code must always obey her leader," he told her in a condescending tone. "She must never question him—"

"The warrior code was given to us by StarClan," Sparkpelt interrupted, her neck fur beginning to bristle again. "But now StarClan has disappeared! And how do you ever expect to connect to them again if you've exiled all the medicine cats?"

Bristlefrost saw Bramblestar begin to swell with fury, his amber eyes smoldering. "It's because of cats like you that StarClan has abandoned us!" he hissed at Sparkpelt. "Cats who did not trust their leaders! But not anymore. Sparkpelt, you are no longer a ThunderClan cat. You are *exiled*!"

Sparkpelt's eyes widened in dismay, but before she could respond, a scratchy voice piped up. "A good warrior doesn't follow their leader off a cliff."

Bristlefrost turned to see Graystripe stepping forward through the ring of cats who surrounded Bramblestar and Sparkpelt. "A good leader doesn't expect blind loyalty," he continued. "Firestar certainly never led like that. And neither did you, Bramblestar—not before you lost a life. Only a weak leader demands obedience at any cost. Only a—"

He broke off as Bramblestar flashed out a paw and raked him across the nose, leaving a long bloody scratch. A gasp rose up from the surrounding warriors.

Almost at once Graystripe recovered, drawing himself up so that Bristlefrost could imagine the formidable warrior he had once been. "Bramblestar would never have hurt his own warrior," he meowed. "I don't know who you are . . . but you're not our leader!"

Bristlefrost was amazed at how close the elder had come to the truth. *Surely every cat must see how wise he is!*

"If you believe that," Bramblestar snapped at Graystripe, "then you can leave with Sparkpelt." With a glance at the assembled crowd, he added, "And so can any other cat who doesn't understand *loyalty*."

Blossomfall hesitated before padding forward to stand beside her father, Graystripe. Her brother, Bumblestripe, followed her, and a heartbeat later Cinderheart joined them, along with her apprentice, Finchpaw. Sparkpelt looked at her kit and nodded silently. Bristlefrost saw her own parents, Ivypool and Fernsong, exchange a glance and a few quick words. Ivypool's paws twitched, and for a moment it seemed like she would walk out, but then she shot a concerned look toward Bristlefrost and Flipclaw.

They won't leave without us, Bristlefrost realized. *And even if Flipclaw wants to go, the Clan needs him.*

Then to her amazement her sister, Thriftear, padded up to their parents, gave each of them a quick nuzzle, and joined the cats who were leaving. She shot a swift glance at Bristlefrost, then immediately looked away.

The group of exiled cats headed across the camp toward the thorn tunnel, without another word to Bramblestar. Bristlefrost remembered Tigerstar's words at the Gathering. *At this rate, there'll be more ThunderClan cats wandering the forest than in your camp.*

"Go then, filthy mange-pelts!" the impostor yowled. "Get out and don't come crawling back!" Whirling around, he faced the warriors who remained. "Remember that I expect loyalty," he snarled. "And if any cat knows that a Clanmate is not loyal . . . come and see me."

His tail whipping to and fro, he stalked back to the tumbled rocks and climbed up to his den.

After the exiles had disappeared, Bristlefrost remained staring at the thorn tunnel for a few more heartbeats. She was so shocked by what had happened that she thought she might never move again. At last she forced herself to glance around at her Clanmates, who all looked just as stunned and horrified as she felt. She could smell their fear, spreading over the camp like a poisonous mist.

"I'll talk to him," she meowed, bracing herself.

Climbing up to the Highledge, she could feel her Clanmates' hostility and hear their voices mocking the offer she had made. She didn't waver or look back. She padded toward the entrance of the den and was just about to enter when she heard Bramblestar already talking to some cat.

Not talking . . . arguing.

"How dare you question me?" he snarled. "I'll show you! I'll show them all! I'll make them regret what they've done to me. . . ."

Setting down her paws as softly as if she were stalking a mouse, Bristlefrost edged forward and peered into the entrance. Bramblestar stood with his back to her. His tail was twitching to and fro, while his neck fur was bristling and his ears were flattened.

But no cat was with him in the den.

Her whole body shaking uncontrollably, Bristlefrost backed away.

CHAPTER 19

Shadowsight slid into shelter under a bush at the edge of the exiles' camp. Every day since the Gathering had been dark and dreary, with hardly any respite from the inexorable wind and rain. Now, as darkness fell, the clouds seemed to be breaking up, but the waning moon was weak and pallid, shedding hardly any light over the clearing.

Cats filled the camp: most of ShadowClan, all the exiles, and the surviving members of the rebel group. Shadowsight drank in their mingled scents, but he could see little more than their dark shapes and the occasional gleam of eyes.

Tigerstar was standing on a flat rock beside the stream, his head raised as he addressed the crowd. "I've spoken to Puddleshine," he announced, "and he told me what happened at last night's half-moon meeting. Puddleshine, I think we all need to hear this."

I wish I'd been there, Shadowsight thought wistfully, knowing that he wasn't strong enough yet to travel as far as the Moonpool.

The medicine cat, who was sitting at the base of the rock

where his Clan leader stood, rose to his paws. "I don't believe Flipclaw even knew he should come. But at the meeting, Kestrelflight and Willowshine both promised to let their leaders know about Rootspring's seeing Bramblestar's ghost, how he showed us a blurry form that might have been that ghost, and what Shadowsight claims he saw while he was between worlds," he announced.

"What about the way Alderheart was exiled and Flipclaw was forced to take his place?" Frecklewish asked.

"Yes, that too," Puddleshine meowed. "So earlier today they paid me a visit to tell me how their leaders took it."

"That's good," Crowfeather commented. "What happened?"

"According to Kestrelflight and Willowshine," Puddleshine replied, "Mistystar and Harestar both had . . . spirited discussions with their deputies and their most trusted warriors."

Crowfeather let out a snort of wry amusement. "Spirited, hmm? So how much fur was flying?"

Tigerstar batted at Crowfeather with his tail, though the WindClan cat was too far away for the slap to connect. "That's not helping," Tigerstar growled.

"Tigerstar, let me explain," Puddleshine mewed swiftly. "Apparently Mistystar decided that all the evidence was coming from cats she didn't know well enough to trust, and she couldn't turn on another leader without StarClan's guidance. In the end, she still believes that Bramblestar knows the most about how to get StarClan back."

"And Harestar?" Crowfeather asked.

"He said Rootspring and Shadowsight had always been a bit odd—"

"No argument there," some cat murmured out of the darkness.

Shadowsight didn't know whether to be amused—because he had to admit there was some truth in what Harestar had said—or indignant that his pain and the risks he had taken were being brushed aside like flies hovering over fresh-kill.

"Then Harestar said there were few cats he trusted more than Bramblestar," Puddleshine continued. "And he desperately needs StarClan's favor to return prey to the moor. Both he and Mistystar will still support Bramblestar."

"But what about Alderheart and Flipclaw?" Squirrelflight asked. "Didn't that mean anything to Kestrelflight and Willowshine?"

"They were both shocked by it," Puddleshine told her. "I think that's what made them decide to pass on all the news to their leaders. But it didn't make any difference to Harestar or Mistystar."

"Great StarClan, what will it take?" Crowfeather snarled, while murmurs of frustration and disgust rose up from the other cats.

"That's the problem," Tigerstar meowed, raising his tail for silence. "RiverClan and WindClan believe that their only hope of seeing StarClan again lies with Bramblestar, so they will *never* see the bad in him. There's no hope of winning more allies to our side." He paused for a heartbeat, then added, "It's time to attack—even if we *are* outnumbered. We have to kill Bramblestar."

"No!" Shadowsight instinctively let out the cry of protest. "How could we kill him?" he continued, as every cat, including Tigerstar, swiveled to stare at him. "Bramblestar isn't just some bad cat. He isn't himself. There is something inside him, something evil. But we know from Rootspring that Bramblestar's ghost is still around here somewhere."

Now every cat looked toward Rootspring. Shadowsight expected support from him, but the young warrior avoided his gaze, shaking his head sadly.

"I haven't seen Bramblestar's ghost for a full moon now," he confessed. "I'm afraid he's . . . faded." At last he looked Shadowsight in the eye, and went on. "I'm very sorry to say this, but I'm not sure there *is* a real Bramblestar anymore. Our chance to save him may have passed."

Shadowsight stared back at Rootspring, hardly able to believe what he was hearing. He wanted to protest, to yowl out his fervent belief that there still *was* a chance to restore the real Bramblestar.

But before Shadowsight could utter a sound, the scene in front of him changed. Flames roared upward, cutting him off from the rest of the cats, consuming everything. He recognized the same vision he had received before he killed Bramblestar's body, the one that had convinced the other medicine cats that his visions were real.

In that vision, fire had divided all the Clans. This time, Shadowsight began to move with the flames, through the forest and up onto the moors. He paused, looking down at the Moonpool. As he set paw on the spiral path, the flames around him died, and he let out a gasp as he found himself back in the exiles' camp.

None of the other cats seemed to have noticed anything. Squirrelflight had sprung up beside Tigerstar on the flat rock, arguing with vehement gestures of her tail. "I'm telling you that Bramblestar *can* be killed," she insisted. "Or at least his body can. And then what will happen to the real Bramblestar's spirit?"

"I don't know," Tigerstar growled in response. "What concerns me is the thing inside him. That has to be stopped, once and for all, before it destroys the Clans. We must attack. We have no other choice."

"I understand, Tigerstar," Squirrelflight mewed. "But please—could you just capture Bramblestar, and not kill him? As a prisoner, he couldn't do any more damage, but it would give us a chance to find the real Bramblestar and reunite him with his body." As she finished speaking, Squirrelflight's figure seemed to sag and she let out a long sigh.

It pained Shadowsight to see the brave and determined she-cat so discouraged. He realized that she, too, was beginning to lose hope that the real Bramblestar would ever come back. It made his own hope start to wither like a seedling under the fierce sun of greenleaf.

"Maybe we could take him prisoner," Lionblaze agreed. "But are we right to attack at all? Can we be sure that we're strong enough to defeat the impostor?"

"We're strong enough," Crowfeather growled, narrowing

his eyes at his son. "Just let me get my claws in him!"

"But if we fail," Lionblaze argued, "then our entire rebel group will be wiped out. There would be nothing to stop the false Bramblestar controlling all the Clans."

Instantly cats began to raise their voices in support of one warrior or the other, and for a moment Shadowsight was afraid that the meeting would break up into groups of squabbling cats. Then Tigerstar let out a loud caterwaul.

"Silence!" he ordered. "The time has come to attack! Getting rid of that mangy interloper is worth the risk. We can never be sure we're strong enough, but this is the right thing to do, even if we may not win! We are warriors! Are we afraid of a cat who doesn't even have his own body?"

Yowls of "No! No!" came from the ShadowClan cats around him. The cats from other Clans seemed surprised by Tigerstar's fervent speech, but inspired enough to join in. Even Shadowsight was impressed, though he still felt uneasy about the attack.

Will it feed the flames of my vision, dividing the Clans? he wondered. *Or will it stop them?*

"We are agreed, then?" Tigerstar continued in a quieter voice, once the clamor had died down. "We will attack in two sunrises. And," he added, with a glance at Squirrelflight, "if possible we will take Bramblestar prisoner."

Squirrelflight nodded. "In two sunrises," she repeated, though Shadowsight could see the fear and misgivings in her eyes.

* * *

Fire blazed up around Shadowsight, though he couldn't feel any heat from the flames. He knew that he was lying curled up in his nest in the medicine cats' den, but he also seemed to be hovering over the lake with the Clans' territories spread out beneath him.

Just as in his first vision of fire, the flames were encroaching on the Clans, slowly devouring them. Shadowsight could hear the despairing wails and shrieks of agony of cats trapped in the blaze. The water level fell in the lake, as if some gigantic mouth were sucking it down, and a cloud of steam billowed up, obliterating Shadowsight's vision.

"Help! Help!"

Shadowsight stiffened as he heard the voice, weak and faint as if it had reached him from an immense distance. Somehow he knew it was coming from the Moonpool.

It's . . . it's Bramblestar!

At that moment Shadowsight startled awake in his own nest. Puddleshine was asleep at the far side of the den, letting out gentle little snores. Everything seemed peaceful, but Shadowsight knew that he had been given a task.

I have to find the real Bramblestar. But how do you find a ghost?

He closed his eyes and concentrated. Bramblestar's voice had come from the Moonpool. What did that mean? Was Bramblestar there? What did it mean, to be at the Moonpool as a ghost? Wherever Bramblestar was, he needed help.

A heartbeat later, Shadowsight knew what he had to do.

Shadowsight searched among Puddleshine's herb stores until he found what he needed. For a moment he hesitated, thinking of Tigerstar and Dovewing, and what they would say if they knew what he meant to do. Then he looked at Puddleshine, so close to him, and he remembered his other Clanmates, and the cats of the other Clans, all of them in desperate need. With his resolve strengthened, he chewed and swallowed.

Shadowsight was shocked by how fast the berry worked. Almost at once he felt waves of heat sweeping through him. His throat tightened and he choked, struggling to breathe. Darkness swirled around him, and he felt himself falling.

Shadowsight opened his eyes to find himself in the forest; a pale glow surrounded him, like a bubble of mist. There was no sound or scent of any other cats, and nothing to tell him exactly where he was.

He had been afraid that he would have to make the long trek to the Moonpool, but as soon as he visualized the waterfall cascading down the rocks and into the pool, he found himself standing at the top of the spiral path.

Good, he thought. *It worked!*

Shadowsight padded down the path and approached the water's edge, leaning over to stare down into the pool. *What was my dream trying to tell me?* he asked himself.

Crouching down, he closed his eyes and pressed his nose to the icy surface of the water. At once he could hear the weak voice again. "Help! Help!"

Shadowsight opened his eyes and gasped at what he could

see, deep, deep beneath the surface of the water: Bramblestar's hazy amber eyes, staring at him with a look of desperation. "Help!" the voice came again.

"I must have bees in my brain to be doing this," Shadowsight muttered to himself as he rose and stood poised at the very edge of a rock that overhung the pool. He wasn't a River-Clan cat, and he knew he couldn't swim.

But I'm between worlds. . . . Maybe my ghost can swim? Or maybe a ghost can't drown?

Before his fear could overwhelm him completely, Shadowsight leaped into the waters of the Moonpool. He sank down, down, farther down, his ears filled with the sound of rushing water.

He couldn't see Bramblestar's eyes any longer, and darkness was growing all around him. *Was it all a trick?* Shadowsight wondered. *What if I'm just dying?*

Then, through the darkness, Shadowsight made out something below him: branches growing up from the bottom of the Moonpool, tangled with vines and bramble tendrils. Unable to stop himself, he plunged into the middle of them and felt the vines winding themselves around his legs and tail. When he fought to free himself, the bramble thorns tore at his fur.

Even though in his spirit form Shadowsight didn't need to breathe, panic overtook him and he began to struggle. But his thrashing only weakened him, tangling him further in the thorns. He knew that he ought to go on fighting, but his whole body was crying out for rest. His strength ebbing, he closed his eyes. His body grew limp, and he did not move again.

* * *

As he came to himself, Shadowsight realized that he was no longer in the waters of the Moonpool. He was lying on something soft; the tangling vines and tearing brambles were gone. He opened his eyes and staggered to his paws.

All around Shadowsight stretched massive trees, as far as he could see. Grass covered the ground, with thickets of fern and bramble here and there; in the darkness they looked like huge, crouching animals waiting to pounce.

When Shadowsight raised his head, he could see nothing but blackness beyond the interlacing branches; there was not even a glimmer of light from the moon or stars.

And there never will be, Shadowsight thought, a deep shudder running through his body from ears to tail-tip, for he realized now where he was. *This is the Dark Forest . . . the Place of No Stars.*

Terror swelled inside him as he took in his surroundings. The only light came from thick fungus growing on the trunks of the trees, which let out a sickly, pale glow. The sweetish scent of rotting crow-food filled the air; Shadowsight swiped his tongue over his jaws in a vain attempt to get rid of the taste.

How do I get out of here? he thought. Then he braced himself. He knew that he had been led here for a purpose; all he had to do was discover what that purpose was.

He remembered what the false Bramblestar had said about connections between worlds . . . if a cat was clever enough to find them. *Is this how the impostor got to the lake?*

Shadowsight began to explore, taking a random path

among the trees. Out of the corner of his eye he could glimpse dark flickers, but when he turned to confront the movement, there was nothing there. Distant echoes reached his ears, as if he could hear the voices of cats stranded here. But he couldn't see them; they felt just out of reach.

Once, this place must have been full of cats, Shadowsight thought, remembering the stories the older warriors told of how the first Tigerstar had trained the Dark Forest cats for a battle against the living Clans. Many of those warriors had died in the battle, and now the forest was almost deserted.

But not quite. Shadowsight shivered. *Are any of the survivors here now? Are they watching me?* His pelt prickled with apprehension, but as he padded on, no cat appeared to challenge him. Gradually he grew calmer.

Then through the trees he spotted what at first he thought was a particularly large bramble thicket. As he drew closer, he saw that it was made out of thorn branches and the whippy shoots of saplings, interlaced with vines and bramble tendrils.

It's like a den. . . . Is this where the Dark Forest cats live?

Shadowsight's immediate instinct was to stay far away from the den or mound or whatever it was. It reeked of danger. But then he realized that this might be what he had been sent to find. At the very least, he needed to investigate it.

To begin with, keeping a safe distance, he padded all around the thing in a wide circle. "It can't be a den," he murmured. "There's no entrance."

Venturing closer, he tried to peer through the branches to see if there was anything inside. To his amazement, he spotted the glint of water. *There's a pool in there! Why would any cat build this thing over a pool?*

The chinks in the interwoven branches at ground level were too small to give Shadowsight a good view. Padding around the outside again, he noticed a larger gap a few tail-lengths farther up; letting his spirit form float upward, he hooked his claws onto the branch below the gap and tried to peer through.

An ivy tendril was blocking his view, and without thinking Shadowsight raised a paw to brush it aside. To his surprise, the tendril moved easily, and he was able to drape it over a nearby jutting twig.

Interesting, he thought. *So even though I'm a spirit, I can move things here.*

With the obstacle out of the way, Shadowsight could see the surface of the pool, and he let out a gasp of wonder and amazement. From side to side the whole of the water was glittering with innumerable stars. For a moment he thought it was reflecting a cloudless starry night, but there were no stars above, only the dark tangle of interwoven branches.

"What is that?" Shadowsight meowed aloud. "Is it StarClan?"

Then he realized that if he could truly see StarClan shining from the pool, then the mound he was clinging to must be a barrier.

And if it is . . . is this what is keeping StarClan away from the living Clans? Did a cat build this?

He pushed his paws against the woven branches, then braced himself and heaved at them with his shoulder, but they wouldn't move, and the gap was far too small for him to climb through. At last, exhausted, he gave up, resting his head against the branches that framed the gap. For a few heartbeats more Shadowsight let his gaze rest on the beauty of StarClan. "I will release you," he promised. "I don't know how, yet, but I *will* do it."

Then he let himself drop from the side of the barrier and turned back to the forest, eager now to find a way out.

With no idea which direction he should follow, Shadowsight let his paws take him where they wanted, weaving aimlessly through the trees. He tried not to look too deeply into the shadows, or try to imagine what might be waiting to drop onto him from the branches above.

He had lost count of how long he had been wandering in the pallid light of the fungi when he thought he heard a faint cry coming from somewhere ahead. He halted, angling his ears forward to listen.

The cry came again, and now Shadowsight could distinguish the words. "Help! Help me!"

Bramblestar was calling me from the Moonpool, he thought with quickening excitement. *That could be his voice!*

Without hesitating, Shadowsight set off toward the sound, picking up the pace until he was racing along with his tail streaming out behind him and his belly fur brushing the grass. The cries grew louder, and at last he could work out where they were coming from: a vast oak tree covered in fungus and lichen, with vines hanging from its branches like the tails of crouching predators.

Shadowsight halted, his chest heaving for breath as he stared at the tree. His first thought had been that he must free any cat in danger under this starless sky, but now he wondered whether the voice was a trap.

How could Bramblestar's spirit have ended up here? he asked himself.

More cautiously now, he prowled forward, encircling the tree from a few fox-lengths away. On the far side he spotted a wide gash in the trunk, blocked by branches crisscrossing from one side to the other, with brambles, twigs, and debris shoved into the gaps. The voice was coming from behind the barrier.

"Help me!"

I was right—I know that voice! Shadowsight realized, a thrill of excitement pulsing through him from his ears to the ends of his claws. "Bramblestar?"

"Yes, it's me!" There was sudden hope in the voice behind the barrier, though it was still very weak. "Who's there?"

"It's Shadowsight. Wait—I'll get you out."

Sliding out his claws, Shadowsight began to tug at the branches, but they were all too heavy for him to move. *What I need is a couple of strong warriors!* Instead he began to claw at the bramble tendrils, ignoring the thorns that caught in his fur and pierced his pads. When he had dragged away several of the tendrils, Shadowsight tore at the smaller debris until he had opened up a narrow gap at the bottom of the gash in the trunk. Peering through it, he spotted a hunched tabby shape and the gleam of intense amber eyes.

"It is you, Bramblestar!" Shadowsight exclaimed. "Can you get out through here? I don't think I can move the heavy branches."

"I'll try."

Shadowsight was doubtful as he watched Bramblestar's spirit trying to squeeze himself through the tiny space, remembering what a big cat he was in the living world. But somehow the ThunderClan leader managed to haul himself into the open, where he collapsed, wheezing.

"Thank you, Shadowsight," he gasped when he could speak. "I thought I would never get out. I was too weak to move that stuff, and getting weaker."

"But how did you get in there?" Shadowsight asked eagerly. "Which cat—"

Shadowsight broke off as, without warning, he felt his legs begin to shake. Losing his balance, he fell to the ground. He could hear voices echoing from far away.

"Puddleshine! *Do* something!"

"I'm fetching yarrow."

Bramblestar scrambled to his paws and came to Shadowsight's side. "What's the matter?" he asked anxiously.

Shadowsight tried to respond, but his belly was convulsing. Bitter bile rose up into his throat. All around him the trees of the Dark Forest were fading, and he could make out the shadowy outlines of more cats bending over him.

"I'm . . . waking up!" he gasped out.

"Then take me with you!" Bramblestar meowed urgently.
"I can—"

The rest of the ThunderClan leader's words were lost on
Shadowsight's next breath. His eyes flew open and he found
himself sprawled on his side in the medicine cats' den. A pool
of vomit lay on the ground beside him, speckled with the
bright red spots of the deathberry he had eaten.

Somewhere nearby he could hear his father yowling.
"Shadowsight, what have you done?"

With difficulty Shadowsight managed to sit up. He was
frustrated to be dragged away from Bramblestar's spirit just
when he was on the point of learning what cat had stolen
Bramblestar's body, but very glad to be back home. He could
still smell the stink of rotten fungus, but he was safely away
from the grim territory of the Dark Forest.

Blinking, he saw Puddleshine crouching at his side, a leaf
of yarrow in his claws. Tigerstar was standing over him, his
horrified gaze fixed on his son.

"It's okay," Shadowsight reassured his father. His throat
hurt and his voice was hoarse. "I knew what I was doing. And
now I know what's keeping StarClan away."

CHAPTER 20

✤

Rootspring crouched beneath an arching clump of ferns a couple of
tail-lengths from the ThunderClan border. His head raised,
he parted his jaws to taste the air for fresh ThunderClan
scent. As long as he didn't cross the border, he hoped that he
wouldn't be in trouble if he was caught here.

*But I'd still have a problem explaining just what I'm doing. I'd rather
not be seen by any ThunderClan cats.*

He had been crouching beneath the ferns for so long that
his legs were starting to stiffen and ache; he knew it might be
difficult if he had to make a quick escape to avoid the rival
Clan. But as much as he wanted to stand up and stretch, he
forced himself to stay in hiding, waiting for Bristlefrost.

Rootspring was beginning to wonder whether he was ever
going to see *any* ThunderClan warrior, but finally the long
grass on the other side of the border parted and a cat came
into view. It wasn't the cat Rootspring wanted to see, though:
It was the false Bramblestar, heading along the border.

Rootspring tensed as he watched the dark tabby tom, noticing that his pelt looked dull, as if he hadn't groomed it in the

last moon. He couldn't relax until the impostor padded safely out of sight and his scent began to fade.

Where is he going? he asked himself, then gave his pelt a shake to dismiss the question. *It isn't time to confront Bramblestar yet, not until Leafstar and Tigerstar agree. I'm not here for Bramblestar.*

Once he was certain that the ThunderClan leader had left, Rootspring crept a little closer to the border, scanning the territory for any sign of Bristlefrost. Eventually he spotted her, winding her way through a clump of elder bushes, with Molewhisker and Hollytuft following her. They were clearly a hunting patrol; Rootspring's jaws began to water at the scent of the prey they carried.

When she was only a couple of fox-lengths from the border, Bristlefrost halted and dropped the vole she was carrying. All three cats looked uncomfortable; Rootspring was too far away to hear what Bristlefrost was saying, but she seemed to be giving the two older warriors instructions.

Since the other warriors had their backs to Rootspring, he risked rising to his paws and padding a bit closer, bushing out his fur to make himself as big as possible.

Come on, Bristlefrost—look at me!

Finally, Bristlefrost's gaze fell on him, and her eyes widened slightly. Rootspring gestured with his tail for Bristlefrost to meet him up a nearby tree, but the pale gray she-cat looked back toward the ThunderClan warriors. To Rootspring's relief, she didn't give him away.

Now that he had moved within earshot, Rootspring could make out what Bristlefrost and the others were saying.

"We've hunted well," Bristlefrost meowed. "You can take the prey back to camp."

"Aren't you coming with us?" Hollytuft asked. Her voice sounded a little cold.

Bristlefrost shook her head. "I just remembered that Flipclaw asked me to bring back a few sprigs of chervil, if I could find any."

"Okay," Molewhisker responded, exchanging a glance with Hollytuft. "We'll see you back at camp."

He and Hollytuft collected their prey, including Bristlefrost's vole, and headed off in the direction of the ThunderClan camp. Bristlefrost stood looking after them until they disappeared into the undergrowth.

Meanwhile, Rootspring crept toward the tree, setting his paws down as quietly as he could, and leaped up onto the lowest branch, hiding himself among the leaves while he waited nervously to see if Bristlefrost would join him.

Finally he heard her clawing her way up the trunk, and then he spotted her clambering onto the branch beside him, struggling to get her balance as the branch dipped under their combined weight.

"Have you got bees in your brain, showing up like this?" she asked him. "If Bramblestar had seen you when he was out on his walk . . ."

"Yeah, about that," Rootspring mewed. "Where was he going?"

"I have no idea." Bristlefrost twitched her whiskers irritably. "Or what he's doing. I—"

"Never mind him, then," Rootspring interrupted. "It's you I'm concerned about. Every cat, except maybe Squirrelflight, seems to think you're a traitor." He hesitated for a heartbeat before asking the question that had been buzzing in his brain ever since the meeting. *Even though I'm dreading what her answer will be.* "Did you betray us to that fake leader?"

Bristlefrost let out a hiss of indignation. "No, I did not!" she retorted. "Honestly, Rootspring, I promised Squirrelflight I would protect Bramblestar's body. That why I didn't help attack him. I'm still on your side. I'm just trying to help from inside ThunderClan. I never wanted him to name me deputy, but I figure at least it'll be easier to defeat the mange-pelt if there's a cat who's close but working against him."

Rootspring found that he believed every word, even though he guessed that many cats wouldn't. *They might think that if she would betray Bramblestar, she would betray the rebels, too.* He wasn't sure what to say; at last he broke a long and awkward silence by shifting his paws to pull himself a little closer to her. "So you're *not* a traitor to the Clans?"

"Of course I'm not!" Bristlefrost snapped. "And it really hurts that you of all cats could think that of me. It wasn't too hard to fool the fake Bramblestar, but I would have thought *you* knew me better than that. I would never have thought so badly of you. . . ."

Rootspring felt as though his belly were falling all the way to the ground, but at the same time his spirits were soaring. *She's on our side after all!*

"I'm sorry for doubting you," he meowed. "But I didn't

know what to think. If I didn't like you so much, I wouldn't have felt so angry when it looked like you had turned on me and the others."

Bristlefrost's eyes widened. "You like me? Even after . . ." Her voice died away.

Rootspring felt as if his pelt were on fire from embarrassment, but he managed to meet Bristlefrost's suddenly softened gaze. "I can't help it," he muttered.

"You know why that could never happen, right?" Bristlefrost's gentle voice sounded impossibly loud in Rootspring's ears. "This whole terrible situation the Clans are in is because of codebreaking—and that includes cats from different Clans getting together. That's always been against the warrior code."

"Yes, I know," Rootspring began. "That's why I would never have said anything. . . ." His words dried up like a puddle under the sun of greenleaf as he realized the meaning of what Bristlefrost had just said. "Does that mean you . . . you like me, too?" he blurted; forcing each word out was a massive effort, but he had to ask the question.

Bristlefrost didn't reply for a moment, instead bending her head to give her chest fur a few embarrassed licks. "Yes . . . yes, I do have feelings for you," she admitted at last. "But what can we do about it? Nothing." She closed her eyes briefly as if in pain. "There's no way it can go anywhere."

Rootspring heaved a sigh from deep within his chest. *I know she's right.* But it hurt so much to hear her say it.

Even as the thought settled in his mind, the twisty feeling in his belly told him that he didn't like having to accept it. Shaking his head clear of his tortured thoughts, he added, "We have something bigger to worry about. Tigerstar is going to lead an attack on ThunderClan tomorrow."

Bristlefrost stared at him with a sharp intake of breath. "Tomorrow? I didn't expect it to be so soon."

"Tigerstar would have liked it sooner," Rootspring told her. "And you might have to be the cat who saves the fake Bramblestar's body. We can't let it be destroyed—if we do, the real Bramblestar might never be able to return."

"I'll have no problem keeping an eye on the impostor," Bristlefrost mewed ruefully. "He seems to like having me around right now, for some reason." Her voice grew wistful. "I'll be so glad when all this strife is over," she sighed. "When the Clans can go back to normal, bickering about territory, not disputing the meaning of the entire warrior code."

Rootspring nodded. "Yes, things will be different—they'll be better, once we've sorted all this out."

Bristlefrost paused briefly, tilting her head to look at him. "Better how?" she asked. "Do you mean, maybe the rules will be looser, things will be . . . possible then, that aren't possible now?"

Rootspring hadn't meant that, but he was not about to tell Bristlefrost so. He realized she was talking about *their* future, and he wanted to know what she would say next. "What if they were?" he asked hopefully.

"Maybe if we both survive this battle, we can be together on the other side," she suggested.

"Yes!" Rootspring responded eagerly. "Maybe we can."

But he saw that Bristlefrost's eyes were full of sadness, as though she knew, deep down beneath her hopeful surface, that nothing would be that easy. Rootspring knew it, too. He leaned closer to Bristlefrost until his head brushed her shoulder, and for a moment they sat side by side, not needing to speak. Basking in the warmth of her pelt so close to his, Rootspring realized that they might not have a future. But right now they were together, and for the moment, that was enough.

Rootspring had just returned to the SkyClan camp and chosen a mouse from the fresh-kill pile when he spotted Blossomheart and Nettlesplash emerging from the fern tunnel, with the false Bramblestar trailing just behind them. He watched curiously as they headed toward Leafstar's den.

"Leafstar!" Blossomheart called. "We have a visitor."

The SkyClan leader poked her head out of her den, her ears flicking up as she spotted the impostor. Padding into the open, she asked, "Where did you find him? Not on our territory, I hope?"

"He was walking along the border," Nettlesplash replied. "He asked to speak to you."

Rapidly gulping down his mouse, Rootspring eased himself a little closer to hear what was going on. More of the SkyClan warriors were gathering, too, alert but not threatening, as the two leaders confronted each other.

"What do you want?" Leafstar asked.

"I've heard rumors that Tigerstar might be planning an attack on ThunderClan," Bramblestar replied. "Do you know anything about this?"

For a moment Rootspring's chest throbbed with panic, as he wondered whether Bristlefrost could have betrayed the rebels by passing on what he had told her. *No, that's impossible,* he reassured himself. *I trust her—and besides, she hasn't had time to find Bramblestar and tell him.*

"I've heard nothing," Leafstar responded curtly.

Bramblestar stared at her for a long moment, as if he was looking for a sign that she might be lying. Then he nodded. "There's nothing to worry about for any of us, because there's no way ShadowClan can take on the combined might of ThunderClan, RiverClan, WindClan, and SkyClan—is there? And if ShadowClan is planning an attack soon . . . there's still time to surprise them."

Murmurs of astonishment and doubt came from the assembled warriors. At the sound, Bramblestar's eyes widened and he turned to rake them with a shocked stare. Rootspring wondered if any other cat could see that the impostor was faking his emotion.

"Leafstar," the ThunderClan leader asked, "I *can* count on you pledging your warriors to support me in a battle with ShadowClan? SkyClan isn't *sympathetic* toward the codebreakers, is it?"

His head swiveled around again to gaze at the warriors, and at that moment he spotted Kitescratch. His jaws gaped open this time, Rootspring thought, in genuine amazement.

He pointed at Kitescratch with his tail.

"This cat was involved in the attack on me," he meowed accusingly. "Why hasn't he been exiled?"

Several of Kitescratch's Clanmates raised their voice in protest, but Bramblestar overrode them. "Look at him!" he yowled. "He's missing the fur from one shoulder, one ear is torn, and he has a bad wound down one side. Where do you think he got those?"

The reddish-brown tom couldn't meet his gaze. "I—I got them fighting an owl," he mumbled.

Bramblestar kept on glaring at him, and Leafstar gave him a stern look as she asked, "Is that true, Kitescratch?"

For a few heartbeats Kitescratch gazed helplessly at Leafstar, then shook his head. "I did go with the others to attack Bramblestar. But I—"

"Enough!" Bramblestar growled. His shoulder fur bristled and he slid out his claws, approaching Kitescratch with menace in his eyes.

But Leafstar stepped forward, blocking Bramblestar with her tail. "Kitescratch," she mewed, "you know what you have to do."

To begin with, Kitescratch looked confused, glancing from his leader to the fake Bramblestar and back again. Rootspring could see the moment when understanding hit him: His head and tail drooped as he turned slowly away and trailed miserably out of the camp.

Tinycloud ran a little way after him, then halted and turned back. "That's not fair!" she exclaimed.

More yowls of shock and dismay supported the white she-cat's outburst. Rootspring stared at Leafstar, unable to believe that she would give in so easily.

"Are you going to let another Clan's leader give orders in our camp?" Sparrowpelt demanded.

"Yeah, who does he think he is?" Macgyver asked.

Leafstar ignored the protests from her Clan, except to wave her tail for silence, and gradually the clamor died down.

"So, I can count on you, Leafstar?" the impostor repeated. "Together we can hit ShadowClan hard, before they have time to defend themselves."

Leafstar fixed a level gaze on him, and her voice was calm as she replied. "You should know where I stand, Bramblestar. The honor of the Clans is very important to me."

Bramblestar responded with a curt nod of satisfaction. "Then we'll attack at dawn." Waiting only for Leafstar to dip her head in assent, he turned and stalked out of the camp.

Rootspring could feel tension tingling in the air after the ThunderClan leader had left. No cat wanted to look at Leafstar, and yet none of them moved away to get on with their duties.

"Bramblestar is out of control," the deputy, Hawkwing, meowed, flexing his claws. "Throwing his weight around like he's the leader of *all* the Clans."

"Quite true," Leafstar agreed. "Hawkwing, go after Kitescratch and tell him to come back. Just make sure that Bramblestar doesn't see you, if he's still hanging around."

"*Yes!*" Rootspring hissed, hearing a murmur of approval

from the rest of his Clanmates.

Relief flared in Hawkwing's eyes at his leader's order. "Right away, Leafstar!" he responded, before bounding across the camp and plunging into the fern tunnel.

Leafstar looked after him, and when she spoke, her voice was a low, insistent growl. "No other leader tells me what to do with my own warriors." With a sweep of her tail she gathered her Clan closer to her. "SkyClan will be fighting in tomorrow's battle," she told them. "But we will fight on the side of ShadowClan and the rebels. We must warn them now."

Yowls of acclamation erupted from the SkyClan warriors, so different from their protests of a few moments before. "Leafstar! Leafstar!"

"I've tried to stay out of this conflict," Leafstar continued, "but I won't hesitate anymore. We may have had our troubles with Tigerstar in the past, but he was right about this false ThunderClan leader and the Clans' current problems. Now I have to pick a side," she concluded, "and it's time to stop Bramblestar!"

CHAPTER 21

♣

Dawn mist still lay heavy across the lake as the cats of ThunderClan headed along the shore and crossed the border into SkyClan territory. Bristlefrost shivered as the chilly droplets soaked into her pelt. She felt uneasy being at the head of the group, padding along at the false Bramblestar's shoulder, sensing the resentful gazes of her Clanmates as she assumed the position of deputy.

Her reluctance to be part of this fight was growing with every paw step she took toward ShadowClan. Since talking to Rootspring the day before, Bristlefrost was well aware that every cat could assume she was willing—even eager—to follow Bramblestar's orders and attack. How had Bramblestar learned that ShadowClan was planning to attack him? It seemed like he had known even before Bristlefrost did, but she knew the rebels would assume she had told him. She glanced sideways at the false Bramblestar. Did he have some source of information she didn't know about? Maybe some other cat among the rebels?

They must all think I'm a traitor. . . . And what in StarClan's name will I do when the fighting starts? She hadn't forgotten her promise to protect Bramblestar's body.

As the ThunderClan cats drew close to the Shadow-Clan border, Bristlefrost heard the sound of many paw steps approaching rapidly from behind. Stiffening with tension, she whirled around, half expecting an attack from the rear, only to see the figures of Mistystar and Harestar looming up out of the mist, with their Clanmates following.

Bristlefrost relaxed, huffing out a sigh. *Thank StarClan! It's only RiverClan and WindClan. The mist must have masked their scent.*

The two Clan leaders padded up to the head of the group to join Bramblestar, giving Bristlefrost the chance to slip backward by a couple of tail-lengths. She had hoped to feel better once she got away from the impostor, but instead her sense of foreboding grew.

By the time the attack force reached the ShadowClan border, Bristlefrost felt as if she were going to burst from mounting tension.

ThunderClan is supposed to be honorable and upstanding, she thought wretchedly. *That's what we're known for! And here we are, about to launch a sneak attack on another Clan, which hasn't done anything to harm us.*

Bramblestar drew his followers to a halt just on the Sky-Clan side of the border, and paused for a moment, looking over the heads of the other cats.

"No SkyClan, I see," he murmured. "I suppose I will have to punish Leafstar for her treachery another day, but we still have the advantage." Gesturing with his tail, he instructed the other leaders how to position their cats to attack the

ShadowClan camp from every side. "Those mange-pelts will have nowhere to run," he growled.

Under his direction, the cats of all three Clans spread out into a loose half circle as they crossed the border and padded through the trees toward the ShadowClan camp. On the way, the mist began to clear, and a gray dawn light filled the forest as they approached the barrier of bushes that surrounded the hollow.

Silently the three Clans padded up the slope and thrust their way through the bushes at the same moment, almost encircling the camp. Bristlefrost expected that the Shadow-Clan cats would still be sleeping, except perhaps for the dawn patrol making ready to set out.

She was wrong. Her belly lurched as she looked down into the hollow and saw Tigerstar standing in the middle of the camp with all his warriors around him. Their shoulder fur was bristling and their eyes glittered with fury.

They've been warned!

Tigerstar stalked out from the group of his warriors and headed toward Bramblestar, who strode down the slope to meet him at the edge of the camp. "What is all this about?" he demanded.

Bramblestar froze for a moment in utter shock, but rapidly recovered himself. "It's obvious why StarClan seems to have abandoned the living cats," he snarled. "All the codebreaking, especially here in ShadowClan. You're the only Clan that has resisted my decrees."

"How do you get to make *decrees* for another Clan?"

Tigerstar sneered. His eyes narrowed as he cast a cold gaze around him at the invading cats. "This alliance of three Clans is going to drive out all of ShadowClan to please the spirits of our warrior ancestors?"

"That's right," the false Bramblestar replied, his calm, confident voice sending a shiver through Bristlefrost.

Tigerstar looked unimpressed. "I'm not going anywhere, and neither is my Clan," he meowed. "If you and the other leaders really want to dishonor StarClan with this attack, fine, go right ahead. But know this: Any warriors that Thunder-Clan, WindClan, or RiverClan lose in this battle will have died for nothing."

Bristlefrost was aware that some of her Clanmates had begun to shuffle uneasily as Tigerstar spoke, his words giving them something to think about. Her muscles were tense, and she drove her claws hard into the ground, expecting that at any moment the waiting cats would explode into battle.

As the two hostile leaders faced each other, with their muscles bunched to spring and their teeth bared, a new scent washed over Bristlefrost, and she heard the sound of many cats scrambling up the slope outside the ShadowClan camp. A few heartbeats later the warriors of SkyClan appeared. They thrust their way through the bushes and between the encircling warriors of the other Clans, and began to pad down into the camp. Leafstar was in the lead, and dipped her head coldly to Tigerstar and Bramblestar as she halted beside them.

"Better late than never," Bramblestar grunted.

The ShadowClan warriors were eyeing the newcomers

warily; Bristlefrost could see the anxiety in their wide eyes and twitching tails. How could Leafstar have decided to fight for Bramblestar? It had seemed like she was on the rebels' side! *Now it's four Clans fighting against one,* she thought with an inward groan. *ShadowClan will be destroyed.*

"Greetings," Leafstar mewed crisply, glancing from one leader to the other. "I see there's no hope of peace between you."

"No hope at all." Bramblestar's voice was smooth and rich, almost a purr, filled with satisfaction at the appearance of more warriors on his side.

Tigerstar confronted Leafstar with a level gaze. "I hope you're happy with your decision," he meowed.

"Very happy," Leafstar replied. Then, to Bristlefrost's utter astonishment, she whirled to face the attackers. "Now!" she yowled.

Instantly her warriors spun around and launched themselves at the other Clans. For a couple of heartbeats the ThunderClan, RiverClan, and WindClan cats were so taken aback that they remained motionless, staring as cats they'd thought would be their allies leaped at them with bared teeth and flashing claws.

It must have been Leafstar who warned Tigerstar! Bristlefrost thought in exultation. *She did believe us! ShadowClan isn't alone!*

Then the battle engulfed her, and all she could think of was how to defend herself. She didn't want to hurt any cat, but she had to make her Clanmates believe she was still loyal to

Bramblestar. And she had to make sure that his body stayed alive.

The ShadowClan warriors had plunged into the battle along with SkyClan, so the whole camp was heaving with tussling, screeching cats. Bristlefrost backed up toward the bushes, though more than once she was carried off her paws by a heavy body slamming into her, or felt a stray claw rake through her fur.

She tried to dodge around Dewspring, but as Mousewhisker charged at him, the SkyClan warrior stumbled back into Bristlefrost and rolled over onto her as he lost his balance. Bristlefrost felt her legs buckle painfully, and she fell to the ground beneath the fighting cats. All the breath was driven out of her, and her face pressed into the earth.

With both warriors on top of her, Bristlefrost was afraid her legs would be crushed. She tried to wriggle free, but though she strained her muscles, all she could do was wave her tail helplessly.

"Bristlefrost!" Mousewhisker yowled. "Help me pin him down!"

But I'm *pinned down!* Bristlefrost thought, heaving vainly at the weight of the sturdy gray tom. For all her pain and discomfort, she was relieved: She couldn't help Mousewhisker, however hard she tried, but he wouldn't suspect that she was trying to avoid the fight.

At last the two wrestling cats rolled clear, leaving Bristlefrost to stagger to her paws and shake dirt and debris out of her pelt. Glancing around, she spotted some of the secret rebels from WindClan and RiverClan, and saw that they were doing the same as she was: trying to stay out of the fight as much as they could, or lashing out with claws sheathed as they tried to protect their injured Clanmates.

Bristlefrost was edging toward the shelter of the bushes when she saw Bramblestar fighting his way through the writhing mass of warriors, batting cats aside as he stalked determinedly toward Leafstar with fury smoldering in his eyes.

"Traitor!" he screeched. "You think you can get away with this?"

Leafstar was standing with her paws on Stormcloud's shoulders, pinning him down. "The only traitor is you, Bramblestar!" she yowled in reply. "You are a traitor to StarClan, after all you've done."

In answer, Bramblestar flicked his tail toward Shellfur and Leafshade. "Attack that treacherous mange-pelt!" he ordered, angling his ears toward the SkyClan leader.

But the two ThunderClan warriors turned their backs on Bramblestar. Both fixed their attention on two Shadow-Clan warriors who were prowling toward them. It was clear to Bristlefrost that they had heard their leader; they were just refusing to pay attention to his command.

"That's against the code!" Bramblestar yowled. "I told you to fight—and a leader's orders have to be obeyed!"

The ThunderClan leader let out a snarl of frustration and bunched his muscles to spring, though Bristlefrost wasn't sure whether he meant to attack Leafstar or his own warriors. But at the same moment a path opened up among the wrestling cats to reveal Tigerstar. His chest was heaving and he was bleeding from one shoulder, but there was a challenge in his eyes as his gaze locked with Bramblestar's.

Dread tingled through Bristlefrost from ears to tail-tip. Everything seemed to slow down around her as Bramblestar took a pace toward the ShadowClan leader.

"It will be *your* defeat that brings an end to this time of treachery and shame," the impostor growled. "Once you're deposed, everything will be put right."

The two leaders advanced on each other, paw step by paw step. *Now what am I supposed to do?* Bristlefrost wondered help-lessly. *I promised Squirrelflight that I would keep Bramblestar's body safe. Am I supposed to fight Tigerstar to protect the impostor?*

But before the two Clan leaders could reach each other, more cats leaped between them in a blur of fur and claws.

"The exiles!" Bristlefrost gasped.

Lionblaze and Squirrelflight joined the battle, Twigbranch and Finleap just behind them. Bristlefrost caught a glimpse of Crowfeather with more cats swarming after him, cutting off her view of the Clan leaders. She spotted Berrynose, too, fight-ing his way through the crowd to the spot where Bramblestar had disappeared.

Before he could reach his Clan leader, he came face to face with Tawnypelt. The ShadowClan she-cat hesitated for a heartbeat, perhaps unsure which side Berrynose was on. When he swiped at her with outstretched claws, she ducked under the blow and raked her claws across his throat and belly. Berrynose let out a shriek and collapsed, writhing.

Horrified, Bristlefrost leaped down the slope to help him, while Tawnypelt whipped around and hurled herself into a fight between Molewhisker and Hawkwing. But the press of fighting warriors cut Bristlefrost off; she found herself swaying to and fro in the crowd, unable to make any progress.

Then a space cleared; Bristlefrost drew breath, only to be forced backward as Lionblaze and Harestar rolled over and over, their legs wrapped around each other, their claws sunk deep into each other's fur. They broke apart right in front of Bristlefrost, scrambling to their paws and spitting furiously.

For a moment the two cats seemed evenly matched. But Lionblaze was strong and rested, while Harestar was already tired from fighting. He lashed out at Lionblaze, but the blow missed the golden tabby warrior by a mouse-length. Lionblaze slid deftly aside and sprang up onto Harestar's back. Instantly Harestar reared up on his hind legs, but he couldn't dislodge Lionblaze. The ThunderClan warrior curled a paw around Harestar's neck, claws aiming for his throat.

"No! Stop!" Bristlefrost yowled.

Even if Lionblaze had heard her, it was too late. His claws sliced through Harestar's fur to the flesh of his throat, and blood gushed out. The WindClan leader let out a choking gasp and slumped to the ground. His body twitched a few times, his eyes glazed over, and he lay still.

Lionblaze had leaped away as Harestar fell. Now he stood staring at the body, blood soaking the paw that had struck the killing blow. Bristlefrost thought he looked shocked that he had killed a Clan leader.

Silence was spreading around Harestar's body, like ripples from a stone thrown into a pool, as cat after cat realized what had happened. The fighting gradually died down as warriors who moments before had been tearing and clawing at each other drew closer to the dead WindClan leader and stood shoulder to shoulder in mingled horror and grief.

"Stop!" Bristlefrost heard Crowfeather call. "Harestar is dead." The cats around sheathed their claws and turned to fix their gazes on the WindClan leader's body.

"A Clan leader has lost a life," Hawkwing murmured. "Is he gone forever?"

Bristlefrost wished some cat could answer that question. Now that they knew that the real Bramblestar hadn't returned to his body, they all realized that no leader had lost a life and returned since StarClan had disappeared. If StarClan had truly abandoned them, Harestar wouldn't return.

What will happen to WindClan now?

There was a disturbance in the crowd as Nightcloud shouldered her way through and stood beside her dead leader, throwing her head back and letting out a yowl of grief. More WindClan warriors followed her, thrusting Lionblaze aside and forming a circle around Harestar. Lionblaze looked sick with guilt and horror.

"Please," Bristlefrost heard Hootwhisker whispering. "Please come back!"

A heavy silence followed. Bristlefrost watched, full of

mounting dread, until she saw a ripple pass through Harestar's body and he raised his head, letting out a panicked gasp. All the cats, from all five Clans, let out murmurs of shock and relief.

Harestar scrambled to his paws, his wide eyes flashing fearfully. "What . . . what happened?" His gaze rested on Crowfeather, and he pressed himself against his deputy, as though there had never been harsh words and the threat of exile between them.

"Is it really you?" Harestar asked.

"Yes, it's me. You're on Clan territory." Crowfeather assured him. "You're not in StarClan anymore."

Bristlefrost watched as Harestar gazed around, seeing the eager expressions on the faces of the assembled warriors, clearly waiting for him to confirm that he *had* been in StarClan. Shakily he raised a paw to his throat to feel that Lionblaze's wound had already closed up. He shook his head, his whole body shivering.

"I was in StarClan's hunting grounds," he rasped. "But I heard only distorted voices, and saw only the haziest figures, no more than a blur. Our warrior ancestors were still there, but it was like they were fading into nothing. . . ."

Bristlefrost turned to look for Bramblestar; every other warrior was doing the same. Soon she spotted him, standing to one side in the shadow of a thornbush. His gaze was fixed on Harestar, his amber eyes full of anger and disbelief, the revived leader apparently the last thing he'd wanted to see.

"That's not what you said when you returned from StarClan," Crowfeather challenged Bramblestar. "You said you spoke to them."

Bramblestar gave his pelt a shake and thrust out his chest, recovering his usual arrogance. "No cat should question me like this," he hissed, stalking forward until he stood nose to nose with Crowfeather. "You weren't there! I did speak with StarClan. The only reason they're fading now is because of all of you. You insist on not listening to me, so of course the situation is getting worse. What did you expect? StarClan probably rejected Harestar because he's just another codebreaker."

Back to his full strength now, Harestar padded up to Bramblestar, gesturing with his tail for Crowfeather to move back a pace. "I am no codebreaker, and I am no liar," he growled.

"The only liar here is you. You're *not* Bramblestar. You've taken his body, but the real Bramblestar never would have done the things you have."

Bramblestar turned at the sound of Tigerstar's voice. Bristlefrost noticed that cats were gathering around the ShadowClan leader: not just his own Clan, but SkyClan and some RiverClan cats as well. Even some WindClan warriors were moving toward him, convinced by Harestar's revival.

The impostor noticed that, too. "I don't believe what I'm seeing!" he exclaimed, his voice outraged. "Are Clan cats really siding with a leader who harbors codebreakers? Don't you want to see StarClan again?"

No cat answered. Bristlefrost shivered to see the accusing glares they fixed on him.

"Well, you're ruining your chances!" the false Bramblestar blustered. "When I *do* succeed in bringing StarClan back, you'll all be punished—even worse than you are now!"

Tigerstar took a pace forward. "Whether they're fading or not, I'm going to send you to StarClan right now!" he snarled.

Without more warning he hurled himself at the impostor, and the two leaders fell to the ground in one rolling, spitting ball of fur. Bristlefrost stood, appalled, on the edge of the fight. *Tigerstar will kill him! I'm supposed to protect him, but I'd just be ripped to shreds!*

The watching cats edged backward to give the battling leaders space as they bit and clawed at each other. At first they were silent in shock; then they gradually began to call out encouragement.

"Tigerstar! Tigerstar!"

Fury at hearing every cat yowling his enemy's name seemed to give Bramblestar extra strength. He swiped both forepaws at Tigerstar, startling the younger warrior. Taken aback for a moment, Tigerstar was too late to stop Bramblestar throwing him onto his back and slashing at his belly. Tigerstar finally forced him off and leapt to his paws, cuffing Bramblestar's ears with his forepaws. But Bramblestar took the opportunity to throw his weight at Tigerstar's vulnerable belly, forcing him onto the ground again. Bramblestar stood over him, his eyes gleaming.

Bristlefrost's belly lurched with fear as Bramblestar raised a bloody paw, his claws extended, to strike the blow that would send Tigerstar to StarClan.

But the impostor never struck. Instead he froze, staring at something behind Bristlefrost. She turned to see the crowd of cats parting and Squirrelflight thrusting her way to the front.

"You're . . . you're alive?" Bramblestar choked out.

While he was distracted, Tigerstar heaved himself up and scrambled out from underneath his opponent. Springing to his paws, he slashed his claws at the side of Bramblestar's neck. As blood trickled from the wound, Bramblestar tried to rear up, aiming a clumsy blow at Tigerstar. Avoiding the blow with ease, Tigerstar butted the impostor's side with his head; Bramblestar's legs crumpled and he fell to the ground.

Tigerstar stood for a few heartbeats, watching his opponent's blood seep out and pool in the dirt, then set one heavy forepaw down on the impostor's neck while he raised the other to strike the killing blow.

"No!" Bristlefrost exclaimed, instinctively racing to Bramblestar's side.

Squirrelflight was there before her. "No, don't kill him," she meowed. "We agreed, remember? We need him. If his body dies before the real Bramblestar's spirit can return, who knows what happens then? Bramblestar could be lost forever!"

Tigerstar looked down at the defeated form of the impostor, whose eyes were closed, his chest heaving weakly. The gleam of battle was still in the ShadowClan leader's eyes, and for a moment Bristlefrost wasn't sure what he meant to do.

Eventually, Tigerstar nodded. "I won't kill his body," he announced. "But I'm not letting this cat walk free."

"You're right," Squirrelflight agreed. "We'll take him prisoner instead. Once he wakes up, we can question him, and get to the bottom of exactly what's going on here."

Tigerstar dipped his head respectfully to the ThunderClan deputy. "Shadowsight!" he called. "Come here and see to this lump of crow-food." Then he turned and stalked off, summoning the other leaders to follow him with a whisk of his tail.

All around the camp the exhausted warriors were breaking up into groups, Clan mingling with Clan, some of them looking embarrassed as they spoke with cats they had been fighting not long before. Though Bristlefrost could hear some of them apologizing for how they had been deceived, for letting their Clanmates be exiled, she couldn't help wondering if every cat was ready to forgive.

How many new grudges were planted today?

Bristlefrost watched as Shadowsight appeared out of the crowd with a pawful of cobwebs and started applying them expertly to the wound in Bramblestar's neck. She tried to feel relief that her leader's body had been saved, and because it seemed that the Clans weren't at war with each other anymore. Then she saw the bodies lying still on the floor of the camp, their Clanmates beginning to cluster around them.

Oh, no! Berrynose . . . Rosepetal . . . Sandynose . . . And there were others that she couldn't identify from where she stood. Her relief was swallowed up in a wash of sorrow.

This didn't feel like the beginning of a better time. Not with so many cats dead. Not with ThunderClan's leader still missing.

CHAPTER 22

Shadowsight crouched in the medicine cats' den, chewing up the last of his store of comfrey to make a poultice for Bramblestar's wounds. Tigerstar had told him that he must keep the ThunderClan leader alive at any cost, and while he had stopped the bleeding, he sometimes felt that Bramblestar was about to slip away for good. Already he had almost exhausted the herb store in his efforts to keep the impostor alive.

It seems like all I can do is pray to StarClan. Or will that do any good? I saw how they were imprisoned. And Harestar said that StarClan was fading, barely there anymore.

Bramblestar had begun to stir as his consciousness returned, when Squirrelflight slipped into the den and stood looking down at him, deep concern in her eyes.

"How is he?" she asked.

"He'll be fine," Shadowsight assured her, though he wished he felt more confident when he said it.

"I must have bees in my brain," Squirrelflight murmured. "I want so desperately to lie down beside him, to try to keep him strong, except . . . that's not my mate, is it? Not really. I'm so confused. . . ."

Shadowsight didn't know how to respond. *I'm a medicine cat. I'll never know anything about the love between mates. So what can I say to her now?*

"I promise I'll do whatever it takes to keep Bramblestar alive," he meowed at last.

"Thank you," Squirrelflight replied.

She was turning to leave the den when Bramblestar stirred again and his eyes flickered open. "Squirrelflight!" he called out in a pained, wheezing gasp. Then he mumbled something else that Shadowsight couldn't make out.

"What did you say?" Squirrelflight asked curiously, turning back to him.

Bramblestar's chest heaved as he fought to breathe, and he finally managed to force out a few more words. Now Shadowsight could understand him.

"I came back . . . for you."

The effort had been too much. Bramblestar's body sagged and his eyes closed as he lapsed back into unconsciousness.

"Is he dead?" Squirrelflight asked, her eyes wide with alarm.

Shadowsight bent over the ThunderClan leader, placing a paw on his chest and sniffing around his muzzle. "No, he's alive," he mewed at last. Straightening up, he added, "Squirrelflight, what did that mean? 'I came back for you'?"

For a moment Squirrelflight seemed completely confused, gazing up at the roof of the den and back down at Bramblestar's motionless form. "I'm starting to think there's something *familiar* about this fake Bramblestar," she murmured. "But I can't quite put my paw on what it is, or who it might actually be. I do know one thing, though," she added, meeting Shadowsight's concerned gaze. "I have a terrible feeling about all of this."

She left the den, and with a last look at the impostor, Shadowsight followed her out to see the devastation still strewn about the camp. Countless moons seemed to have passed since the Clan had roused before dawn, and yet sunhigh was still a little way off.

The camp was still full of warriors from the other Clans, moving their fallen Clanmates to their burial places. Pain clawed at Shadowsight's heart as he spotted Strikestone and Frondwhisker being carried into the center of the camp so their Clanmates could sit vigil for them that night. Warriors from WindClan and RiverClan were lifting Smokehaze and Softpelt, ready to bear them home. Meanwhile Puddleshine was passing from one cat to another, checking on the wounds they had received in the battle. All the cats were grieving and exhausted, and after a moment Shadowsight couldn't bear to go on looking.

So many warriors dead or injured because of that evil thing inside Bramblestar.

Instead he glanced across the camp to where his father was deep in conversation with the other leaders and their deputies. Shadowsight noticed Bristlefrost hovering awkwardly on the edge of the group, clearly wishing she were anywhere else.

Tigerstar looked up and, spotting Shadowsight, beckoned him with a whisk of his tail. Shadowsight bounded over to join him, and Squirrelflight followed.

"How is that piece of fox dung?" Tigerstar demanded as Shadowsight halted in front of him.

No need to ask who he means! "I've treated his wounds," Shadowsight replied, "but he's not doing as well as I'd like. There's still a chance he might not make it."

Tigerstar nodded. "This means we have a big decision to make about the future of ThunderClan," he told the others. "It still has a leader, but he's in no fit state to lead—and he can't be trusted. It also has a deputy who is clearly too young to take over the leadership."

"Oh, thank StarClan!" Bristlefrost breathed out; she looked almost giddy with relief. Squirrelflight blinked at her affectionately, and even Tigerstar looked amused. *I'm glad they've realized she was never on the impostor's side,* Shadowsight thought.

"Squirrelflight, you're the obvious choice to lead Thunder-Clan now," Tigerstar continued. "What do you think?"

Squirrelflight shook her head uncertainly. "I don't know. . . . Strictly speaking, I'm not even a member of ThunderClan anymore, since I was sent into exile. Besides, Berrynose—"

"Berrynose is dead," Tigerstar interrupted. "And the impostor had no authority to exile you or any other cat, or to replace you as deputy."

"Please, Squirrelflight," Mistystar pleaded, stretching out a paw toward her. "You are ThunderClan's true deputy, and every cat in the forest trusts you."

Squirrelflight ducked her head with embarrassment at the RiverClan leader's praise, seeming more embarrassed still as the other leaders and deputies murmured their agreement.

"Very well," she mewed. "I'll do it for the good of the Clan—but only temporarily, until we get the real Bramblestar back. Bristlefrost," she added, turning to the pale gray she-cat, "I'm sorry, but I don't think you ought to be deputy. I'm going to choose Lionblaze."

"Oh, don't be sorry, Squirrelflight!" Bristlefrost burst out. "I never deserved to be deputy, and I'm sure StarClan would never have approved, no matter what the false Bramblestar said. I'm just not ready. I'm so glad to step back for a cat who's truly worthy."

Squirrelflight took a pace toward her and touched noses with her. "I'm sure you have a bright future in our Clan," she mewed.

A lighter mood settled over the assembled cats as the paws of ThunderClan returned to the right path.

"I think we should hold a Gathering tomorrow night," Tigerstar suggested. "We all need to figure out how we should best move forward, now that we have the impostor under control."

Relief flooded through Shadowsight. It seemed that everything was working out at last. But then his gaze rested on the medicine cats' den, and he couldn't help wondering.

Is it really over?

He felt his paws carrying him back to the den, as if something was drawing him there. Stepping in, he padded up to the sleeping Bramblestar and looked down at him. He almost felt the evil wafting off the impostor, filling the den like a damp wind.

While Shadowsight was standing over him, Bramblestar's eyes suddenly snapped open, narrowing as his gaze fell on the medicine cat.

He recognizes me. . . .

The impostor opened his jaws and spoke, but not in the voice of Bramblestar, the one Shadowsight had always heard at Gatherings. Instead it was the voice he remembered from his visions.

"I won't be thwarted," he told Shadowsight. "You saved my life, and because of that, you have ensured my success. Because once I'm back to full health, I'll be able to bend any cat to my will. . . . Just ask that skinny black cat with the yellow eyes."

For a moment Shadowsight wasn't sure what the impostor meant. *Surely it can't be . . .* Then, with a gasp of amazement, he realized that Bramblestar must be talking about Spiresight, though he had no idea how the two spirits could have met.

Before Shadowsight could question Bramblestar, the impostor went limp again and his eyes closed.

Shadowsight still had no idea who the spirit inside Bramblestar might be, but he knew one thing. *The Clans' troubles aren't over yet.*

CHAPTER 23

❧

Rootspring poked his head into the medicine cats' den to see his father, Tree, flexing his injured leg. "It feels fine," Tree told Frecklewish.

The medicine cat sniffed at the poultice she had placed on Tree's wound; Rootspring caught the clean tang of horsetail.

"It seems to be healing well," she meowed. "But I would stay off it for a day or two. Come back and see me if it starts swelling or feeling hot."

"Yes, I think I'll give tonight's Gathering a miss," Tree responded. With a wry look at Rootspring, he added, "You can't imagine how upset I am about that."

Rootspring stifled a snort of amusement. "I'll stay behind and keep you company, if you like," he offered.

"No, you must go," Tree insisted. "Like it or not, you have an important part to play in the Clans right now. You need to be there."

Rootspring twitched his whiskers doubtfully. *Being important is overrated, if you ask me.* But he had to admit that his father was right.

"Okay," he sighed.

He headed out into the clearing, and Tree limped after him. "Good luck," he mewed to his son.

"Thanks, I'll need it. Just make sure you get a good night's sleep."

"Your mother will see to that." Tree whisked his tail in farewell and padded off to the warriors' den.

The sun had set, and Leafstar was already waiting beside the fern tunnel along with the cats she had chosen to go to the Gathering. "There you are, Rootspring!" she exclaimed as he joined his Clanmates. "We've been waiting for you. We can't go without you; I have a feeling we're going to need you tonight."

Just what Tree said, Rootspring thought, his paws tingling with apprehension. *Am I ever going to get to be just a normal warrior?*

When Rootspring padded up the shore of the Gathering island and pushed his way through the bushes into the clearing, most of the other Clan cats were already there. They seemed shaken by what had happened, glancing nervously from side to side. He wouldn't blame them for half expecting another fight to break out, yet they were mingling with one another instead of bunching up into groups divided by Clan.

Rootspring had hardly had time to take that in when he noticed something else: Around the edges of the clearing lurked the spirits of the cats who had died in the battle. A shiver ran through Rootspring from paws to tail-tip.

They should have gone to StarClan—but they're still here.

Rootspring had always been told that when a warrior died,

his spirit would join StarClan and be at peace, but these were crouching with every muscle tensed, their fur bristling and their eyes wide and scared as they looked around the clearing. Some of them were gazing forlornly at their living Clanmates, who couldn't see them.

Slipping cautiously along the line of the bushes, Rootspring looked for the real Bramblestar's ghost, but there was no sign of him, not even when Rootspring had covered the entire clearing twice to be sure he hadn't missed the ghost leader.

After the battle on the previous day, Rootspring had managed to speak briefly with Shadowsight.

"I found Bramblestar's spirit trapped in a hollow tree in the Dark Forest," the young medicine cat had explained. "Once he was free, he should have been able to return."

"But I haven't seen him," Rootspring had responded. "Have you?"

Shadowsight had shaken his head. "His spirit is out there somewhere—but where?"

Now Rootspring was almost ready to despair. *Will the real Bramblestar ever return?*

He had to give up his search as the four remaining Clan leaders, along with Squirrelflight, leaped into the tree and Tigerstar let out a commanding yowl. "Cats of all Clans, the Gathering has begun!"

Leafstar rose on her branch and took a pace forward, as if she was about to take charge. Rootspring half expected Tigerstar to object, but he remained silent, and every cat turned to listen to the SkyClan leader.

"This has been a terrible time for the Clans," Leafstar began. "I'm sure we can all agree that we've made some dreadful mistakes. I know there are wounds on our bodies and in our spirits that will take some time to heal, but now is not the time for revenge or retribution. And now is definitely not the time for punishing cats for past wrongdoings."

Harestar murmured agreement, dipping his head respectfully to the SkyClan leader. "Bramblestar was a false leader and a bad cat," he pointed out, "but it *is* possible that StarClan disappeared because we've all broken the code so many times. It wouldn't be a bad idea for us all to start sticking to it more closely. Maybe if we do, StarClan *will* come back."

Rootspring felt his heart clench painfully at the WindClan leader's words. *Bristlefrost thought things might get easier, but it sounds like she was wrong.* Harestar seemed totally haunted by his journey to the abandoned StarClan and his encounter with the fading warrior spirits.

Tigerstar straightened up, standing tall at the end of the branch he had chosen. Rootspring guessed that he was trying to dominate the Gathering as much as Bramblestar had instinctively done in the past.

"I respect StarClan as much as any cat," he meowed. "But if I'm honest, I trust them well enough to know when a cat has lived a good and honorable life. All the cats accused of codebreaking may have violated the rules, but can you truly say that there was darkness in their hearts?"

A ripple of unease passed through the Gathering. "What are you saying?" Crowfeather demanded. "That we should change the warrior code?"

"Or ignore it altogether?" Lionblaze added. "That's madness! StarClan will never come back then!"

Rootspring realized for the first time that the exiled Crowfeather had taken his place as deputy on the roots of the Great Oak, and that Lionblaze, who must be the new ThunderClan deputy, was sitting by his side. Glancing around, he saw that the other exiles were in the clearing, too.

It's good to see them back where they belong, he thought, feeling a little encouraged.

"That's what the false Bramblestar *wanted* us all to believe," Tigerstar responded to Lionblaze's objection. "But isn't it clear now that everything he told us rose from his malice? Frightening us into believing that StarClan was angry with us was just a tool he used to control us all."

"How do you know that?" Mistystar asked. "After all, no cat can deny that we have heard nothing from StarClan for moons now."

"I don't know for certain," Tigerstar replied. "But when Shadowsight traveled as a spirit into the Dark Forest, he saw glittering stars trapped in a pool, as though StarClan was somehow being kept away from their hunting grounds."

"What?" Rootspring saw Harestar's eyes widen and his ears angle forward as if he couldn't be sure he had heard right. "With all due respect, Tigerstar, that sounds like a load of thistle-fluff! Stars trapped in the Dark Forest? Driven out of their hunting grounds? Tigerstar, I was *there*, in StarClan's hunting grounds, and so were the spirits of our warrior ancestors.

They were faded and in distress, but they were there."

Leafstar stretched out her tail to the WindClan leader in a calming gesture. "Medicine cats' visions shouldn't always be taken literally," she meowed. "There's no reason to believe that Shadowsight's experiences in spirit form are any easier to make sense of than omens from StarClan."

While she was speaking, Tigerstar's shoulder fur gradually bushed up, and his eyes glittered with fury. "What do you know about it?" he snarled, words pouring out of him like a flooding stream. "It was Shadowsight who traveled to the Dark Forest, nearly killing himself to do it. It was Shadowsight who was nearly murdered by the false Bramblestar, Shadowsight who endured your scorn for sharing the visions he believed were from StarClan. When will any of you bee-brains listen to my son? He's telling us how to get StarClan back!"

His voice rang out across the clearing, and for a few moments after he had finished, every cat was stunned to silence. Mistystar was the first to speak, dipping her head respectfully to the ShadowClan leader.

"Tigerstar, just now you might be too angry at everything that happened—at the unfair accusations leveled at yourself and Dovewing, and your kits—to be truly thinking clearly."

"I agree." Squirrelflight, who had so far listened to the leaders in silence, spoke up. "Shadowsight's contributions have been very valuable," she continued, "but even if what he said is true, that doesn't tell us how to defeat whatever lies in Bramblestar's body. To beat him, we must figure out who he is."

"Yes!" Harestar turned an enthusiastic gaze onto Squirrel-flight. "You know Bramblestar better than any of us. What do you think?"

Squirrelflight paused for a moment, clearly in deep thought. "He said . . . he came back for me." For a few heartbeats longer she went on thinking, then shook her head, her shoulders drooping. "I'm still not sure. . . ."

The Clan leaders broke out into the same old argument, about StarClan and why they had disappeared. Rootspring felt a tingle of foreboding in his paws. *After all we've been through, are we just going to start up the same fight all over again?*

"Well," Tigerstar meowed at last, "at least all the exiled cats can go home again."

"I'm not sure," Mistystar responded, to Rootspring's surprise. "Icewing and Harelight, come and stand here at the foot of the Great Oak."

Rootspring watched in confusion as the two warriors Mistystar had named emerged from the crowd of their Clanmates and stood side by side, gazing up at their leader with uneasy expressions. *What is Mistystar thinking?* he wondered. *Icewing and Harelight were never exiled.*

"I believed that you were loyal RiverClan warriors," Mistystar meowed, pain in her blue eyes as she looked down. "Yet in the battle I saw you fighting against your Clan. You disobeyed my orders. Even now that I know the false Bramblestar was evil, I must send you into exile."

The two warriors gaped at their leader, too stunned for the moment to protest or defend themselves.

In the silence Mothwing rose from her place beside the other medicine cats. "Mistystar—" she began.

"Mothwing, I see that I was wrong to exile you," Mistystar interrupted. "I am sorry for it. You are welcome to return to RiverClan."

"No, Mistystar," Mothwing retorted; a gasp went up from the cats who surrounded her at the single word. "I will never feel welcome in a Clan where warriors are exiled unjustly. Icewing and Harelight risked their safety and their lives to oppose the evil presence inside Bramblestar. We should be thanking them, not sending them into exile. Besides," the medicine cat continued, "I chose to be a RiverClan cat, and I have served my Clan faithfully, and yet you drove me away because of my birth, which I had no control over. It will be hard for me to forget that."

For a heartbeat Rootspring thought that Mistystar wavered, her jaws parted to speak, and yet no words came out. Then she took a deep breath and spoke. "Then Mothwing, Icewing, Harelight—you are no longer RiverClan cats."

"That's not fair!" Icewing exclaimed. "Okay, we did fight on ShadowClan's side, but Mothwing never did anything wrong."

"Yeah, can't we even atone somehow?" Harelight asked.

Mistystar's only reply was a lash of her tail.

Rootspring could feel shock passing through the Gathering like ripples from a stone thrown into a pool. *How could Mistystar do this to her medicine cat and two loyal warriors? And where are they expected to go?*

"Mistystar, are you sure about this?" Leafstar asked. "We

are all taking our exiles back and forgiving them. Harelight and Icewing were only trying to do what they thought was right. Fighting in the battle must have been the hardest decision they have ever had to make."

"And they made the wrong decision." Mistystar's blue eyes were full of distress, but her tone was unwavering. "They must bear the consequences."

The other leaders exchanged regretful glances, but there was obviously no point in arguing further.

"In that case," Tigerstar announced eventually, "they had better come with me to ShadowClan. They will always have a home there."

Sharp cries of shock rose up from the assembled cats. "Who are you, and what have you done with Tigerstar?" Needleclaw muttered into Rootspring's ear.

Meanwhile, Tigerstar announced that the Gathering was at an end. A stunned air had fallen over every cat as the crowd began to break up into their separate Clans, ready to go home.

Mistystar was the first leader to leap down from the Great Oak and summon her Clan with a whisk of her tail. She led them off with a determined stride toward the encircling bushes, leaving the three exiles standing clustered together as they watched their Clanmates leaving without them. Icewing took a pace toward the ShadowClan cats, then halted.

It's still too strange for them, Rootspring thought. His belly twisted with compassion as he watched RiverClan go. *I wonder if the Clans will survive this,* he added to himself. *How can things possibly feel this terrible, after such a great victory over the fake Bramblestar?*

The other leaders had jumped down to gather their Clans when Squirrelflight suddenly let out a loud yowl. "Wait!"

She raced back to the Great Oak and leaped back into the branches. Even from a distance, Rootspring could see that her green eyes were wide and bright, with a lurking trace of horror.

The dispersing cats slowly halted, turning to look curiously up at her. A few RiverClan cats who had already vanished into the bushes pushed their way back into the clearing.

"Don't worry," Tigerstar called out, looking over his shoulder at Squirrelflight. "We won't hurt Bramblestar's precious body."

But Squirrelflight shook her head. "That's not it," she responded, her voice hoarse. "I *know*."

"Know what?" Jayfeather asked crankily. "For StarClan's sake, come out with it. We're all tired."

"I know who has taken over Bramblestar's body!"

Rootspring gaped, hardly able to believe what he had just heard. Around him, all the cats were letting out exclamations of confusion and surprise.

"And," Squirrelflight continued, "if I'm right, it's even worse than we thought."

CHAPTER 1

Swiftcub pounced after the vulture's shadow, but it flitted away too quickly to follow. Breathing hard, he pranced back to his pride. *I saw that bird off our territory,* he thought, delighted. *No rot-eater's going to come near Gallantpride while I'm around!*

The pride needed him to defend it, Swiftcub thought, picking up his paws and strutting around his family. Why, right now they were all half asleep, dozing and basking in the shade of the acacia trees. The most energetic thing the other lions were doing was lifting their heads to groom their nearest neighbors, or their own paws. They had no *idea* of the threat Swiftcub had just banished.

I might be only a few moons old, but my father is the strongest, bravest lion in Bravelands. And I'm going to be just like him!

"Swiftcub!"

The gentle but commanding voice snapped him out of his

dreams of glory. He came to a halt, turning and flicking his ears at the regal lioness who stood over him.

"Mother," he said, shifting on his paws.

"Why are you shouting at vultures?" Swift scolded him fondly, licking at his ears. "They're nothing but scavengers. Come on, you and your sister can play later. Right now you're supposed to be practicing hunting. And if you're going to catch anything, you'll need to keep your eyes on the prey, not on the sky!"

"Sorry, Mother." Guiltily he padded after her as she led him through the dry grass, her tail swishing. The ground rose gently, and Swiftcub had to trot to keep up. The grasses tickled his nose, and he was so focused on trying not to sneeze, he almost bumped into his mother's haunches as she crouched.

"Oops," he growled.

Valor shot him a glare. His older sister was hunched a little to the left of their mother, fully focused on their hunting practice. Valor's sleek body was low to the ground, her muscles tense; as she moved one paw forward with the utmost caution, Swiftcub tried to copy her, though it was hard to keep up on his much shorter legs. One creeping pace, then two. Then another.

I'm being very quiet, just like Valor. I'm going to be a great *hunter.* He slunk up alongside his mother, who remained quite still.

"There, Swiftcub," she murmured. "Do you see the burrows?"

He did, now. Ahead of the three lions, the ground rose up even higher, into a bare, sandy mound dotted with small shadowy holes. As Swiftcub watched, a small nose and whiskers poked out, testing the air. The meerkat emerged completely, stood up on its hind legs, and stared around. Satisfied, it stuck out a pink tongue and began to groom its chest, as more meerkats appeared beyond it. Growing in confidence, they scurried farther away from their burrows.

"Careful now," rumbled Swift. "They're very quick. Go!"

Swiftcub sprang forward, his little paws bounding over the ground. Still, he wasn't fast enough to outpace Valor, who was far ahead of him already. A stab of disappointment spoiled his excitement, and suddenly it was even harder to run fast, but he ran grimly after his sister.

The startled meerkats were already doubling back into their holes. Stubby tails flicked and vanished; the bigger leader, his round dark eyes glaring at the oncoming lions, was last to twist and dash underground. Valor's jaws snapped at his tail, just missing.

"Sky and stone!" the bigger cub swore, coming to a halt in a cloud of dust. She shook her head furiously and licked her jaws. "I nearly had it!"

A rumble of laughter made Swiftcub turn. His father, Gallant, stood watching them. Swiftcub couldn't help but feel the usual twinge of awe mixed in with his delight. Black-maned and huge, his sleek fur glowing golden in the sun, Gallant would have been intimidating if Swiftcub hadn't known and loved him so well. Swift rose to her paws and greeted the great lion affectionately, rubbing his maned neck with her head.

"It was a good attempt, Valor," Gallant reassured his

daughter. "What Swift said is true: meerkats are *very* hard to catch. You were so close—one day you'll be as fine a hunter as your mother." He nuzzled Swift and licked her neck.

"*I* wasn't anywhere near it," grumbled Swiftcub. "I'll never be as fast as Valor."

"Oh, you will," said Gallant. "Don't forget, Valor's a whole year older than you, my son. You're getting bigger and faster every day. Be patient!" He stepped closer, leaning in so his great tawny muzzle brushed Swiftcub's own. "That's the secret to stalking, too. Learn patience, and one day you will be a *very* fine hunter."

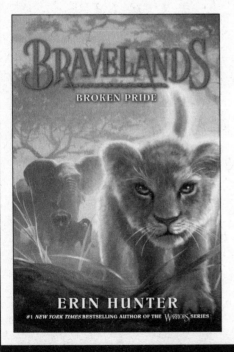

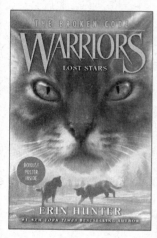
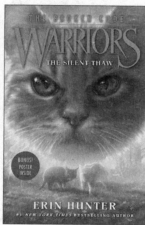

WARRIORS

How many have you read?

Dawn of the Clans
- ○ #1: The Sun Trail
- ○ #2: Thunder Rising
- ○ #3: The First Battle
- ○ #4: The Blazing Star
- ○ #5: A Forest Divided
- ○ #6: Path of Stars

Power of Three
- ○ #1: The Sight
- ○ #2: Dark River
- ○ #3: Outcast
- ○ #4: Eclipse
- ○ #5: Long Shadows
- ○ #6: Sunrise

The Prophecies Begin
- ○ #1: Into the Wild
- ○ #2: Fire and Ice
- ○ #3: Forest of Secrets
- ○ #4: Rising Storm
- ○ #5: A Dangerous Path
- ○ #6: The Darkest Hour

Omen of the Stars
- ○ #1: The Fourth Apprentice
- ○ #2: Fading Echoes
- ○ #3: Night Whispers
- ○ #4: Sign of the Moon
- ○ #5: The Forgotten Warrior
- ○ #6: The Last Hope

The New Prophecy
- ○ #1: Midnight
- ○ #2: Moonrise
- ○ #3: Dawn
- ○ #4: Starlight
- ○ #5: Twilight
- ○ #6: Sunset

A Vision of Shadows
- ○ #1: The Apprentice's Quest
- ○ #2: Thunder and Shadow
- ○ #3: Shattered Sky
- ○ #4: Darkest Night
- ○ #5: River of Fire
- ○ #6: The Raging Storm

Select titles also available as audiobooks!

HARPER

An Imprint of HarperCollinsPublishers

www.warriorcats.com • www.shelfstuff.com

SUPER EDITIONS

- ○ Firestar's Quest
- ○ Bluestar's Prophecy
- ○ SkyClan's Destiny
- ○ Crookedstar's Promise
- ○ Yellowfang's Secret
- ○ Tallstar's Revenge

- ○ Bramblestar's Storm
- ○ Moth Flight's Vision
- ○ Hawkwing's Journey
- ○ Tigerheart's Shadow
- ○ Crowfeather's Trial
- ○ Squirrelflight's Hope

GUIDES   FULL-COLOR MANGA

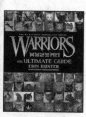

- ○ Secrets of the Clans
- ○ Cats of the Clans
- ○ Code of the Clans
- ○ Battles of the Clans
- ○ Enter the Clans
- ○ The Ultimate Guide

- ○ Graystripe's Adventure
- ○ Ravenpaw's Path
- ○ SkyClan and the Stranger

EBOOKS AND NOVELLAS

The Untold Stories
- ○ Hollyleaf's Story
- ○ Mistystar's Omen
- ○ Cloudstar's Journey

Tales from the Clans
- ○ Tigerclaw's Fury
- ○ Leafpool's Wish
- ○ Dovewing's Silence

Shadows of the Clans
- ○ Mapleshade's Vengeance
- ○ Goosefeather's Curse
- ○ Ravenpaw's Farewell

Legends of the Clans
- ○ Spottedleaf's Heart
- ○ Pinestar's Choice
- ○ Thunderstar's Echo

Path of a Warrior
- ○ Redtail's Debt
- ○ Tawnypelt's Clan
- ○ Shadowstar's Life

A Warrior's Spirit
- ○ Pebbleshine's Kits
- ○ Tree's Roots
- ○ Mothwing's Secret

HARPER
An Imprint of HarperCollinsPublishers

www.warriorcats.com • www.shelfstuff.com

Don't miss these other Erin Hunter series!

SURVIVORS

Survivors
- ◯ #1: The Empty City
- ◯ #2: A Hidden Enemy
- ◯ #3: Darkness Falls
- ◯ #4: The Broken Path
- ◯ #5: The Endless Lake
- ◯ #6: Storm of Dogs

**Survivors:
The Gathering Darkness**
- ◯ #1: A Pack Divided
- ◯ #2: Dead of Night
- ◯ #3: Into the Shadows
- ◯ #4: Red Moon Rising
- ◯ #5: The Exile's Journey
- ◯ #6: The Final Battle

SEEKERS

Seekers
- ◯ #1: The Quest Begins
- ◯ #2: Great Bear Lake
- ◯ #3: Smoke Mountain
- ◯ #4: The Last Wilderness
- ◯ #5: Fire in the Sky
- ◯ #6: Spirits in the Stars

Seekers: Return to the Wild
- ◯ #1: Island of Shadows
- ◯ #2: The Melting Sea
- ◯ #3: River of Lost Bears
- ◯ #4: Forest of Wolves
- ◯ #5: The Burning Horizon
- ◯ #6: The Longest Day

HARPER
An Imprint of HarperCollinsPublishers

www.shelfstuff.com

www.warriorcats.com/survivors • www.warriorcats.com/seekers